WRITE TO THE END

A Lex Stall Mystery
Manhattan's Tenacious Female Detective

MARK L. DRESSLER

© 2023 Mark L. Dressler – all rights reserved.
Published by Satincrest Press, USA
ISBN: 978-0999062340

Editor: Heather Doughty – HBD Edits
Proofreader: Joshua Suhl
Formatting: Liz Delton
Cover Design: Jeanine Henning – JH Illustrations
Author Photo: Jessica Smolinski

CHAPTER 1

It was as if author Essex Westbrook had written the ransom letter himself.

We have your wife. $100,000 will get her back. Instructions to follow.

The truth is that those words were penned in a forgotten fiction novel he once wrote, but this time they were real. Svetlana had been kidnapped.

⬥

MARCH 31, 2019

Essex Westbrook and his wife, Svetlana, resided on the twenty-sixth floor of the Grand Truman Hotel located on West 30th Street between 6th and 7th Avenues. Penn Station, Madison Square Garden, and Herald Square were all within walking distance.

The author emerged from his office after typing two chapters of an unfinished manuscript and walked to the wet bar, located against the wall nearest the living room's extension. Avoiding the dining table, he held a bottle of scotch.

Svetlana, ten years younger than her fifty-nine-year-old husband, stopped him from pouring a pre-dinner drink. "I ordered meals from the restaurant downstairs. A glass of wine will go nicely with our supper."

"Very good. I'll put a bottle of chardonnay on the table."

After doing so, he sat there with his wife until a restaurant staffer knocked on the front door. Svetlana opened it, and aromas of freshly cooked edibles caught Essex's senses. The white-aproned server wheeled in a cart, placed the silver-domed plates in front of the diners, and revealed two savory-smelling meals. "Enjoy," he said.

Svetlana thanked him before he left the room.

Essex reached for the saltshaker, and his mouth watered as he gazed upon his thick, juicy, medium-rare slab of filet mignon. Red potatoes and asparagus accompanied the steak. Svetlana's plate of seared Atlantic salmon was served with the same sides as her husband's dinner, perfectly arranged. The hungry author then opened the bottle of chardonnay, filling their glasses.

After savoring their Sunday evening dinners, they finished of wine. Svetlana stacked the empty dishes on the nearby cart, took it out to the hallway, and called the restaurant to have it picked up.

The author rose from his chair. "Please excuse me, I'm going to continue my new manuscript. I will try to write to the end."

"It's still nice out. I am going for a walk."

"Can you bring me coffee?"

"I will."

Before retreating to his office, he looked at the mantel above the gas fireplace to admire the Author of the Year Award he'd received two weeks ago. His book, *The Last Corpse,* earned him that foot-tall, bronzed, opened-book memento, which also had the year 2018 and his name etched into it.

Sitting in a comfortable chair, he switched on the goose-necked lamp that sat on his mahogany desk a few inches from the computer. Scrolling to page 288 of the unfinished work, the author began tapping the keys as if they were Steinway ivories.

Svetlana returned a few minutes after eight o'clock, quietly set a cup of black coffee beside the laptop and walked toward the bedroom. Engrossed in the manuscript, he didn't hear the sound of running water from the bathroom tub where Svetlana readied herself to take a relaxing bath.

The author continued writing. When he glanced at the clock, it read 2:15 a.m., he saved the finished document. The last sip of cool coffee coated his throat as he shut down the computer.

Essex Westbrook donned his blue striped pajamas and was

careful not to wake his sleeping wife, sliding under the covers and feeling her warmth, not knowing that he may never be this close to Svetlana again.

Chapter 2

Westbrook was a homebody and preferred to spend most of his time inside, venturing out only when he deemed necessary.

The author awakened at 8:15 a.m., and the other side of the bed was unoccupied. Svetlana often took early morning walks, bringing back coffee from a local café just as she had last evening.

Yawning as he made his way to the master bath, he gazed at Svetlana's picture on his nightstand and admired her beauty. After completing his perfunctory activities, he entered the main living space where he pulled back the curtains and enjoyed the sunlit Manhattan skyline. Thoughts of breakfast occupied his mind, but he chose to wait until Svetlana came back with coffee.

The next part of his routine was to head toward the front door to retrieve the morning newspaper. He noticed a white envelope lying on the green carpet. There were no markings on the outside, and he wondered if this was an April Fools' message that Svetlana had strategically put down where he'd find it.

Curious, he removed the envelope's contents and froze as he digested those eerily familiar words.

We have your wife. $100,000 will get her back. Instructions to follow.

Was the dastardly demand indeed real? He recognized this was not Svetlana's writing and wondered how the envelope got there.

After making several unsuccessful attempts to connect with her cell and leaving unanswered messages, his fear rose to panic.

Tucker Rutledge flashed in his mind, only Tucker Rutledge was a figment of the author's imagination. Tucker Rutledge didn't exist.

4

Tucker Rutledge's wife never existed. They were merely characters in the author's poorest selling book *Greta's Gone,* which was written almost ten years ago. That unheralded story never reached the *New York Times* bestseller list, and it was one he never liked to talk about.

Tucker's wife, Greta, was gone, and now Svetlana had apparently disappeared. Westbrook's imagined characters and Svetlana had become intertwined. The same fictitious ransoming words Essex Westbrook had written were now as real as life. He knew his wife was in danger.

Chapter 3

Monday mornings were never routine for Manhattan's tenacious detective Lex Stall, and this day's awaiting surprise was one the seasoned sleuth could not have expected.

After making her usual stop at Starbucks for a cinnamon latte, she drove her 2015 Corolla into the Central Park Precinct parking lot. This station had been home to the detective's unit for over a year while renovations were being made to the 19th Precinct on East 67th Street.

This spring day, she wore a recently purchased gray pantsuit and white blouse. Her dark, shoulder-length hair moved slightly with the breeze as she walked with hot coffee in her hand, weapon tucked into her hip holster. She looked toward the stable at the end of the lot. Lex's favorite horse, Butterscotch, spent her off-duty hours there when not patrolling Central Park. She opted to allow her four-legged friend to finish breakfast and instead walked up to the second-floor squad room.

The silvery tiled floor was a shade different from the walls of the inornate workplace. And there were no posters or pictures on the walls, but there was a rectangular chalkboard next to the water cooler. A chart of detectives names, shifts, and active cases had been filled in by Captain Pressley. Brightly lit cubicles in the detective spaces were adjacent to a separate glassed-in office that housed their boss.

Lex passed the interview and meeting rooms, as well as the lavatories, on the way to her desk. The smell of flavored coffee accompanied her as she sauntered toward her partner, Gil Ramos. However, she couldn't escape Stanley Hutchinson, known as Hutch, a senior detective who liked to remind Lex she was the only female around. "Morning, sexy," he said to his attractive, shapely coworker.

She continued walking toward her partner while snarling at Hutch. "Grow up."

Gil was seated with his tan sport coat wrapped around the back of his chair. "I heard the old dirtbag."

She placed the hot cup on her desk. "I know. He's harmless though. When are you going to stop eating those things?" She pointed to the doughnut in his hand. "You're looking a little...." Not wanting to say the word *fat*, she instead uttered, "Robust lately."

"Hey," he said, "be nice. And that big latte must have a lot of bad stuff in it. You're lucky you don't blow up like a balloon."

She took a sip before sitting. "Moderation and diet. I'm not sure you know those two words."

Gil smirked. "Give me a break. I walk my dog every morning and evening." He finished the heart-clogging snack and drank his coffee. "So how is Stefan?"

"He's fine. We saw *The Phantom of the Opera* Saturday night."

"When's the wedding?" He held a napkin in one hand.

Lex sneered at her partner, who was five years older than her not quite forty years. "Will you stop asking? We haven't been dating that long, and one bad marriage was enough. It will take a lot of convincing for me to stand at the altar again. Those pieces of divorce papers can be deadly weapons, especially when attorneys get into it." That memory stirred up unimaginable hostilities. "I should know. Even though I'm the one who had my lawyer serve Jon papers, those legal hounds dragged up everything including his affairs. And then he had the audacity to file that nasty custody petition." Lex breathed hard. "If I wasn't such a lady, I'd say my ex should have been castrated."

Gil cringed at the reference to severing testicles. "Ouch."

Lex saw his face curl. "I'm glad I have Liz."

"She's a good kid."

"Thank you. Lex took another drink of coffee while noticing the old-fashioned flip calendar on her partner's desk. "It's April, you know."

7

Gil wiped his face and advanced the calendar. "Happy now?"

"Happier. How is your better half, Ray-Ann?"

"Great. I took her to the Metropolitan Museum, and then we ate at in Spanish Harlem at Hector's El Barrio. The paella is to die for."

"The museum." Lex smiled. "Well, look at you. It's about time you started getting some culture in your life."

"Yeah, Ray-Ann has been bugging me to take her there."

Lex cradled her cup. Referring to a previous case, the murder of museum curator, Fredrike Cambourd, she said, "You know, we got the killer, but I'm still intrigued by the unsolved aspect of that case, especially the tie-in to Boston's Gardner heist. Neither the FBI nor anyone else has found those stolen paintings."

"Look at the bright side: you would have never met Stefan if it weren't for us having to visit his gallery during our investigation."

"That's true. Save my seat."

Gil nodded. "You and that ladies' room. If I had to go as much as you, I'd be in diapers."

She left the cube and reappeared minutes later. Finishing her coffee, she said, "I have a feeling something will come along to ruin our day."

Her instinct was correct. She had no sooner gotten those words out of her mouth when Captain Pressley entered the detectives' workspace. The brawny, six-feet-tall, deep-voiced, balding boss, who had commanded the detective squad for nearly a decade, was about to make their day. "Ever heard of Essex Westbrook?"

Without hesitation, Lex asked, "The author?"

"Who?" Gil looked confused.

Lex shot a glance at her partner. "You need to pick up a book every now and then. He's a best-selling mystery writer who earned the Author of the Year Award a couple of weeks ago."

"Will you two ever stop bickering?" Pressley was all business. "Listen, a call from him came in to downtown earlier. It appears his wife has disappeared."

"Kidnapped?" Lex uttered curiously.

"He has a ransom note."

"And murdered?"

"There is no evidence of that yet."

"Why involve us?" Lex asked. "We're homicide."

Pressley tapped the wall of the cube and looked through Lex's glasses into her brown pupils. "Because you're the best damned detective in Manhattan, and this could be high profile."

"Thanks. That's what we get for being so good," Gil said.

Pressley shifted his attention to Gil. "Was I talking to you? I said she's the best detective in town. Now get over there. Westbrook lives at the Grand Truman."

"Never been there," Lex said. "I know where it is, though, near Penn Station and Madison Square Garden. The last time we had a hotel case was the one at the Roosevelt, and you remember how that ended up." Lex was referring to a murder that had occurred inside a guest room. There was enough evidence to arrest the killer, but there was never a conviction.

"I remember," Pressley said. "Your boy, Rusty, managed to contaminate evidence, and it botched the case. You still haven't gotten beyond it."

Rusty Brainerd, the lead CSI examiner, blew that case on technicalities because of his sloppiness. "Damn right. He couldn't get prints from an elephant."

"Go," the captain ordered his detectives.

Downstairs, Lex said, "I'm going to pay Butterscotch a visit."

"Now?"

"Just get the car."

An attendant was mucking the enclosure as Lex entered the horse quarters. Bales of hay were stacked in one corner. She walked to the dark brown mare in an already cleaned section. The four-legged friend seemed to recognize her. "Going for a walk in the park today?" she asked the alert horse while scratching its head.

Hearing her partner beep the squad car horn multiple times, Lex got the not-so-subtle message. "Gotta go, girl. See you later."

She got into the vehicle and buckled up. Gil asked, "Just what is it with you and that horse?"

"I guess I never told you about my horse."

"Come on, you had a horse?"

"Yes. When I was a little girl, my father would take me to his cousin's farm in Litchfield, and there were horses as well as goats and chickens. I used to ride a tawny brown mare like Butterscotch. She was named Honey, and when I was eleven, the horse died. I never forgot her."

Chapter 4

The detectives were bound for the Grand Truman in an unmarked Chevy squad car. As they approached Macy's, Lex looked over at Gil. "What are you giggling at?" he asked.

"Nothing." She couldn't remember the last bloodless crime scene they had been to.

"Don't tell me, *nothing*. What gives?"

"I still can't believe how uncomfortable you get at some crime scenes. The odors, blood. With your queasy stomach, how'd you ever get through the academy?"

Gil swung toward his partner. "Funny, Lex. Who said this one is a crime scene? All we have is a missing person."

She knew he was right. "Good observation. It's not a homicide, at least not yet, unless we happen to find a dead body."

"And I hope we don't."

As their vehicle passed Madison Square Garden, Gil said, "I haven't been to a Knicks game in almost two years, not since Darryl and Dwight left for college." His twin sons were named after two former New York baseball players and had earned athletic scholarships to Florida State University. "I hope they make it. Maybe the Mets will sign them."

Lex took out her cell and called Westbrook, identifying herself. She detected nervousness in his voice. "My partner and I are on our way to your residence."

The author huffed. "Okay, but I need to tell you the elevator code."

"What did he say?" Gil asked after Lex hung up.

"The man is antsy. He gave me an elevator password to input into the lift's code box in order to travel up to his floor."

Gil pulled into the circular drive, lowered his window, and displayed his badge to a mid-twenties looking male whose shirt indicated his name was Victor. The red uniformed employee politely said, "I'll be happy to park the car for you."

Gil hesitated and Lex prodded her partner to hand over the fob, so he did.

As she and Gil walked toward the revolving front door entrance, Lex got a close view of the mostly glass structured hotel, as well as a stone bust of Harry S. Truman situated a few feet from the valet stand.

Proceeding to the hotel entrance, a similarly clad doorman stepped aside, allowing the detectives to enter the lobby through one of two wide revolving doors. The moment she was inside, Lex surveyed the space, beginning with a crystal chandelier. The white marbled floor contrasted the gold and red-striped wallpaper adorning the walls with shelled sconces lighting the room. The registration counter and concierge station were to her right. All employees wore uniforms matching the valet and doorman. A seating area was up a small flight of stairs, as was a restaurant and bar.

A concierge was standing next to a full baggage cart as the detectives approached the elevator. Stepping aside to let them into the lift, he asked, "What floor are you going to?"

"Twenty-six," Gil said. "We're here to see Mister Westbrook."

"Do you have his access code?"

Lex observed the employee's name tag. "Thank you, Cedric, I do." She entered it as instructed.

The elevator stopped on level five, and the concierge exited the lift. "Have a nice day."

The door closed, and Lex read the listings on the control panel. "Level two is where the ballrooms, meeting venues, and management are located. The spa and gym are on three."

Upon reaching the author's floor, they exited opposite the Westbrooks' suite, and Lex was surprised he opened the door as quickly as he did.

Westbrook, clad in black pants, a plain blue dress shirt, and slippers, asked them to sit on the spacious, plush couch. The man's grayish hair looked as if he'd run his hands through it several times, and he wore a grimace on his face.

The detectives introduced themselves, and the fidgeting author picked up a glass from the table next to the couch.

Before sinking into the sofa, Lex studied the open-concept floor plan. A living room adjoined the dining area with a large table, credenza, and wet bar. She assumed the hallway led to the kitchen, lavatory, and bedrooms. Taking another few moments before sitting, she noticed the prestigious award the author had received that was sitting on the mantel. She also recognized artwork hanging on the walls as paintings by Matisse and Miró and knew they were reproductions because she had seen the originals at the museum.

"We understand your wife is missing," Lex said.

Westbrook grimaced. "I don't understand it. She never returned this morning."

"I can see you are very upset," Lex said. "What happened this morning?"

Westbrook veered toward his wet bar and retrieved the ransom letter, shoving it in front of the female detective. "Read this."

She saw the inscription and showed it to Gil. "When and how did you receive this letter?" he asked.

Westbrook took a deep breath and retrieved a white envelope from the dining table. "It was inside this. It appears someone slid it under the door."

"May we have that?" Lex asked. He started to hand it to her. "Please put it back on the table. Do you have a Ziploc bag?"

"I think so. Why?"

"That envelope and letter may have prints other than yours, and I want to see if we can have them analyzed."

"Right. Of course. I'll be right back."

Westbrook retrieved a plastic zippered bag, and Lex took a pair of latex gloves from her purse and put them on, carefully placing the evidence inside. She pointed to a framed photo on a table. "Is this a recent picture of Svetlana?"

Trying to remain poised, he uttered, "Yes."

Lex silently studied Svetlana, admiring her coiffed ash-brown hair and blue eyes. Addressing the sad-faced author, she again asked, "What exactly happened this morning?"

"How do I know? She's been kidnapped."

The doorbell rang, and the author rose. Walking purposefully to open the door, he was slightly relieved when he saw his guest. "Joshua, the police are here."

The man, wearing a black suit and striped tie entered. Addressing the detectives, he said, "Hi. I'm Joshua Recker, Mister Westbrook's attorney."

"Nice to meet you," each detective said.

Recker put his briefcase down and took a seat. "What the hell happened?"

Lex said, "That's what we hope to find out."

Bewildered, Westbrook said, "I don't know. Svetlana takes walks and usually returns with coffee, but she never came back." He started to move toward the wet bar.

Recker tried to stop him. "Hold it. Come back here."

The author's uneasiness was apparent to Lex as he disregarded the attorney and refilled the glass with liquor.

She held her glasses in her hand momentarily, then put them back on before asking him to elaborate. "Please tell us everything. Start with when you woke up and realized she wasn't here."

"I'm sorry. I don't usually drink this early."

His hands began to shake as he set the drink on the table in front of the couch. Lex didn't buy that comment about not imbibing this early.

"I was up until about two a.m. last night writing and then went to bed. Svetlana goes for morning walks and always brings back coffee. When I came in here to get the paper, I spotted the envelope."

"What time was that?" Lex asked.

"Eight-thirtyish. I called her a few times and left messages, but she never called me back."

"And then you phoned police headquarters?"

"No, I called Joshua, and he advised me to report it."

"Any idea who might have sent that note?"

"No, but I know I offended a few authors with my award."

Lex swung toward the mantel. "I was aware of you being named Author of the Year."

"Thank you, but that designation came with a lot of flak."

Westbrook lashed out, "Sons of bitches. I know a couple of authors at the awards presentation felt they were slighted and deserved the award. Chandler Browning and Eldridge Gladstone. Goddamn Browning actually accused me of plagiarism."

"How well do you know them?"

"Browning, he's a pompous ass, and Gladstone thinks he's Robert Ludlum. The three of us have the same agent, Lydell Lawrence."

"How unhappy are Browning and Gladstone?" Gil asked.

Westbrook slammed his fist on the bar. "Christ's sake, they're just jealous bastards who think I didn't deserved the honor."

Lex wanted to gather more information and it was obvious Westbrook had contempt for his colleagues. "Can you think of anyone else? Any of her friends or acquaintances who might have a bone to pick, so to speak?"

"Jesus, no. I can't think of anyone who didn't like her."

"So, you haven't noticed any strange behavior, phone calls, emails?"

"Her? She doesn't even use email."

"What about you?"

"Nothing abnormal."

"Have you noticed anyone following you or Svetlana? From what you said, she walks every morning, so someone had to know that."

The beleaguered man, often reluctant to step out of his comfort zone, said, "I don't know, but I have to get the money."

A single ping sounded, and Westbrook looked at his cell.

Svetlana is safe for now. You have forty-eight hours to get the money.

"May I have your phone?" Lex asked.

He handed it to her.

"I'm curious." She checked the phone for information about the caller. "I think it's a prepaid number." She handed it back to him. "Send a reply. Say you need more time, and you must talk with Svetlana."

"Do it," Recker advised.

Westbrook heeded his attorney's advice and texted back.

I can't get the money that fast. I want to talk to Svetlana."

Lex nodded in approval.

Seconds later came a response.

Perhaps you didn't understand. Svetlana is okay for now.

She may not be after forty-eight hours has elapsed, get the money! That's it.

Wait for instructions. Don't let her die.

"They are not joking around. I have forty-eight hours. He chugged his drink, the alcohol clearly burning his throat as he exhaled, and said, "I have to get the cash."

Lex warned, "Getting the money now isn't wise."

He raised his voice. "Are you saying this is some kind of scam?"

"Hardly. That message said you had forty-eight hours, and instructions will follow. We should wait until you are contacted again. When they contact you, ask...demand to talk with Svetlana."

"Demand? They won't listen to me!"

Lex tried to take his mind off the situation. Even though she hadn't read his novels, she said, "I am a fan of yours. Your books are very good."

"Thank you. I finished my next one last evening."

"May I ask what it's called?"

"I have a couple of titles in mind. As of now it's untitled. Sweat glistened on his forehead. He hastily left the room and returned with a medium-sized, plaid suitcase, and marched toward the front door.

Lex faced Recker. "Stop him. His behavior is irrational."

Recker yelled, "No. The detectives are right. Shut the door and get back here."

Westbrook opened the door. "I haven't got time for this." Shaking his fist, he forcefully said, "Bullshit. I'm doing it now."

Recker again pleaded, "Listen to the detectives."

The incensed author stepped into the hall and pressed the elevator button.

Gil yelled, "Wait. You can't go alone. I'm coming with you."

There was nothing the attorney or Lex could do.

Recker said, "I'm going back to my office. Call if you need me."

CHAPTER 5

Lex was alone, so she took the opportunity to inspect the living quarters for signs of foul play.

An empty coffee cup sat near the computer inside the office. A bookcase contained an array of books, and next to it was a small couch. Peering out the window, she saw Penn Station, Herald Square, and a distant glimpse of Macy's.

She moved to the desk, leaned over the author's chair, and browsed files on the computer including a manuscript; in fact, she saw several items of interest. Opening his email messages, the last couple from Lydell Lawrence caught her attention. They indicated some kind of conflict between the agent and author.

Across the hallway was a spacious bedroom. Lex spotted a pink robe, presumably Svetlana's, hanging from the walk-in closet door. A wall-mounted TV was opposite the unmade king-sized bed, the remote on a dresser. On one nightstand, she noticed a diary with Svetlana's name etched into the cover. Opening it and turning to the last few pages, she saw the most recent entry was two days ago. A notation at the bottom read: *The Letter*.

The curious detective stepped into the lavatory and inspected the hamper as well as a linen closet. A large rectangular mirror hung above dual sinks and a medicine cabinet was on the adjoining wall. Studying the notorious hiding place for narcotics, she saw no evidence of drugs.

In the galley-style kitchen, she observed nothing out of the ordinary except a personalized coffee maker with Essex Westbrook's name on it.

Next to the wet bar were a few pictures sitting on the credenza. Lex recognized the one of Svetlana. Two other photos were of the Twin Towers taken before the September 11 terrorist attack. There was also a photo of the memorial with the names of victims inscribed into it. Lex saw the name Margaret Westbrook and wondered if she was possibly his sister, mother, or former spouse.

There were no scuff marks, pulls in the carpet threads, debris, or any obvious indication of foul play.

Lex thought about the ransom note and how Westbrook said it got there. She remembered the management office was on the second floor. The elevator brought her down, and she followed the arrow on a wall sign that led her to her destination.

A young woman looked up from her desk and asked, "May I help you?"

"I'm looking for the manager," Lex said.

"Clark Fullerton will be right back. I'm Betsy Halloran, the assistant manager. In the meantime, is there something I can do for you?"

Lex saw no need to explain to Betsy why she wanted to speak with Fullerton. "I'll wait if you don't mind."

"Please have a seat. And your name is?"

"I'm Lex Stall, and it's a private matter."

"I see."

A tall, mid-fiftyish man dressed in a business suit entered the reception area. Betsy said, "This lady, Miss Stall, is waiting for you."

Proceeding to his office, he said, "Come in."

Lex shut the door and took notice of the manager's workplace that was decorated with pictures of several famous New York sites including the old Lindy's, Stage Door Deli, and Radio City Music Hall. "I'm Detective Lex Stall with the NYPD." She displayed her badge. "I assume there are cameras all over the hotel."

Clark nodded. "Why are you asking? Has a crime been committed?"

"We're not sure. Svetlana Westbrook is missing."

The manager leaned forward with his hands on the desk. "What?"

"Let me explain." Lex informed Fullerton of what she knew.

"Please keep this quiet for now. We don't know who brought the envelope containing the ransom note up to the Westbrooks' suite. I'm hoping a video will show that person."

"This is unbelievable."

"If you can retrieve videos from this morning, specifically the twenty-sixth floor and the lobby, that would be very helpful. What I'm looking for might have happened between six and nine a.m."

"I'll be right back."

While waiting, the always curious detective noticed the expensive looking ebony desk and wondered how Gil and Westbrook were making out at the bank. A few minutes later, she heard footsteps, and the manager walked in.

"I have them." Fullerton held two disks in his hand, sat at his desk and inserted a video into his computer.

Lex came around to his side as they watched the twenty-sixth-floor footage. "There," Lex said when she saw Svetlana, dressed in purple sweats, leaving at 7:02 a.m. The video kept rolling and then at 7:37 a.m., she pointed at the screen. "Hold it. Who is that?"

Fullerton said, "That's Tomas, one of our valets."

"He's sliding an envelope under the door. Can you get him in here? He should be able to tell us something."

"Oh no," Fullerton said, "I hope it's not what it looks like."

"Please have him come here right now."

The manager called the valet stand and asked that Tomas come immediately to see him.

The wait for the valet seemed like an hour to the detective, but it was only nine minutes before the uniformed employee entered.

"Close the door and have a seat," Fullerton said. "This is Detective Lex Stall. She has a question or two for you."

Lex said good morning to the young man, whom she took to be in his early twenties and asked, "Did you deliver an envelope to Essex Westbrook earlier today?"

"I did. Why?"

"Where did you get the envelope, and who told you to deliver it?"

Tomas glanced at Fullerton. "I don't understand. What's wrong?"

Lex drew the valet's attention back to her. "I didn't say anything was wrong. Please tell me about the envelope. Was it yours?"

"Mine? No. A man in a limo handed it to me and asked that I deliver it to Mister Westbrook."

"A man in a limo? Explain that."

"This black limo pulled up. A guy with a beard and wearing a fedora-type hat rolled down the rear window. He said they were running late for the airport, and handed me the envelope, asking me to deliver it to Mister Westbrook. And along with the envelope, he gave me a hundred-dollar bill."

Lex was aware of the need for an elevator code. "So, you know the code in order to get up there?"

"Yes."

"How is it that you know the code?"

Fullerton commented. "A while ago, I gave it to him because he found Westbrook's keys on the ground and brought them up to him."

Lex switched back to the man in the limo. "Have you seen him before?"

"No, never."

"What about the driver?"

"I couldn't tell. The window was rolled up, and it was tinted dark."

"What time was that?"

"Around seven twenty, maybe a little later. What's this all about?"

"It's about that envelope. Why did you slide it under the door instead of handing it to Mister Westbrook?"

"I knocked, and he didn't answer. I knew Misses Westbrook had left and thought maybe he wasn't there or was still sleeping."

That answer intrigued Lex. *I didn't see him knock in the video.* She looked into the valet's eyes. "Are you sure you knocked on the door?"

"I think I did."

Her cell phone rang, and a quick glance revealed a call from Gil. "Excuse me. I have to take this."

"We just left the bank and will be back soon," her partner said.

"I'm with the hotel manager. I'll fill you in when you get back. I have to finish here." She ended the call and focused on the valet.

"Would you like to see the video? I don't think you knocked."

Tomas squinted. "Maybe I didn't. Hey, the guy gave me a hundred-dollar bill."

Continuing to keep her focus on him, she asked, "Did you observe anything unusual about Misses Westbrook this morning?"

He sat quiet for a few seconds as if he were thinking. "I don't know if this means anything, but she always goes east toward Broadway, but today she went west toward the train station."

"Are you sure?"

"Yes."

Lex excused the valet and shifted toward the manager. "We need another video. I want to look at the limo."

Fullerton retrieved the recording and again inserted the disc. Playing it, the limo came into view.

There was no clear look at the bearded man, but Lex did see him handing the envelope and money to Tomas. Then the car drove off. "The license appears to be shaded. We'll never make it out. I'd like to take these disks. Do you mind?"

Fullerton handed them to her.

"Thank you. I'm going to see Mister Westbrook. You've been very helpful. And please don't say anything to anyone at this point, including Betsy. As soon as this news gets out, the media will be all over it."

She left and waited for the elevator door to open. When it did, Gil and Westbrook were inside.

"Hey," Gil said. "Are you hitching a ride?"

They rode up to the twenty-sixth floor. After entering the residence, Lex opened her purse, taking out the disks. "This one is a video of the letter deliverer."

"Who the hell was it?" Westbrook demanded as he set his suitcase full of money beside the dining table. This is heavy."

"You better sit," Lex said. "It was Tomas."

"The valet?"

"Yes, I spoke with him." Lex explained what he'd told her. "Were you aware that Svetlana always walks east when she leaves here?"

"No."

"Well, according to Tomas, she does. But for some reason this morning, she went west." Lex held the disks. "One shows Tomas delivering the envelope. Another shows the limo and the man who gave it to him."

Lex surmised whoever was behind this apparent kidnapping knew Svetlana's habits and somehow lured her into going a different direction, but who and how? Had she gotten a call or message to be somewhere at a given time? "You're aware Svetlana kept a diary, aren't you?"

"What? You snooped in our bedroom?"

Lex nodded. "I'm sorry, but I was looking for any clue that might tell us what happened. Yes, I read a couple of pages and noticed she skipped yesterday. Is that normal?"

"How the hell would I know? That's her private journal."

Lex conceded, "That's true. The last thing she wrote was 'The Letter.' Does that mean anything to you?"

"Hell, no."

Lex dropped the diary talk. The observant detective took a gander at framed pictures on the credenza. "I saw those 9/11 photos."

Westbrook bowed his head and pointed to the photo of a woman about his age. "Worst day ever. That's Margaret, my first wife. She was on the twenty-second floor of the north building."

"You have my condolences," Gil said.

"I'm so sorry," Lex added. Having seen the bothersome emails, she had one more thing to ask Westbrook. "I apologize, but I also saw a couple of messages on your computer between you and your agent. You two appear to be having some kind of conflict."

"You got that right. I'm firing him. He stole money from me. I need a drink."

"I see. Is there anything else you can tell us?"

He stood at the wet bar and poured liquor into a tumbler. As soon as sat, Lex stared at him and asked, "Does Svetlana have family?"

"Not really. She came from Russia after her father passed, and her mother has remained there. No siblings."

"What about your personal lives? Your marriage, friends, affairs, or arguments?"

The tone of his voice let Lex know he resented that query. "I know what you're asking, and I know it is none of your business. I suggest you leave now."

"Don't be so hostile!"

"Look. I'm tired and in no mood to answer more questions."

"Have it your way." Lex made sure he saw her card on the table. "We'll check back early tomorrow morning, but if you are contacted before then, call the precinct."

"I'll be awake all day and night." He raised his glass. "Me and Johnnie Walker will be okay."

The detectives left him to his friend and Gil asked Lex, "Did you find anything?"

"No. And I didn't see anything that would suggest foul play. No signs of narcotic abuse…the only substance addiction appears to be his alcohol consumption."

Once they were back in the hotel's lobby and exited through the revolving doors, Lex saw Victor who was standing at the valet stand. When she and Gil approached hm, Lex asked, "Where is Tomas?"

"He'll be right back." The valet made the detectives aware of the young couple standing to the right of the entrance. "He's getting their vehicle."

"Did you see Svetlana Westbrook this morning?"

"No, ma'am."

"What time did you get here?"

"Tomas was already here. I showed up at nine."

Tomas exited the garage, slowly driving a Lexus. After getting out, he opened the doors for the apparent newlyweds. "Have good day," he said.

Lex watched Tomas but remained quiet as Victor retrieved the squad car, and the detectives left the Grand Truman.

Chapter 6

The Buick Gil owned remained in the driveway of his Queen's home. While he was on the job, he preferred riding the train to and from the precinct.

Lex, on the other hand, was not a fan of crowded subway cars, so her five-year-old Corolla provided her transportation. Avoiding rude drivers, buses, and pedestrians, who seemed to enjoy the challenge of crossing streets by not utilizing crosswalks and daring vehicles to move out of their way, forced her to be alert all the way to and from the precinct.

Her return to Waverly Place at times was frustrating. Although windshield stickers and signs reserved parking spaces for residents, it didn't mean people always obeyed the rules.

There was an open spot a few doors down, in front of the house that had belonged to her alcoholic neighbor. A year had passed since Sheila, a friend and a woman who many times stayed with Liz when Lex had to leave at an odd hour committed suicide. "Rest in peace," Lex said.

She walked up the five steps to her front door, found the mailbox to be void, and proceeded inside. Her adopted cat, once named Van Gogh, greeted her. Realizing the pet was female, she and Liz renamed her Cassatt. The feline followed Lex into the kitchen where Liz had stacked the mail. Not seeing her nearly seventeen-year-old daughter, the mother yelled, "Liz, are you upstairs?"

"I'll be right down."

The young girl who was the spitting image of her mother, entered the room. "Can we go to John's?"

"Pizza? Not tonight. I don't mind going to Bleecker, but let's get something lighter."

Lex reminded her daughter she had scored 1490 on her SAT exam. "We need to start thinking about college choices."

"I know. Shannon did almost as well, and she's thinking about Rutgers or Penn State."

"Have you thought about any schools?"

"Not really, maybe Yale."

"Did you feed Cassatt?"

"Nope. I'll do it, and then can we go?"

Lex picked up the mail, the usual pile of bills and unwanted ads. One envelope looked to be her monthly child support payment from her ex, Jon. She left it unopened on the table. "I'm going up to change."

After putting on casual clothes, she placed her gun into a dresser drawer and was ready to dine out. While walking to a village café, Liz said, "I know we're going to the record shop after we eat."

Lex grasped the girl's hand. The old store, once her deceased father's, she couldn't forget. "I'm glad you understand my visits. It was hard to tell you things you might not have wanted to hear about your grandparents and me, but you had to be told."

"I know, Mom."

The hard-to-explain truth was that Lex had been raped as a teenager by a classmate and didn't tell anyone except her parents. Her mother never understood, blamed her daughter, and grew distant. It was Lex's father who nurtured her, and they still communicated with each other in a surreal way.

When he died a decade ago, an employee purchased the business and until recently, it was still operating. Although forty-five rpm vinyl records were not to be seen, albums had begun to come back in vogue. The shop was now sadly vacant, but Lex still felt a magnetic urge to stop, gaze into the window, and have a chat with her father.

After dining at a local café, Lex and Liz walked to the empty windowed shop. Lex stood in front and exchanged words with her deceased father. *"Dad, I hope you're not as sad as I am. The old store is no longer open.*

As usual, she heard his voice. *Yes, I know, dear. I knew it couldn't last forever, just as I couldn't. It's okay.*

I still miss you, Dad. Liz and I are fine.

Turning to face her daughter, Lex said, "We can still make *Jeopardy*."

"Mom," Liz said, "I have something to tell you. I'm happy you are dating."

"Thank you, sweetheart. It's taken a while. Stefan and I enjoy each other's company, though I don't know what the future will bring."

Once the women were home, Liz hit the TV remote to watch *Jeopardy*, while Lex opened the envelope she had left on the table. Her divorce and subsequent custody battle with her ex left the two at bitter odds.

Expecting payment, she read the enclosed note.

Lex, I hope you understand. I'm a little behind right now. Julie's funeral cost was steep, as you can imagine. I'll make it up to you, but I can't afford the $700 right now. Please don't pursue legal action or keep Liz from me.

Lex sighed. Cancer had taken Jon's second wife, Julie, in a matter of months, leaving him solely to raise Adam, Liz's five-year-old half-brother. The understanding, sympathetic ex-wife and mother folded the note and put it in her purse. Bitterness aside, she went into the den to watch *Jeopardy* with her daughter. Liz correctly guessed the final answer, unlike any of the contestants and Lex said, "You should try out for the show."

Liz laughed. "I don't think so. Not me. Dream on, Mom. I'm going upstairs."

A pinging on Lex's phone indicated Stefan was calling. "Hi," she said.

"How are you?"

Lex smiled. "Fine. I'm still thinking about the musical and how much I enjoyed it."

"I did too. And I loved serving you breakfast in bed."

"Uh-huh, so that's why you took me to see the Phantom...just to get me into bed?"

There was a moment of silence before Stefan answered. "You are the detective, and you can take me to jail any time. Besides, I didn't hear any complaints."

"I guess it's too late now, but the bacon could have been crispier."

Stefan laughed. "Okay, so my cooking needs improvement." He paused. "Listen, today I took in a new artist, and I'd like to do a showing. I'd love for you to attend."

Lex flashed back to a little over a year ago when she stepped into the Stefan Martine Art Gallery where the suave owner seemed to have an attraction to her from the start. A few weeks later, Stefan invited Lex as his date to an artist showcase, and she accepted his ask. "I don't see why not."

"When can I see you again?"

"What did you have in mind?"

"Dinner at Mastrangelo's."

"That sounds nice."

"Saturday night."

Lex hesitated. "Can we make it the following Saturday? I want to spend this weekend with Liz."

"Understood."

The call ended, and Lex had a notion to call Jon, but she put the cell down, picked up a pen and notepad, and wrote to her ex.

Jon, I feel for your loss and promise to allow you to get through this rough time. Don't worry about the support for now. Liz loves you and Adam very much, and I won't say anything about this to her. With respect, Lex

GRETA'S GONE

Tucker Rutledge, one of the wealthiest men in Westport, Connecticut, liked to drive around town in his silver Maserati Gran Turismo; his wasn't the only one in the neighborhood, but the *TUCKIT* license plate was unmistakable.

Never the best-dressed man, with his rugged appearance, he appeared to be more suited to a Chevy pickup. Tucker failed to complete high school, and never held down a meaningful job. His Swedish mother left his father years ago and severed contact with them after moving back to Stockholm. Despite his history, money wasn't an issue. Hence the car.

Greta, his trophy wife, shared their fenced estate by Long Island Sound. A year ago, it belonged to Tucker's father, Trenton. The patriarch's hedge fund business was prospering, but a Cessna accident took the man's life. The deed was recently legally transferred to Tucker.

Ironically, Tucker and Greta weren't far away when the crash occurred. Having completed his forty hours of flight training in that very aircraft, Tucker was driving to pick up his pilot certificate from his instructor, but the Cessna he had learned to fly was gone.

An investigation into the crash determined the ailerons had been in the wrong position, causing the mishap. Tucker accused the local airport mechanic, Eddie Franco, of sabotaging the airplane. Police Chief Harrison Weiss investigated the accident but couldn't substantiate Tucker's allegation.

Tucker had Greta, the estate, fancy cars, money, and a buddy named Sal. Dogs, cats, really any type of pets were taboo. His vice was cocaine.

His long hair and goatee were trimmed every week at the local barbershop. He preferred that place rather than the stylish, upscale unisex salon across the street. Instead of shelling out upward of eighty dollars, he gave his hair trimmer twenty-five but routinely handing the mostly bald barber an extra fifty. Tucker was that way...cheap but rich.

The one thing that annoyed him was the attention Greta received from males. Tucker couldn't help but notice and wished he could take a gun to every drooling, horny guy's balls.

He also knew deep down that Greta was only with him because of the money. If she left him, she would take a huge settlement with her. There was no prenuptial.

One April night, they made love and went to sleep satisfied. The next morning, Greta left in her jogging clothes at 6:10, the sun beginning to rise over Long Island Sound. She veered off the main path onto a narrow dirt trail. That was her biggest mistake.

That's when Tucker's nightmare began.

He had just gotten out of the shower. The sound of a text echoed from his cell phone resting on the bathroom counter. It was 7:10 a.m. He read the message in disbelief.

We have your wife. $100,000 will get her back. Instructions to follow.

CHAPTER 7

Lex loved her job and despite Hutch's unnecessary digs, she liked the detective most of the time.

Toting her coffee and walking toward her cube, she heard his familiar voice. "I bet your boyfriend loves the perfume."

She didn't respond to the Cinnabar comment. "That reminds me: this coffee is expensive. I need to ask for a raise. By the way, you look like you're down a few pounds."

"Only five, but it's a start." Hutch pointed to his young, in-shape partner. "It's his fault. And as of today, there are no more doughnuts in here."

She nodded at Benzinger. "Good job."

The junior detective added, "I don't think Gil is a happy camper."

"In case you haven't noticed, he's always an unhappy camper."

Benzinger added, "You should have seen him when Pressley told him about the doughnuts. I thought he was going to shoot the captain."

"Well, I'm glad I wasn't the one to tell him." She paused. "Is anything happening with the park killing?"

Most crimes in Central Park were purse snatchings, tourist robberies, and muggings. Fights sometimes broke out where combatants had to be contained in the small lockup downstairs that was usually occupied by drunks.

However, the public space was not immune to killings. Six days ago, two men snatched the purse of a young college student as darkness set in. She apparently resisted and was struck by one of the thugs before they ran off with their take. Gwyneth Lancaster, a student at Fordham University and from Warwick, Rhode Island, died when she fell on the stone steps at one of the park's entrances.

Benzinger said, "All we have is what witnesses told us and fingerprints on the strap of the stolen purse. They could be hers or one of theirs or both. There are also footprints, looks like sneakers, sizes ten and eleven. I'm hoping a video shows up."

"Good luck." Lex continued to her cubicle and set her drink on her desk.

Moping, Gil said. "I heard. They told you about the morning snacks."

She sat, took a sip of coffee, and grinned. "I think you will survive."

Pressley wandered into their workspace. "Have you tagged the envelope and letter yet?"

Gil retrieved the baggie with the items inside. "They will be marked for evidence, and we'll get them down to Police Plaza. "

"Prints are probably not going to be obtained," Lex commented. "It's a self-sealing envelope and doesn't appear to have been licked. Since it was delivered by hand, there's no stamp. I'd be shocked if any prints other than the valet's and Westbrook's were on it. We have no idea who is demanding the ransom, and we have no assurance that Svetlana is alive."

Pressley nodded. "You realize, at this point, Svetlana isn't even considered a missing person."

"Technically, that's true." Lex moved to the squad room.

"Here she goes again," Gil said. "What pearls of wisdom will she come back with?"

A few minutes later, she was back and sat. "I'm more than curious. Why did Svetlana walk in the opposite direction? Was she instructed to do so? Was she meeting someone? How many people are involved in the kidnapping?" Lex's lips pressed together, producing a slight frown. "It's possible she might have known her kidnapper. That leads to the next question: was she really taken by force?"

Pressley crossed his arms. "We don't know, but we can't send out red flags until we find out what they are planning."

Gil said, "The media will be all over this when the word gets out."

"True, we need to keep the chief informed with what's happening before this story leaks."

Pressley retreated to answer his ringing desk phone, and Lex saw the surprised look on his face as he spoke. Excitedly, he waved to his crew to join him. He sat back in his chair and announced, "You won't believe this, but I was just told something that should make you all happy." He waited a moment. "We're staying here."

"What did you say?" Lex smiled.

"I said we're staying here. The renovations at the nineteenth are done, but they decided to move the Major Crime Unit in there, so you and Butterscotch can continue your love affair."

"Any chance I can transfer to the horse patrol?" Lex jokingly asked.

Pressley pointed to her partner and pivoted toward Gil. "I suggest from now on you call him Mister Ed."

Lex ribbed, "Sorry, you're not as handsome as Mister Ed, but I guess I'm stuck with you."

Leaving their boss, Gil said, "Thanks, Lex. But I do have one thing that old horse also has." He didn't complete his sentence.

"And just what is that?"

He grinned at her. "A nag for a partner."

Lex flirtatiously winked at him. "I'm going to the ladies room."

"It's all yours. You're the only one who uses it."

"Start thinking. All we have, as of now, is a missing person. The only other people who know anything are the hotel manager, Recker, and the valet, so the news could get out soon. Call Westbrook while I visit my place of solace."

"I'll wait until you return so I can put him on speaker."

"Fine."

As soon as she got back to their cube, Gil made the call and Westbrook answered on the third ring. "I was about to call you."

Lex heard his tense, almost hyperactive voice. "I got a package a little while ago."

"What kind of package?" Gil asked.

"I found it at my door. Come take a look. There's a note too. Please get over here."

"What is in the package?" Lex asked.

"Bags, leather bags. Satchel-like. You need to see for yourself."

Gil said, "Lex and I will be at your suite in about twenty minutes or so."

Realizing they had to get the Ziplock bag with the envelope and letter downtown, Lex picked it up and said, "Westbrook needs us."

Gil suggested, "What about having Benzinger take it?"

"Good thinking." Lex took the evidence and approached Pressley. "We're going to Westbrook's now. How about having Benzinger take this Ziplock downtown?"

Pressley agreed. "I'll get him on it. You keep me in the loop."

CHAPTER 8

Exiting the elevator on the twenty-sixth floor, the detectives took a few steps toward Westbrook's suite, and Lex noticed a cart in the hallway that was moving toward a unit down the corridor. The woman steering it was dressed in a loose white outfit appeared to be a cleaning lady. The hotel employee stopped and looked back when Lex caught her attention. "Excuse me," the curious detective shouted.

"Yes?"

Lex approached her and asked, "Did you just clean the Westbrooks' suite?"

"Not today, ma'am. Mister Westbrook gave me the laundry bag and said to move on."

Lex noted the name on the uniform. "Addie, how often are you here?"

"Every Tuesday. I need to move on to the Kimballs."

"Just another minute and I won't bother you. I take it you have keys or a master key to all of these units?"

"Yes. ma'am. They go back to Mr. Fullerton when I'm done."

"Thank you," Lex said.

The detectives neared Westbrook's. "You don't think she had anything to do with the kidnapping do you?" Gil asked.

"I seriously doubt that."

Gil knocked on the author's door and when Westbrook opened it, his cell phone was to his ear. "You can't be serious. You knew I was severing our relationship."

Lex listened and watched him carefully.

"Really? You can't do that. I'm in control now." A minute later, Westbrook shouted, "Go to hell!" He closed the phone, wiped his brow, and took a deep breath as he inched closer to his liquor stash.

"Was that your agent?" Lex asked.

He poured himself a drink. "Yes, Lydell Lawrence. I should say...my soon-to-be former agent. Contract, my ass." The author went to the dining table and pointed to the delivered box.

Gil moved to the carton and removed the contents. "It's a satchel alright."

Lex saw the black Naugahyde bag with an over-the-shoulder strap. "I know what it's for. The money." She read the enclosed note. *$100 bills. Fill the bag and wait for instructions.*

The author chugged his scotch and raised his already agitated voice. "They better contact me soon."

At that moment, Westbrook's phone beeped, and he looked at the text message. "They know you're here, and they want more money."

Lex and Gil each read the text.

Cops, you got cops.

Not a good move.

Cops just cost you another $100 grand. You have until the end of today to get the money.

Instructions will come later.

"Oh shit," Gil said.

"They have spies watching us who could be from inside the hotel or outside." Lex instructed Westbrook, "Send them back a message. Tell them if they want the money, the cops stay, and you need to talk to Svetlana."

"But they'll kill her."

Lex had no idea if what she was about to say was true, but she had to calm him down. "I think not. If they want to get paid, they will not harm her."

Westbrook spoke as he texted: *I must see Svetlana.*

Seconds later, he got an answer and showed the orders to Lex.

Get the money, fill the bag, and then you can see her.

Otherwise, she will be dead.

Tomorrow at noon, her alarm will sound, and then the clock will run out.

Lex saw the scariest part of the message.

Don't let her die.

She noted this message had come from a different number than the previous one. "It's another phone. Now I know they're using prepaids. No two messages will come from the same one."

Fearing the worst, he reiterated, "They're going to kill her. I know they will."

"Please sit, at least for a moment," Lex suggested. "What about the gym? Does Svetlana utilize it?"

"She's a walker. Once in a while, she goes there when it's cold out. It's mostly for guests anyhow."

"Did she act any differently in the past few days?"

"Not that I'm aware of."

Lex squinted. "What exactly do you mean? She either did, or she didn't."

"I said no."

That's not what he previously answered, but Lex continued, "And she never mentioned her diary and that note about a letter?"

"Again, I don't know anything about it."

Gil rubbed his chin. "We want to talk to the neighbors."

"They have nothing to do with this. The old couple, Benton and Claudia Kimball, are retired. He owned a travel agency. They're okay. Anderson Flanagan is a Wall Street trader. He's hardly around."

Lex saw the fidgeting author grow more impatient as he peered toward the suitcase.

"Are we done? I'm going to my bank." He rose, went to the bedroom, retrieved Svetlana's suitcase, and broke for the door.

"Please don't go," Lex pleaded.

"It's my problem. Not yours."

That irrational comment made Gil stand. "Damn it! Wait for me."

Lex watched them leave and then attempted to query the neighbors. However, when there was no answer to the ringing doorbells, she surmised neither were home.

Almost an hour later, Westbrook and Gil returned with another hundred grand. "Done," Westbrook said. "I need a drink."

Lex politely held up her hand. "Please. I'd appreciate it if you could refrain from the alcohol for now."

He huffed. "Okay, but I need to tell them I have the money."

"Fine," Lex said. "But again, insist on seeing and talking to Svetlana."

Westbrook initiated the text and appeased Lex by reading it aloud. "I have the extra cash. Your turn. Now I need to see and speak with Svetlana before you get the money."

Seconds later, a message alert sounded. "They've written back. Oh no! The picture they sent is quite disturbing!"

Lex and Gil looked over his shoulder at the message and photo.

Congratulations. Now wait until tomorrow and get rid of the cops.

Westbrook enlarged the picture of the tired Svetlana. When he moved the focus to the long arm with a gun pointed at her, his body cringed. He handed his phone to Lex and marched toward the liquor stash. "You have to go. They want you out."

Both detectives saw the photograph. Lex whispered to Gil, "I believe there may be bugs here."

Westbrook asked, "What are you discussing?"

Lex said. "Mister Westbrook, Please stay in the kitchen for a few minutes."

"Why?"

"Just do it."

When he was out of the living space, Gil moved toward a lamp on the wet bar and inspected it. He shook his head sideways indicating to Lex that this lamp was clean."

"I have something, " she softly said. "Take a look at this."

Gil stood next to her at an end table beside the couch. In a low voice she said, "Under this lampshade."

"Clever," he whispered. "These things are so small."

The curious Westbrook didn't stay out of their way long. "What are you doing?"

Lex pointed to the lamp and stood next to him, speaking into his ear. "They can hear us. I'm sure there are other listening devices planted here."

Curiously, Lex walked into the office and saw a table lamp. This one too was bugged. Rejoining Gil and Westbrook, she confirmed her suspicion.

Westbrook bowed his head. "Damn it, what a fucking mess." The troubled author yelled, "Forget it. I should just hand the cash over and be done with it. I may be sorry I ever called the police station."

Knowing they were not alone, Lex said loud enough for the kidnappers to hear, "Look, I know they want us gone. Is that what you want as well?"

"Yes, leave me alone. I'll handle this."

Lex pretending to be angry, raised her voice. "Listen, you can do whatever you want. If you'd like us to back off and never come back, that's your choice."

"And I'll do what the hell I want to do. Get out!"

Lex walked toward the door with Gil and said, "One last time: if that's what you really want, then we're gone. Don't call us if you decide to cry wolf."

The detectives left and Gil asked, "Are you serious about backing off?"

"Not at all. I want the kidnappers to believe we don't care and aren't coming back."

"So, what's your plan?"

Lex was quiet for a few seconds. "As of right now, I don't have one, but we will have to get his place debugged."

CHAPTER 9

Lex pondered what the detectives next step would be and came up with a plan to discuss with Gil and Westbrook.

Her workspace was barren when she walked into the squad room, and she heard her beloved comrade. "Morning," Hutch said. "I like the hair. Always had a thing for ponytails."

Glancing at him while winking, she said, "Thanks."

"I see Gil hasn't shown up yet."

"He's at Queens Medical Center."

Lex uttered, "He's where?" She saw Pressley eyeing her.

"Come in," he called out.

"What the hell happened?"

"Your bumbling partner was walking his dog this morning, and they had a run-in with another dog. He pulled his hand back and got bitten by the pug. Gil has a cut with teeth marks and is waiting to get checked out. He said the ER is crowded, and it may take a while for him to be seen." Pressley pointed at Lex. "Looks like you're it today."

She sighed. "And that's why I have a cat. It poops in the litter box and doesn't have to be walked in all kinds of weather."

"Sit down," Pressley said. "What's new with Westbrook?"

"He's a mess. The kidnapers want us out and so does he, so we agreed to leave him alone and whatever happens, happens."

Surprised, Pressley said, you what?"

Lex frowned. "I had to. The place is bugged, and I want the kidnappers to think we bowed out. I have to contact Westbrook before he does anything stupid."

39

Pressley leaned forward. "How the hell are you going to do that without the kidnappers knowing?"

Her mind was in motion. "I can call the hotel manager, Clark Fullerton, and have him ask Westbrook to come downstairs. Then Westbrook can call me using the manager's phone so we can talk."

"That sounds like it could work."

"It has to be done."

"Go for it."

She went to her desk and before contacting Fullerton, she called Gil. "Nice going," she said.

"Hey. Sorry. Pugs can be aggressive. At least my dog is okay."

"Are you going to live?"

"Funny, Lex. I'm still waiting. This emergency room is like a bakery, and my number hasn't been called yet. Ray-Ann stopped the bleeding, most of it. My hand is bandaged. It stings a little, and I hope I don't need stitches. I'm guessing I'll get a rabies shot."

Lex heard waiting room chatter in the background. "I know you spoke with Pressley and told him about us staying away from Westbrook."

"It's hard to hear but go ahead. Have you thought of anything?"

"Yes."

"Hold on a second. I'm going to a less congested area." He stood against a wall in the corner. "What are you planning?"

Lex shared what she had in mind.

"I have to go; my number was called."

Lex, still holding her cell, was ready to put her strategy in motion, and she phoned the hotel manager. "Good morning, Detective."

"Good morning. I have a favor to ask. I'd like you to get Essex Westbrook into your office immediately. When he gets there, call me back. It's urgent that he and I speak."

"I don't understand. Why not call him yourself?"

"It's complicated. I have a good reason and will let you know after he is there. Do not mention me."

"Okay. What shall I tell him?"

Lex without hesitating said, "Tell him a mail carrier is waiting for him with a letter from the IRS that he has to sign for. It has an urgent sticker."

"That sounds hokey, but I'll do it."

"Phone me as soon as he gets there."

Lex paced the squad room for ten minutes before sitting at her desk. Her patience was growing thin. *Where is he?*

Another five minutes elapsed until her cell beeped. "Hi," she said.

"Detective, Mister Westbrook is with me."

"Put him on."

Westbrook took the phone. "What's this about?" he asked. "There's no mailman and furthermore, there's no letter from the IRS."

"Listen, I wanted to get you away from your place. The fact is we are not going away, but I don't want the kidnappers to know it. Have they contacted you again?"

"Not yet."

"Don't do what you said. Hold onto the money."

"Why should I listen to you?"

Lex huffed. "Because I am going to get Svetlana back."

Begrudgingly, he agreed to her demand.

"After you are contacted, call me but not from inside your suite. Step into the elevator and then dial my number. Hopefully, they will give you a drop site."

"Elevator? Do you know how bad the reception is there?"

"True. Go into the hallway to call me. Text if you have to."

"But how can I be sure Svetlana will be safe?"

"Trust me, they want the money, not her."

"I have to get back upstairs."

"Put Fullerton back on." The manager identified himself again. Westbrook left. "Sir, you heard part of the conversation." She explained the rest to him.

⚊

He paced his living room, holding a glass of liquor. It was nearing noon, and his nerves were fraying as he tried to make sense of it all. He looked down at the street from his window, unable to hear the noises. The always bustling city traffic and pedestrians silently packed the roads and sidewalks. In an effort to take his mind off his wife, the distraught author walked to his den, opened the laptop and brought up his new novel, still a work in process.

Self-editing was always a chore, a necessary task and he began to make changes to chapter one. Twenty pages into the story, it was nearing two p.m. He saved the material before stepping away and browsing the bookcase. *Greta's Gone* stared back at him, and he imagined Tucker Rutledge for a few seconds, ruing the day he created the couple.

The author still hadn't received a message, but he knew he couldn't call the detective from inside, so he stepped into the hallway to phone her. "Detective, I still haven't heard anything. What should I do?"

"Where are you?"

"In the hallway. I'm a little edgy."

"I'm guessing they may contact you later, maybe this evening. I think they want to make sure you haven't been in touch with us. I hope you haven't blown our cover."

"This is killing me. What if they want the money tonight?"

"Call me immediately if they do."

The day ended without any word from the kidnappers.

GRETA'S GONE

Greta Rutledge started her morning by downing an energy drink. She wore exercise clothes and a headband. In the dawn light, she trotted the peaceful path and picked up her pace. Halfway into the jog and without warning, two people quickly accosted her, covered her eyes, and bound her mouth shut. She did not see her attackers. They carried her to a waiting vehicle while she tried to wiggle free. Greta was swiftly shoved into the car's back seat. One person drove; the other sat beside her and tied her hands and feet so they couldn't move.

Hearing other vehicles, she knew they had gotten onto the interstate. The getaway car kept rolling. Scared and dazed, she mumbled.

"Shut up," a male voice said.

She again mumbled and began to fidget, trying to free her hands.

"You're a feisty one," he said. "Shut up. You're not breaking free. We'll be there soon."

Twenty minutes later, she was extracted from the vehicle and escorted inside. The kidnappers unmasked her and removed the tape from her mouth. The natural log walls communicated they were in a cabin. "Who the hell are you?" she asked. "What's this all about?"

The female kidnapper said, "You'll find out soon."

"I have to go to the bathroom."

"Come with me," the female accomplice said. "I'll untie your hands, and then you'll be a little more comfortable."

Greta was shaking as she went to the lavatory. The view out the window revealed nothing but trees and sky. Coming out of the bathroom, she asked, "Where are we? What's happening?"

The male started to retie her hands. "Hold it," he said. "These jogging clothes need to go, and she's still sweaty."

"She is," the accomplice said. "I have a few things she can wear, but first I'll get her into the shower."

"What do you want?" Greta asked.

"Just take off those clothes, and you can take a shower."

She hesitated.

"Now," demanded the male as he pointed a gun at her for the first time.

Greta began undressing. When she was naked, she was escorted to the shower.

"Nice tits," he said. "Ass too."

"Shut up," the woman said. Greta noticed wedding bands and guessed they were married.

After showering and changing into the clothes provided, Greta, her head spinning and confused, asked, "Why am I here? What do you want?"

"As I said, you'll find out soon enough. And in case you're wondering, there aren't any neighbors within a mile," the male said.

Chapter 10

Lex gave Gil a smirk when she saw him sitting at his desk and facing her. "I knew you were going to the dogs."

"Good thing it wasn't a boxer, or I might have had a black eye."

"You look fine to me," she said.

"I'm okay. It could have been worse. Where's my doughnut?"

"Sorry about that but I'm kind of on the wagon too. I'm trying to cut back on Starbucks."

Pressley, standing nearby, asked Gil, "How's the hand feel?"

"A bit achy. I took some Motrin. It could have been worse."

"Your partner will take good care of you."

Lex broke into a small laugh. "Sure, I will."

As Pressley walked away, Gil asked Lex, "Any word from Westbrook?"

"Not yet."

"He does understand we are still with him, right?"

"Yes, but I'm not sure I trust him, and I can't call him." She pointed to a printout on her desk. "That's the lab report on the envelope and letter. As I suspected, the envelope shows prints from Tomas and Westbrook only. And Westbrook's were the only ones on the letter."

"Par for the course."

Lex resorted to her habit and began walking around the squad room. *The money drop can't be far, and it may be a public area. Maybe a bar or restaurant. Penn Station is nearby. Then again, it could be anywhere....*

Returning to Gil, she said, "I'm betting the drop site will be a

45

public area, right out in the open. They're brazen, and I think they want to rub our faces in it. Regardless of what he's been told, I think they know we haven't disappeared. And the ruse about backing off and having Westbrook contact me from the hallway is probably of no value. I'm betting they contact him soon."

"What if they don't? Or what if they do? He could pay them, and we could have a crazed author."

⚔

Westbrook had nightmares about the kidnapping and sulked. Finally, the nervous author received the message he'd been waiting for.

Shove the money inside the satchel and go to Washington Square Park.

Sit on a bench on the opposite side of the arch and water fountain.

At 3:00, you will get another message.

He frantically typed his response. *When will you free Svetlana?*

The reply: *After we've counted the money, she will be set free.. DO NOT BE LATE!*

Westbrook texted. *I got rid of the cops.*

The author stared at the Naugahyde bag and started to call the female detective. He quickly put the phone back in his pocket before stepping into the hallway.

"I've got the satchel filled with money," he said when she answered her phone. "They instructed me to go to Washington Square and sit on a bench opposite the arch. Three o'clock sharp. I told them I got rid of you."

"Good. Do exactly what I tell you." Lex detailed the next step.

"You have to be kidding," he said. "How do I do that?"

"Carefully. Look, Washington Square is my neighborhood. Go to the park and don't look for us. We'll be there to observe the area and you."

"Who else will be there?"

Lex knew he would not like her answer. "Us as well as the usual park patrollers. Go back inside and wait before taking a cab. Be there early."

Inside his residence, he stared at Svetlana's picture. The clock next to her photo ticked while he followed the detective's suggestion, waiting impatiently until it was time to leave.

▲

Pressley invited Gil and Lex into his office. She said, "My hunch was correct. The drop site is Washington Square."

"A busy park," Gil said.

"Yes, it will be a hornet's nest. We'll be looking for the queen bee, but I still don't like it. Why there and why mid-afternoon? It doesn't make sense."

"It never does." Pressley strongly urged the detectives to enlist help. "I think we should plant some yellow jackets there."

"No," Lex said. "A special squad will clear the park and scare them off. I told Westbrook uniformed police are always there, and I don't want the square to appear any more guarded than usual." She reiterated, "I still don't feel right about this. They are smart, and I believe they know we will be there. Will the pickup person be armed? Will he or she be on a bike? A motorcycle? Will it be a jogger? They know those choices would be too risky. Something is off."

▲

Westbrook was fighting the temptation to visit the enticing wet bar when his phone rang. It was Joshua Recker. "What's going on?" the lawyer asked. "Anything happening?"

"Josh, I'm a wreck. They want me to hand over the money this afternoon."

"Where?"

"I need to be at Washington Square at three."

"What about Svetlana?"

"They said they will let her go after counting the cash."

"What about the detectives?"

"They'll be there, and so will the usual police patrol."

"Anything I can do?"

"I guess not. I'll let you know after the exchange is made."

"Okay. I have to be in court anyway. I'll talk to you later."

As soon as the author ended the call, he thought better of his craving and retreated to the couch without booze.

The clock kept ticking. At 1:45 p.m., making sure he would be early, he picked up the satchel and flung the strap over his shoulder. He stood at the elevator and as the door opened, he heard, "Wait for us." The voice belonged to his neighbor, Benton Kimball. The seventy-nine-year-old retiree and his wife, Claudia, approached the car. The elderly couple walked slowly, and Westbrook waited as patiently as he could. *Don't be late,* he kept hearing. Finally, after what seemed like an hour, but in reality was about thirty seconds, the Kimballs got in.

"It looks like you're bound for a ranch," Benton said, referring to the satchel hanging over the author's shoulder.

"It's just a new carry bag."

The lift started down and stopped three times to pick up guests before arriving at the lobby. He hastily exited, and said to his neighbors, "Have a nice day."

The shaking author approached the concierge. "Nice bag," Cedric said. "Are you alright?"

"I'm fine. Please get a cab for me."

With the satchel on his shoulder, he reached into his pocket and handed Cedric a ten-dollar bill.

"Thank you, sir. Go outside. Your ride will be here in a minute or two."

He waited and while peering down the driveway, he began to sweat. Two minutes later, a yellow vehicle stopped, and Victor opened the rear door for the passenger to get in. The author instructed the driver to take him to Washington Square.

The taxi left the hotel and went up 5th Avenue. Midway there, the passenger saw visions of his imaginary character, Tucker Rutledge. He drifted into the world he had created. *What are you waiting for Tucker? Hand over the damned money!*

Nearing the square, the driver said, "Almost there."

Westbrook snapped back to reality and grabbed the Naugahyde case. Exiting the cab, he paid the driver and toted the satchel across his body. The park was bustling as usual with tourists, neighborhood people, strollers, dogs on leashes, children, a couple with stringed balloons, and picture takers. A policeman was patrolling the area on foot.

Paranoia set in while walking around the circular fountain. The unsteady author was sure he was being followed. Sitting in the warm sunlight on an unoccupied bench made him feel uncomfortable, and a wrenching chill zipped through his body.

He looked at his watch. The 'don't be late' threat was no longer in play. He tried to remain calm by casually observing the sea of humans to his right and left. He also saw the commonplace flocks of pigeons wandering the grounds, as well as the homeless-looking man famous for having a strange relationship with these birds. Somehow he always had popcorn or something else to feed the scavengers.

Westbrook saw a few children in the play area and the fenced in dog park, which was alive with hounds. It seemed like a normal day as nothing appeared to be out of the ordinary.

▲

Lex and Gil stepped within the park limits and casually strolled around the fountain, pretending to be tourists. "He's on a bench. I see him," Lex said.

Gil spotted the author. "He's looking around."

The bright sun bothered her eyes, so she switched to sunglasses. They casually passed in front of the kidnappers prey, and Lex knew Westbrook had seen them. "All we have to do is wait. It's quarter to three now. It should happen soon," she said.

Gil flexed his injured hand. "What do you think?"

"I think I still don't like it. It's way too crowded. Something's not right. I can feel it in my bones. A biker? A pedestrian? A gang of kids? An armed gunman? None of that makes sense."

CHAPTER 11

The detectives stood near a tree, several yards from Westbrook. An ice cream vendor was in one corner of the park, and business was snappy. His bicycle and white uniform were definitely throwbacks, reminding Lex of the Good Humor days. "They may not even show. This could be some sort of test," Lex uttered.

Gil agreed. "It is weird."

"And make no mistake about it. They know we are here."

Five more minutes passed, and the detectives continued scouring every direction. Lex stared at the waiting Westbrook as he espied the time on his cell phone. At exactly three p.m., Westbrook stood, walked over to a grassy area, and laid the satchel on the ground. Then he stepped back.

"That must be the drop area," Gil said. "I should have taken a Motrin. My hand is throbbing."

The detectives were on alert, but there was still no indication of an intruder. "If it's going to happen, it has to happen soon," she said. "Be ready."

"This is strange, Lex. The bag is just sitting there. Anyone could take it."

At that moment, a woman with a carriage and a leashed dog tied to it neared the bag. "That can't be the pickup," Lex said. "We have to get them out of there."

"What if it is?"

Lex hastily walked toward the woman and dog. "What's his name? He looks friendly. May I pet him?"

"Piper," the startled woman said. "He's friendly."

The dog wagged its little tail as Lex bent and whispered to the woman, "You need to walk away from here right now. I'm a police officer. Just go. Now!"

"What about that suitcase?"

"Don't ask. Please go."

When the area was cleared, except for the satchel, Lex moved back to Gil while staying alert. "It's three o'clock. Where are they?"

Looking around again, Gil said, "I don't see anything unusual."

Lex grabbed her partner's arm. "Something is happening. Westbrook is darting toward the satchel."

The detectives rushed to him. "It's a fake," he said. "I just got a text. We've been set up." He showed Lex the message.

Glad you can follow instructions.

Be back here at 3 a.m. with all the money in the bag.

Westbrook replied: *You better let her go.*

Texting back, the demand was: *Sit on the same bench and set the money by the fountain.*

You lied. There were cops.

P.S. Hope you like the present waiting for you at your residence. Don't let her die!

Lex let out a breath. "This was a test. I had a sixth sense about this." She pivoted toward the area where the bag had been. "Obviously, the kidnappers are cagey. There's no telling how many there are."

Gil said, "I'll call Pressley on the way back to the Grand Truman."

Lex looked at Westbrook. "Let's get you back home."

Victor greeted them when they arrived at the hotel. "Mister Westbrook, there's a package for you. It was delivered less than an hour ago. Cedric has it."

"Thanks," he said.

After retrieving the delivery, Lex examined the return address on the small box. "This is no help. I know the location. It's the Bronx Zoo. This is a false return identification."

When they got upstairs, Westbrook opened the box and there it was: Svetlana's wedding ring. Westbrook held it and cringed. "They're going to kill her. I need a drink."

"Have a drink, but please, only one," Lex said. "I want someone to stay here tonight. We have to be back at Washington Square by three a.m."

Westbrook said, "No. I don't need a guard or roommate, and they know cops will be there."

"Right," Lex said, "and for some reason, I doubt we will scare them. I still want someone to stay with you."

Gil said, "I'll stay. Might as well. It beats taking the train back from Queens. I'll call Ray-Ann. I know she'll be thrilled, but it's not the first time."

Westbrook protested. "Does he have to?"

"It will be fine." Lex assured him.

"Easy for you to say."

Lex was ready to leave the two men and said to Gil, "I'm going to the precinct."

"When was the last time you drove a department vehicle?"

Lex walked toward the door. "When was the last time you walked a dog without getting bitten?"

Gil ignored the sarcastic jab as Lex opened the door and said, "I'm not taking the squad car. You need it. I'll have Victor hail a cab for me."

When the taxi dropped her off at the precinct, she paid the driver, walked into the building, and headed straight to Pressley's office. "We have a long night ahead of us," Lex said.

Baffled by what Lex had told him, he raised his hands up. "That's an understatement." .

"After vehemently protesting to have someone stay with him, he conceded, and Gil is staying with him."

"Good idea. Listen, I am calling downtown to arrange for a SWAT unit to be there."

"I don't think it will matter because we are not a secret, and they will be anticipating a police presence. And for some reason, they don't care. Why? What are they up to?"

"I agree, but what if they plan to take the bag and Westbrook? I want to get a SWAT team there; they know what they're doing."

A tired Lex said, I have to go home to get some sleep."

"Get going."

Chapter 12

His unanticipated company stayed and kept the author and Johnnie Walker apart.

"I'm going to make coffee."

"Make mine black," Gil said.

Several minutes later, Westbrook handed the detective a hot drink. "Are you hungry?" Gil asked.

"A little. You are making me nervous, but I can order something from the restaurant downstairs."

Twenty minutes later, food was delivered, and the twosome sat at the dining table eating chicken. Not quite finished, Gil put his fork down and pushed his dish aside. "I can't eat any more. Three o'clock will come soon enough."

The pent-up kidnappers target left the table, his meal barely eaten. "I'm putting the plates outside and having them picked up."

Gil slouched on the couch to watch TV while the author went into his office and with only the hall light keeping the room from total darkness, he reclined in his high-back chair and closed his eyes.

Gil was still awake, afraid to sleep and an hour before they had to leave, he when into the office and shook Westbrook, waking him up. "We have to leave here in an of hour."

Westbrook yawned. "I'm okay. I'll wash my face and get ready."

When it was time to go to Washington Square, Westbrook retrieved the satchel from his bedroom, donned a Calvin Klein zip-up jacket and held onto the Naugahyde bag that would inject an unexpected element to the kidnapping.

ᴀ

Lex had little sleep as she wrestled with how the transaction might happen. *SWAT or not, the kidnappers have something up their sleeve. What is it?*

Earlier, Lex informed Liz about having to leave in the middle of the night, but she didn't say why. Talking about her job to her daughter was not something she often did.

The detective's alarm woke her at 2:00 a.m. She pulled the cord on her nightstand lamp to shed some light. The tired Lex went into the bathroom to prepare herself for the Washington Square adventure. The mirror reflected bags under her weary eyes, but she managed to finish freshening up.

Wearing jeans, a tee shirt she'd purchased at a Fleetwood Mac concert a few years ago, sneakers, a jacket and sporting her gun, she left her home, not knowing what to expect.

Entering the night's darkness, she decided not to walk and got into her car, which was parked under a streetlamp. Upon approaching her destination, the suspicious detective couldn't see the SWAT team, and parked her car.

Washington Square was eerily quiet, and Lex observed two benches occupied by sleeping people she assumed were homeless.

There was a slight breeze, and a full moon, accompanied by stars. Lex stood near a tree and rubbed her hands together.

Westbrook wasn't in sight, nor was Gil. The buildings across the street had lights on in a couple of windows. Focusing on the road, she noticed a car pulling up, and Westbrook got out. The author was carrying the satchel as he strode to a lonely bench. He sat, closely guarding the sack. Lex knew Gil had driven and wondered where he was going. She reached for her phone and called the detective. "Hey, where are you?"

"Parking the car. Be there in a few minutes."

Lex waited and was startled when Gil tapped her on the shoulder. "Sleep much?" he asked.

She flinched and took a breath. "Don't scare me like that! This better be the real thing. I could use a cup of coffee."

"I already had some. It feels so eerie here. Anything could

happen."

Lex pointed to the occupied benches. "We're not exactly alone. And doesn't it bother you that the kidnappers know we are here? Hiding is doing nothing. It's not right, I tell you."

Gil browsed the area. "Do you know where the SWAT team is?"

"No. I just hope they are here."

Gil shook his throbbing wrist. "My hand doesn't appreciate being up this early either. It's a little achy."

Lex checked her phone. "It's time."

"Nothing is happening," Gil said. "I don't get it."

Lex again scoped out the square. "Nothing. We may have been taken again."

Suddenly, Westbrook rose and carried the satchel to the fountain and then walked back to the bench. The trees were still, and the only disruptive sounds came from the street where every few minutes a car or two cars passed by. "I don't see anyone suspicious. What the heck is going on?" Lex said.

A couple of minutes later the stillness was interrupted by a whirring noise. Two bright lights appeared above. Lex raised her eyes and was dumbfounded.

"What the hell?" Gil muttered as a foreign object neared the money bag. "A drone?"

Before they could react, the flying craft swiftly swooped down and lifted the sack from the ground. It rose in the same manner and flew away with the satchel.

"Holy Christ," Gil said. "What just happened?"

Lex quickly took out her phone and in the darkness attempted to video the drone as it flew away. "We couldn't have foreseen this."

Westbrook approached them, holding out his phone. "I have a message."

Lex grabbed it to see what had been sent.

We know your cop friends are just as surprised as you.

We'll contact you after we count the money.

The SWAT commander rushed to the scene. "We were expecting a human to do the job," Vincent Scalderone said. "It all happened so fast, but we couldn't just shoot it out of the air. The whole neighborhood would have wakened to gunfire."

"I videoed it as it flew away," Lex said. She checked her phone and viewed the footage. She sighed. "Well, this is pretty useless."

Lex called Pressley, who was at the precinct, and told him about the unthinkable act that had occurred. "Are you serious?"

"Stunned. I don't know what to do."

"It's late. I suggest you get home and be here early in the morning."

"It is morning. We'll all see you later."

"What are we doing?" Gil asked.

 We're getting out of here," Lex uttered. "You get him back to the Grand Truman."

"Yeah, and then I'm driving the squad car home."

▲

The author was lying in bed, half asleep, when his phone beeped. It was six a.m., and the kidnappers had sent an angry message.

What the fuck did you do, you asshole?

Nice of you to hand us a satchel full of bath towels.

That just cost you another 50 grand. Get us the money.

Don't let her die!

Chapter 13

By eleven a.m., Lex, Westbrook, and Gil were somehow at the precinct, seated with Pressley. To the left of the captain was a dark suited, short haired, clean-shaven man. FBI agent Neil Gerstein acknowledged the detectives. "If you're wondering why I'm here, it's because we have been asked to get involved in the kidnapping."

Lex looked at Pressley. "Did you request the help?"

"No. They did downtown. Chief Aguilera asked."

Gerstein said, "You know we usually don't step in unless the crime is defined as a federal offense. As far as we know, this kidnapping hasn't crossed state lines. However, since we've been requested to help, the bureau has assigned me to the case." He said to Lex, "I've been informed about you."

Lex removed her glasses. "What is that supposed to mean?"

He tersely asked her, "What exactly happened?"

Detecting a larger-than-life attitude from the questioner, Lex had fire in her eyes as she sarcastically responded, "Would you repeat that question?"

Pressley quickly intervened. "Let's take this to the meeting room."

Following the captain, they entered the enclosed space, and Gil shut the door. The rectangular table was the perfect size for all five. Lex sat across from the brassy agent.

He derisively said to her, "You heard me the first time. What do you know?"

Lex was forthright and calmly brought him up to date.

Gerstein sighed. "I wish we had been involved earlier."

Raising her voice, she asked, "And what exactly would you have suggested or done had you been informed?"

Gil sat back and listened to the combatants.

Lex's answer drew Gerstein's ire, and his gruffy tone reflected it. "You're out of line."

That remark enraged Lex, and she stood. "I'm out of line?" she shouted.

Pressley pointed at her and commanded, "Sit and calm down."

Lex huffed. "I'm going to the ladies room."

Pressley said, "Go." He then added, as he fixated on the FBI agent, "When you return, Mister Gerstein and you will be cordial. Isn't that right?"

Lex exited as Gerstein nodded his assent. Agitated, she found it difficult to gather herself. The fiery detective headed to the lavatory and returned to the room, a calmer lady.

Gil whispered to her, "Are you okay?"

She didn't answer and paid attention to Pressley's voice. "Listen, it's not every day we have a hostage-ransom situation." He addressed the agent. "I'll make sure you are informed of everything we know from here on out. We can't go back. We have to move forward."

With the tension in the room eased, Westbrook chimed in. "I don't have any idea who they are." He held Svetlana's ring, trying to slide it onto his pinky, momentarily distracted.

Lex said, "We know there are listening devices in the suite. We found two under lampshades." She turned to Gerstein with an appeal. "Can you get a team over there to search for and remove listening devices?"

Her thinking switched to Westbrook's well-being, so she shifted toward him. "Clark Fullerton should be able to accommodate you with a temporary room."

"Oh no, I won't be comfortable there."

Lex looked into his eyes. "There is no other way. You can't stay in your suite."

Grimly, Westbrook assented.

Gerstein said, "I'll take care of the debugging. For now, I need to go back to headquarters."

The detectives and Westbrook remained in the meeting room.

Lex said, "Svetlana never answered her cell phone, and we assume the kidnappers have it." She then faced her partner."Gil, why don't you go with Mister Westbrook to the car. I'll be down soon."

As soon as Lex and the captain were alone, he asked, "What's with the attitude?"

"Gerstein? He grated on me from the get-go with those beady eyes and his pompousness. He jumped right on us, actually me."

"Okay, how about cooling the hostilities?"

"Fine. Listen, I want to get Westbrook's phone records, too, but I didn't want him to know I intend to do that. Here is his number, write it down."

Pressley pointed at his astute detective. "I'll get on it."

She gave her boss a thumbs-up and walked to the parking lot.

Lex's instinct told her there could be trouble brewing at the Grand Truman. As soon as the detectives and the author reached the hotel, she saw several news vehicles near the entrance. "Here we go," she exclaimed. "My favorite people are here."

"We can't do anything about that," Gil said as he carefully drove up the driveway toward Tomas.

The valet said, "Quite a mess with these reporters and cameras."

"That's for sure," Gil replied. "You can park it."

Westbrook and the detectives went into the lobby and were confronted by a reporter with a cameraman to his rear. "No comment," Lex barked. Another local TV reporter approached, and the irked detective shoved this station's cameraman aside. "Get out of here. This is a police matter. A woman's life is in danger."

"Mister Westbrook, what about the ransom money and the drone?" a tall reporter asked.

Lex recognized him from his television reports. "You heard me, leave now."

Gil pulled Lex back and guided her and the author toward the elevator. "Sorry, boys and girls," he said. "We have work to do. I suggest you find somewhere else to hang out."

As soon they exited the elevator, the trio was confronted by additional media people armed with cameras. A microphone was shoved in Lex's face. Before a question could be asked, the riled Lex snapped, "See the elevator? I suggest you get in and press the lobby button. Then get into your van and go back to the TV station.

Who the hell let you up here anyway?"

Benton and Claudia Kimball were standing and watching. "They piled in here a half hour ago and banged on our door," he remarked.

Addressing the Kimballs, Gil advised them to return to their suite.

A reporter not heeding Lex's directive asked, "What do you know about the kidnapping? What can you tell us about the drone?"

Lex grabbed the microphone and threw it toward the elevator. "Now get out of here. Mister Westbrook is exhausted, and we are going inside. Go fetch your mic and get into that elevator."

"You'll hear about this," the angry reporter barked. "The police chief will love to see this video."

Gil pointed to the elevator and adopted a harsh demeanor. "You better leave. I've been with her for a long time, and you haven't seen her when she gets really mad."

The news crew retreated, Westbrook opened his door, and the detectives followed him inside. "Mister Westbrook, we're getting you into a different room now. Gerstein's crew will search for devices."

"Let me gather a few things, like a change of clothes and my laptop. What about the money? Lady, your suggestion of placing towels in the satchel has put Svetlana's life in real danger."

Gil asked, "Where is the cash?"

Lex held her hands up and pointed to the lamp, reminding them that everything they say can be heard."

"In my closet, two suitcases." he whispered. "There's a safe downstairs. Maybe we can store them there."

Lex stepped into the hall and called Gerstein. "Listen, we are at the hotel, and media are here but should be gone soon. We're going to secure Mister Westbrook a room right now."

"Thanks. I'll have a team over there later this afternoon."

Lex checked the hallway and pressed the button to open the elevator door as Gil, toting a suitcase in each hand, and Westbrook holding onto an overnight bag got inside.

Reaching Fullerton's office, the manager rose from his chair and greeted them. "I think it's quieted down. What a swarm of gnats."

Lex said, "We have a team of agents coming to debug Mister Westbrook's suite. Can you provide him with a room for a night or two?"

Fullerton nodded. "I can do that."

Gil pointed to the suitcases. "We understand you have a safe and would appreciate it if they were stored in there."

"What is in them? Gold?"

"Sort of," Gil said. "Just store the bags."

"Okay, let me lock them in the vault." He got up and opened the door behind his desk with a key, revealing the storeroom. "I'll take them." He stationed the luggage in one corner of the safe, locked it, and did the same with the door behind his desk. "Stay here and I'll be back with a room key."

It wasn't long before the manager handed Westbrook a key card that had been programmed for room 810 and handed it to Lex.

"Thank you. We'll let you know when Mister Westbrook can go back upstairs."

They rode with Westbrook to room 810 and made sure he was comfortable before leaving him alone.

The elevator door opened in the lobby where a few newsmen were still hanging around. Exiting the lift, she said to them. "If you don't want to get arrested for loitering, I strongly advise you to get out of here now!" She and Gil walked through the revolving door and minutes later were inside the squad car..

While on their way to the precinct, Lex received a call from Westbrook. "I just got a threatening message." His voice wavered and Lex felt his anger. "They are damned mad they were duped once, and demand the money, or Svetlana will die. Instructions to follow. And just for good measure, they want me to have a good weekend!" Yeah, while they fuck the shit out of her!"

Lex rarely was at a loss for words and was momentarily quiet. "We have no choice. Don't lose my number."

GRETA'S GONE

Tucker had the well-being of his wife, Greta, angering him and he stood frozen in place. All he could do was try to remain calm. Then came the next cell phone beep and message.

Greta is fine. You will receive a number for a Swiss bank account, and you will wire the money to it.

He texted back: I need to see her.

The reply read: You'll see her after we see the money. We'll contact you in 48 hours.

Tucker typed: Bastards.

The last message said: It's her or the money. Your choice. NO POLICE...GOT IT?

Tucker got into his Maserati. Greta's red Porsche Boxster with only 6500 miles on it was still in the garage. His father's Mercedes, which Tucker sometimes used, was in the third space. Images of his wife being held hostage consumed him on his drive to the bank to get the money. He twirled his keys as he got out of his parked car. Entering the bank entrance, he removed an expensive pair of Ray-Ban sunglasses and tucked them inside his shirt pocket, stepped past an ATM and two tellers, and strode directly toward the manager.

Cindy Walker greeted him. "Hi, Tucker. What can I do for you?"

He remained standing. "Ever wired money to a Swiss bank account?"

"We have, but it's not something we do every day. Why do you ask?"

"I may have to wire a sizable transfer from one of my father's old accounts that were transferred to me. Can you take a look?"

"Can you give me an account number?"

"I don't remember it."

"What's your Social Security number?"

Tucker rattled it off, and Cindy found a sizable CD and two money market accounts. "How much are you looking for?"

"Two hundred thousand."

Cindy glanced at the balances. "You're covered." She looked at him with a squint and tilted her head. "I'm curious. Your father's business was investing. Why did he keep funds in these low-interest accounts?"

"I don't know what his thinking was. He did want to have cash around for things like buying cars without liquidating any of his investments."

"I guess that's a reason."

"Thanks, Cindy."

Tucker started to get into his car but glanced across the street at the barbershop and slowly walked over. Tucker's best friend, Sal, was in the barber chair. "Hey, Tucker. Where have you been? I tried to call you," he said.

"I've been busy. Sorry. And Greta had to go to Jersey, Ocean City, for a couple of weeks. Her aunt is ill."

The barber, Frank, who was nearing retirement, waved his white towel after Sal got up from the chair. "Tucker," he said. "Trim it up?"

Sal called out to Tucker, "I have to run. Call me later."

With shorter hair, Tucker rose, paid for the trimming and handed Frank an extra twenty. He took the sunglasses from his pocket, walked to his car, and went home to wait for the next instruction.

Chapter 14

Lex was as mystified as Westbrook and remembered what Gil had said about separating her job from her family life, but it was not as easy for her as it was him.

No sooner had Lex gotten home than the first crisis of the weekend presented itself. It was her adoptee. Cassatt's eyes were cloudy, and Liz was cleaning vomit from the kitchen floor. "She needs to see the veterinarian," Liz said.

Lex picked up the ill cat. "I don't think we need an appointment." She handed Cassatt to Liz after the vomit had been cleaned up. "Give me a few minutes and we'll get her to Doctor Yasick."

Twenty minutes later, they entered the veterinary clinic, registered and waited in the outer office along with four other animals and their owners. Lex spotted a dog across the room. "He's adorable."

The pet's owner looked over and said, "Louie is a Cavalier King Charles. He's here for his shots. That's a nice cat."

"Her name is Cassatt," Lex said. "She been vomiting."

A veterinary assistant pointed to Lex and Liz who was holding their pet. "Let's go to room one."

They went inside, and Cassatt was examined from head to tail. After a urinalysis, it was determined the cat had a urinary tract infection. "I'll give you antibiotics. She should be fine in a few days."

Liz held her furry friend's face to hers. "I'm so relieved it's not serious. You're going to be fine."

They left the clinic and picked up Chinese food for dinner. The Stall women ate while Cassatt napped. After settling onto her couch in the den, Lex called Stefan. "How are you?" she asked.

"Fine. It wasn't the best week. The artist I wanted to preview backed out."

"That's too bad. Earlier we had to take Cassatt to the vet, but she's okay."

"What was wrong?"

"It's a urinary infection, and I have antibiotics."

"What are you doing this weekend?"

"I had planned to spend it with Liz, but she is going to be with Shannon tomorrow so they can go to a friend's birthday party. Sunday, they are going to the movies. That's the way it is with teenagers. I can't wait to go to Mastrangelo's next week."

"Me neither. I have a rich client coming in tomorrow. He was in the gallery about a week ago and had inquired about a seascape painting that an artist from New Jersey, Jeffrey Balding had consigned to me. He balked at the price, and I told him I would talk to Jeffrey."

"What is he asking?"

"Two grand, but he'll come down to eighteen, and the customer is buying it."

"I'm just curious and hope you don't mind me asking. What is the split?"

"Let's just say it's enough to take you to dinner."

"Okay. Are you doing anything Sunday?"

"Well…I kind of have a date…but I can break it."

"Excuse me, a date?"

"Yeah, I'm taking the Jaguar to the car wash in the morning."

"Ah, I see. You certainly have your priorities in order." She paused. "Would you want to come down here Sunday afternoon? It should be a nice day."

"That sounds good. What time?"

"Why don't you get here around noon."

"Book it. I'm in. I'll see you then."

"I'm tired. I'm going to bed."

"See you soon."

Saturday flew by, and Sunday was indeed a nice day. Cassatt

felt better and so did Liz.

It was ten before noon when Stefan rang her bell. Liz was leaving to meet up with Shannon. "Perfect day," he said as he entered the living room. "Hi, Liz."

"Hi," she said and walked to the door.

"I'll see you later," Lex said.

"I should be back around five."

Lex closed the front door after her daughter left. "I didn't mention lunch. Are you hungry?"

"What did you have in mind?"

"Come on. I want to show you something on Bleecker. We can eat a café on the way."

They ate lunch and began strolling as he took her hand. "How did the sale go?"

"Happy to say, I have one less piece of artwork hanging in the gallery."

"My house," she said. "I came back with Liz after my divorce. The house belonged to my parents."

"You said you went to NYU," Stefan prompted.

"I dropped out. That's another story. Lex stopped and stood at a store window that had a 'For Rent' sign posted. "This was my Dad's record shop. There are a lot of memories inside here, and I still imagine him behind the counter. It was called Maitland's then, and it was open until about a year ago."

Stefan peered inside. "You said he died a long time ago."

"He did, but a former employee of his bought the business from my mother."

"Maitland?"

"My maiden name. Alexis Maitland. Everyone always called me Lex." She began to laugh.

"What's so funny?"

"It's my middle name. I was born May 19, so they dubbed me May. I'm lucky I wasn't born in February. How about you? Do you have a middle name?"

"Nothing too imaginative. Joseph."

They moved away from the storefront and continued their walk toward the college. Lex pointed to a dormitory. "When I was attending there, I had a boyfriend. That was his room. He was killed in a robbery at the drugstore that used to be on the corner. That's really the reason I became a detective."

"Wow. You are full of surprises."

"Well, there's one other thing I will tell you. When I was with him, I got pregnant but had a miscarriage. That's when I dropped out."

Stefan squeezed her hand. "Everyone thinks I grew up in France. Not true. We lived in Brisbane, and my father was a cattle farmer. Although I was a terrible painter, I did study art in Paris and decided to come here almost fifteen years ago, after my Mon and Dad died within six months of each other. As for marriage, I never did that." They approached an ice cream shop. "You interested?"

She smiled. "Ever hear anyone refuse ice cream?"

After purchasing cups of creamy treats, they found a bench and sat. "I never thought I'd be dating a cop."

She planted a kiss on his cheek. "I never thought I'd be dating again period after my nasty divorce. I'm so lucky to have Liz."

"She favors you."

"I know, and that's got me scared. She's growing up. It happens so fast."

They finished their snacks and went back to Waverly Place. An hour later, Liz was home. Lex and Stefan welcomed her back, and then Lex walked her boyfriend to his car.

"I'll call you, and I'll make reservations at Mastrangelo's," he said. Then they kissed goodbye.

CHAPTER 15

The weekend passed without word from Westbrook. Lex took that to mean he hadn't gotten another text. The captain was waiting for her. "I see you're empty handed. Step into my office." Pressley dropped into his chair and tapped his desk while staring at Lex, his prized detective. "Now, young lady, why don't you tell me about your tantrum."

Lex knew where the captain was going with his request. Then she faced her boss, giving him a blank look. "Tantrum?"

"Damn it, Lex. You know what I mean."

This thrashing of the press was not her first run-in with the media. There was another incident several months ago with the press. That time she had them forcefully removed from a crime scene by uniformed police, but it was after she had smashed a camera lens.

"Okay. What exactly have you heard?"

Pressley smirked. "They're a little upset with you downtown. The TV station is demanding an apology and reimbursement for the microphone you destroyed. Lex, you can't keep doing these things."

She gave her boss a smug look and tight-lipped smile. "Neither can they." Lex raised her glasses and seamlessly changed the conversation. "The kidnappers are playing a game. What kind of game? Is it about the money? Is it about Westbrook? Is it about Svetlana? Will they kill her?" The veteran detective knew that last statement was the one Westbrook had serious concerns about. "I still don't believe they are killers."

Pressley clasped his hands. "We won't know that until the game is over."

"Yes, may I join my partner?"

Lex abruptly left the room and started walking around the squad room. She heard Gil say, "Uh-oh, she's pacing again."

Indeed, she was in thinking mode. *The spying devices. How did they get into the suite? Who planted them and when? And the limo. The man who handed Tomas the envelope. And Tomas...I want to see that video again.*

She opened the top desk drawer, removed the limo video Clark Fullerton had given her, and took it into the captain. "There are a couple of things we need to know. One is who planted the bugs? Second, that limo bothers me. Play the video, please."

Pressley inserted it into his computer as Gil and Lex gathered around him.

"I don't see anything," Gil said. "We certainly can't make out the guy inside the car."

Lex was sure she'd seen something odd. "Wait. Play it back from the beginning." It ran again and suddenly, she said, "Stop. The man in the car. He gave Tomas the envelope and then handed him a hundred-dollar bill. Did you see that?"

Gil took a closer look. "Yes, the valet took the money."

"Not that. Did you see Tomas's thumb? He gave the guy a thumbs-up. It looks to me as if Tomas knew the guy. He knew what was going on. Look, the man in the car nodded. Damn it. We're going to the Grand Truman, and we're going to have another chat with Tomas."

"Could he have also planted the bugs?" Gil asked.

"It's a possibility."

Pressley said, "I didn't see that either." The captain removed the video and handed it back to Lex.

"Let's go. We have a fish to fry."

"Don't you think we should check in with Westbrook?" Gil asked.

She took out her phone and called the author. He answered and said, "I was about to call you."

"Did you get another message?"

"Yeah, a sarcastic one. They wanted to know if I had a good weekend. And for good measure they said that Svetlana had a good one. Bastards!"

"Alright, we're coming over now."

Gil asked, "What's happening?"

"He got a message. A mocking one about him having a nice weekend, and another about Svetlana."

▲

The unmarked police vehicle pulled up to the hotel's unmanned valet stand. "No one is here." Gil said. "I guess I'll park it in the garage myself."

Tomas appeared as the detectives reached the revolving doors. "You're late," Gil said. I parked it myself."

Lex kept her composure, but she knew nabbing him would be like catching a salmon swimming upstream. Though she pegged the valet as a person of interest, she held off alerting Tomas because she had to talk with Westbrook first.

The detectives walked into the lobby, proceeding to elevator and up to the twenty-sixth floor.

The suite's door was ajar, and Lex knocked. "It's open," he said. Upon entering. Westbrook said, "I didn't get much sleep this weekend, but I am relieved we are now talking in private."

Detecting the author had yet to start indulging in alcohol, Lex didn't wait until he felt the urge. "May I see the text?"

Grabbing his phone, he showed the detectives the message.

Patience. Hope you had a good weekend. And don't lie again about cops.

Svetlana had a nice time.

Westbrook opened his hand, holding Svetlana's ring, and moved toward his wet bar to fill a glass with amber liquid. "Do you want a drink?"

"No, thank you," Lex replied.

Gil rejected a drink too.

The tired author said, "I can't help thinking about them killing her."

Lex observed the terror in his eyes. "I wish I could be more comforting, but there appears to be something more than money going on here. And as I have said all along, I don't believe they are

70

killers. This is a high-stakes chess match. We have to try to outlast them. You need to trust us."

Westbrook rubbed his brow and chugged his scotch, wincing as the burn hit his throat."

Lex asked, "How well do you know Tomas?"

"Tomas Costa, the valet?"

"Yes. What do you know about him?"

"Not much. Why?"

"We have to speak with him again. I'd like him to join us here."

"What do you want to know?"

"We want to know more about his interaction with the limo."

Gil said, "I'll go down and ask Fullerton to have Tomas come here." He left the suite, and Lex watched Westbrook, as he stood almost frozen, peering out the window.

Returning, Gil said, "It's done. Fullerton called him. He should be on his way."

Eight minutes later, Lex heard footsteps and opened the door. "Thanks for joining us, Tomas. Have a seat." She pointed to the couch and watched him move to where she had indicated.

"What's this about?"

"I want to ask you a few more questions."

"Me?"

She pointed at him "Yes, you. Let's start with the fact that when we spoke before, you said you didn't recognize the man who handed you the envelope and the hundred dollars."

"Right, that's true."

Lex stared him down. "Is that true?"

"What are you getting at?"

The intuitive questioner didn't pull any punches and went after her prey. "I think you're lying."

Tomas shifted his body and reiterated, "I don't know him. Never saw him before; never saw the limo either."

Observing a bead of sweat beneath his cap, she briskly asked, "Then why are you sweating?" Lex decided it was time to apply a little pressure. "Don't lie to me. You know him, and you directed Svetlana to go west, didn't you?"

Appearing to have been caught off guard by the queries, Tomas was silent for a few seconds. "No! I swear I'm telling you the truth!"

The detective amped up the heat, concentrating on his demeanor. "May I see your phone?"

The valet started to get up, and Gil raised his hands, signaling him to remain seated. "Not yet. The lady is speaking to you. Answer her."

"Your phone," Lex repeated.

"I left it in my car," he shouted.

Raising her voice, Lex said, "Really? Is your car in your pocket? I know you have the phone on you."

"I need to get back to work."

Lex sternly demanded, "And I need your phone."

Angered by the harsh ask, he replied, "Back off. I didn't do anything."

Keeping up her harsh tone, she said, "Then you won't mind if we look at your phone, right?"

Tomas abruptly stood, ignoring Gil's second attempt to keep him seated. "Like I said, I have to get back to work. My phone is none of your business."

The male detective again held his hands in front of the valet, preventing him from walking toward the door. "You're not going anywhere yet. She's still talking."

Lex stared at him. "You know there are cameras outside. We've studied the video. You gave the man in the limo a thumbs-up, and he nodded back at you. Who is he?"

"He gave me a hundred dollars. I thanked him, and he acknowledged my gesture."

Not convinced Tomas was just doing his job and was innocent, she eased her voice. "Answer my questions, and you can go back downstairs. Who are they? What's the endgame? Where is Svetlana?"

Tomas breathed hard, then tersely answered, "You're wrong! I don't know anything!"

Westbrook appeared to be mesmerized by the female detective and sat silently.

She upped her volume to match the valet's. "I think you do!"

"Are you arresting me?"

"Not yet, but I know you know more than you're telling us. If Svetlana dies, you'll die in prison. I ask you again: who are they…and where are they?"

The valet was adamant. "I told you—I don't know. I need to go do my job."

"Which job? The valet or the stooge?" A frustrated Lex stared at Tomas. "Get out of here, but don't rest too easily."

The ruthlessly interrogated employee hastily exited.

"I was sure he was going to break," Gil said.

"He didn't, but he knows we'll be watching him."

Westbrook asked, "Can't you arrest him? What if he comes after me?"

"No," Lex replied, "we can't arrest him. If need be, I can subpoena Tomas's phone."

"Media people tried to contact me, but I didn't answer my phone."

Lex watched Westbrook pick up his glass. "They can be like leeches. You did the right thing." She paused. "Listen, those devices that were found. Do you have any idea how they were planted? Who else comes in here besides you, and Svetlana.?"

"No one." He paused. "Wait. Svetlana wanted to go on a Caribbean cruise for her birthday last month."

This revelation was news to Lex. "How long were you away?"

"Ten days."

"Do you know who cleaned here?"

"I'm sure it was either Addie, or Berta. You'll have to ask Clark Fullerton who was on then."

"We'll do just that."

"What the hell are they going to do next? They better let Svetlana go." The agitated man looked as if he was about to toss his glass at the fireplace but quickly regained his composure and put the glass on a table.

Lex tried to reassure him. "They said they would contact you again, and they will. Wait."

Chapter 16

Armed with new information, Lex had to find out who cleaned Westbrook's suite. If videos existed, she knew where to obtain them. Betsy's chair was vacant when the sleuths entered the management office, but Fullerton was there, and they approached him.

"What can I do for you now?" he asked.

Not bothering to sit, Lex asked, "Can you tell us who cleaned the Westbrooks' unit while they were on their cruise? You did know they were away, didn't you?"

"Yes, I have to know in case of an emergency. It was a little over a month ago. Why are you asking?"

"We would like to know who might have been inside their unit while they were away."

Fullerton pulled up the assignment list on his computer. "According to my worksheet, Addie cleaned their suite."

"We met her. Tell us about her."

"She's been here since we opened. She was previously at the Waldorf for years."

"May we speak with her?"

"She's off today. She'll be back in the morning."

Gil asked, "May we look at videos from that time period?"

Fullerton put his hands on the desk. "That's not possible because after thirty days, they are recorded over."

Lex had a bad feeling. "Are you saying there are no videos that would show anyone entering the Westbrooks' residence while they were away?"

"It was over a month ago, so that's correct."

Disappointment stung her. "Great, just great." Dejectedly, she said, "Thank you."

The detectives ambled outside to retrieve their vehicle and Lex icily stared at the combative Tomas. "You can get our car," she said.

The valet quickly got the fob and walked purposefully to the garage. When the vehicle appeared, it stopped near the detectives. Tomas stepped out and opened the passenger door for Lex, who was unamused by the silly grin on his face. "Have a nice day," he said as he closed her door.

Gil began to drive away, and Lex said, "I didn't appreciate that clown's remark. I know he's hiding the truth, and we have to break him down."

"How about getting that subpoena for his phone?"

"We may, but I want to give him one more shot before I do."

⚓

Keeping the captain updated, Lex said, "Tomas Costa is a tough cookie. I questioned him."

"Not quite," Gil said to the captain. "She grilled him up and down."

After Lex recapped the inquisition, Pressley said, "Keep on him. And Lex, don't worry about the media. Get out of here."

As she and Gil were on their way out of the precinct, they passed Hutch. "Not very ladylike," he blurted.

Lex abruptly halted, realizing news had spread about her media incident. She was not about to take that barb lightly and pointed to her shoes. "See these?" she harshly asked. "Know what they are?"

"Jimmy Choo?"

"Not quite, they're TBs."

"They're what?"

Lex had daggers in her eyes as she glared at Hutch. "Testicle Busters. You don't want to read the label."

Hutch backed away, as Lex and Gil exited the precinct.

GRETA'S GONE

For three days, Tucker Rutledge agonized about the threatening messages he'd received. The money was ready to be wire-transferred as soon as the bank account number was in his hands. He worried Greta was being abused, and his mind tortured him as he imagined them treating her as a sex toy.

Tucker stared at his phone, wishing, trying to command it to convey a new message. When that didn't work, he opted to seek his medication. His stash was low, but he knew where he could score more cocaine. He got into his Maserati and drove to the hardware store to obtain a fresh supply.

Two hours later, he brought his purchase to his man cave, a room with a large TV and theater seating where he took a hit. That's when a text came in on his cell phone.

Tucker, you may be wondering why we haven't contacted you in a few days.

You have 48 hours to get the money. In 2 days, you will receive the Swiss bank account number. Got it?

Tucker texted back: Who the hell are you? I need to see Greta.

That message prompted a quick response. One that gave Tucker a jolt. He stared at the disturbing picture of Greta, whose hands were tied to a bedpost while she was lying face down, nothing covering her bare buttocks. Words followed.

She's worth every bit of two hundred grand.

Rage tore through him. He knew he had to obey the kidnappers and wire the money, but he couldn't do it yet. He still had to wait for the final instructions with the Swiss bank account number. And the sight of Greta naked infuriated him.

REMINDER TUCKER. No cops if you ever want to see Greta again.

Tucker thought twice about going to see Police Chief Weiss. Instead, he sat back and let the drug do its job.

Chapter 17

Lex was calm as she entered the squad room and stood at Hutch's cube. "Hey. I might have been a little rough yesterday. Look at these shoes."

"Oh no."

"These are Jimmy Choo."

"Nice to know." He gave her a thumbs-up. "They look comfortable."

Empty-handed, she continued toward her partner. "How's the hand?"

"Okay. You seem like you're holding up pretty good without the latte."

"Yes, and I'm not even irritable, am I?"

"You? Irritable? Hell no! Just don't tell the news people that. And how about me? I don't miss the doughnuts." He gave Lex a dour look. "I don't lie very well, do I?"

"No, and neither does Tomas Costa. He's a bald-faced liar."

"You are right, and he didn't seem scared."

"No. I hope Westbrook hasn't started drinking again."

"What if he already has?" Gil shot a questioning look at Lex.

"We can't control his habit."

Right on cue, the antsy voice of Essex Westbrook was the next one Lex heard when she answered her phone.

"It's not happening yet. Their silence is killing me."

"Us too. We're leaving here and coming to see you."

⅄

Arriving at the Grand Truman, Victor was handed the vehicle fob. "Too bad Tomas is out. I'm alone today."

"Is he sick?" Gil asked.

"I heard he has the flu."

Lex asked, "Are you sure?"

"Yeah, Mister Fullerton told me."

"Thank you," she said.

She and Gil approached the elevator. "What are you thinking?" he asked.

"I think Tomas is gone."

As soon as they reached the second floor, Lex saw the manager in the corridor. "Mister Fullerton," she said, "We have to talk with you."

"Sure, I'll be back in a few minutes. I just have to open the ballroom so our staff can arrange tables for a dinner."

Betsy was at her computer. Lex said, "We bumped into Mister Fullerton."

"Yes, he'll be right back. You can wait in his office."

They went in, and Lex again studied the nostalgic pictures on the wall. "The Twin Towers still get to me, and I know they get to Westbrook."

Fullerton walked through his door and asked, "What is it you want to know?"

"Victor told us Tomas called out sick," Lex said.

"He did. He has the flu."

The leery detective asked, "Can you give me his address and cell number?"

The manager opened a cabinet, found Tomas's file, and wrote the information on a piece of paper. Before handing it to her, he asked "What's this about?"

"Nothing, sir. It's for our records. Thank you."

The detectives had what they needed, so when they were in the hallway, nearing the elevator, Lex kept walking. "Where are you going?" Gil asked.

"Toward the ballroom. There's an open area, and I'm going to attempt to contact Tomas." Seconds later, she left a message on his voice mail. "No luck. He's not answering."

"He may be sleeping."

"There's one way to find out. We're going there."

"What about Westbrook?"

"Call and tell him something came up, and we can't visit with him right now." Lex was sure she had alarmed Tomas, and was positive he was either about to disappear, or he had already left town. "I'm sure that liar is on the run. If we're lucky, we may catch him while he is still here."

Chapter 18

Once inside their unmarked police car, Gil said, "Read me the address."

"Washington Heights, Mills Apartments."

Gil drove toward Amsterdam Avenue and later veered left onto West 176th. "Traffic isn't bad. I figure about twenty minutes."

Nearing their destination, Lex spotted a quadrangle of tall brick apartments and a sign that read 'Mills Apartments 3600.' "That's it on the left. He's in building C, unit three-oh-seven."

Gil pulled into a lot outside building D where several other vehicles were parked. The center of the quad had a garden, and a basketball court was off in one corner where several boys were playing a game. The loud rap music coming from a boom box was not Lex's kind of music. Gil said, "Good old shirts and skins."

The multilevel brick housing units had air conditioners hanging from several windows, some rusted, most draped with bird droppings. A few windows were open, a few with no screens, and Lex got a whiff of home cooking.

As the detectives approached building C, Lex heard shouting coming from the basketball court and looked over to see a quarrel in progress. Her instinct was to rush over to break it up, but Gil said, "Let it go. It's nothing. Happens all the time."

She was fixated on their destination when a loud bang rang out, followed by another ear-catching pop. There was no mistaking them as cars backfiring; it was gunfire. Lex saw boys scattering from the basketball court and focused on a body that wasn't moving. "Oh my God. He's been shot." She reached into her hip holster, taking out her Glock 19. The detectives ran toward the court, the music still blaring, as Gil quickly attempted to phone 911. The music was so loud he had to turn off the boombox before making the call.

The victim's blood pooled on the asphalt; his dreadlocks wet from it. The size of the puddle was increasing, most likely from a wound on the back of his head. More red fluid gushed from the bullet hole in the boy's chest. Lex returned her weapon to her holster and knelt to check for signs of life. "His pupils are still. He's not breathing. No pulse. He's dead."

A Ruger had fallen not far from the body. Looking around at the suddenly deserted court, she saw a blood trail. It looks like the other guy was hit." She pointed to an alleyway with two dumpsters. "I wonder if he dropped a gun in one of those trash containers."

"I'm going to check." Gil approached a corner of the court and spotted something in the grass. "There's a cap over here with a New York Knicks logo on it."

"Leave it. I can see casings over here."

"I'll search the dumpsters." After rummaging through the large metal trash containers, Gil returned to Lex and the dead victim. "Those dumpsters are loaded with garbage and have flies roaming around. They smell like a horse crapped in them."

The sounds of approaching sirens bounced off the brick buildings in the quad. Seconds later, flashing red, blue, and white lights from an ambulance and three black and whites lit up the scene. EMTs hurriedly approached the victim. "He's dead," Lex said.

The medics quickly assessed the victim's condition, confirming Lex's observation, and retreated to roll out a stretcher for the victim.

A uniformed sergeant approached the detectives. The name on his black vest read Johnson. Lex, after identifying herself and her partner, told the policeman about their activities.

Gil said, "One weapon appears to belong to the other shooter who ran past those dumpsters. I looked for a gun inside them and didn't spot one."

"Thanks," the sergeant said as several policemen dispersed to scour the area.

News of the incident was quickly spreading throughout the complex, and a small crowd gathered near the court. Police held the bystanders back. As the dead boy was being covered, one man said,

"That's Amare."

The detectives and the sergeant approached the elderly man. "Sir, you know the boy?" Johnson asked.

"Amare Jamison. Lives in my building."

Johnson removed his hat. "Jesus." He commented to the detectives, "He's a bad dude. We picked him up a week and a half ago because he beat his girlfriend after an argument. She's okay. Laticia Cannes has two brothers. I can see where this is going. Damn it, Amare must have been out on bond, and this looks like retribution to me. Our legal system slaps these teenagers on the hand, and they are out almost as soon as they are booked."

Lex pointed to the pavement. "It's all yours," she said.

"We'll take it from here."

Lex said. "We're here on another matter. If you need us, here's my card."

The detectives walked back to do what they had come to do: find Tomas Costa. Once they were at building C, they strode past bike racks where chains attempted to safeguard the bicycles. Several tenants were staring at the basketball court and victim. "Who was shot?" one person asked.

Not wanting to reveal the victim's name, Lex said, "I'm not sure."

Standing at the building's entrance, she heard, "You're cops," from a man with a beard and white hair.

"Yes," Lex retorted. "We're here to see Tomas Costa."

"Tomas who?" the same man asked.

"Tomas Costa, apartment three-oh-seven."

"That's my place," a long-haired, overweight man said.

"Does he live with you?"

"Never heard of him."

"Are you saying Tomas Costa doesn't live here?" Gil asked.

Lex asked the crowd, "Does anyone know Tomas Costa?"

Not one of the dozen people standing there acknowledged the name, and Lex knew they had been taken for a ride, deceived, sent on a goose chase. "Sorry to bother you," she said. "I hope they catch the shooter."

▲

Back at the hotel, the partners decided to split up. Gil made his way to see Westbrook, while Lex sought out Fullerton. She found him at Betsy's desk. "We were just at the address you gave us for Tomas Costa. He's not there and nobody seems to have any idea who he is."

"What?"

"When we got near his alleged apartment, there was a bang and we saw a teenager sprawled on the basketball court. He was dead. The area police said that type of violence is not uncommon there."

Betsy said, "I didn't think 165th was that bad."

"Where did you say?" Lex asked. "We went to Mills Apartments, West 176th."

"That is the address I have on file," Fullerton said.

Betsy chimed in. "The cabinet files? They have not been updated. He moved from there a while ago. He's near Yankee Stadium." She clicked her computer keyboard. "Here's his updated address." She handed a piece of paper to Lex.

"Can you tell me what time he called in sick?" Lex asked.

"About six," Fullerton said.

Lex thanked them both, exited the room and went to see Westbrook.

When she got there, Gil opened the door. "He's not right. He's a madman. He's been drinking and now he's holed up in the office."

Lex stepped to the office's French doors, and quietly opened them.

Westbrook was staring out the window with his back to Lex. Then, facing her, he said, "I'm not in a very good mood. Leave me alone."

Lex allowed her frustration to creep into her tone. "I can see that, and neither am I. What's going on? Gil said you and your agent were arguing."

"God damn right we were. He's countersuing me. And he had the balls to bring Svetlana into the fray."

"Take a deep breath," Lex suggested.

He chugged the remaining scotch from his glass. "It's all getting to me. Bastard kidnappers. Their silence is deafening. What are they doing to Svetlana? I need a Xanax."

"I may need one too. Try to remain calm. They will send a message soon."

"Easy for you to say. And what the hell was so important that you blew me off?"

She knew it wasn't wise to mention their venture to Tomas Costa's alleged apartment. "An emergency call came in and we were sent to assist another detective. Anyhow, we didn't forget you."

"No, but the kidnappers have."

"I doubt it. They're up to something."

"I better find out soon. You'll be the first to know."

"Second to know," Lex said. "We have to file a report now for that incident we got called to. Get some rest."

"Rest? I haven't had any in over a week."

As they were leaving, Gil asked how she made out downstairs with the manager.

"That address Fullerton gave us is an old one. Tomas lives out by Yankee Stadium. Let's go there."

Gil said, "It will be quicker to get uniforms over there. Time is important."

"I'm calling Pressley," Lex said.

She phoned him and relayed the details. Then she said to Gil, "He agrees. He'll ask local uniforms to go there. We can return to the precinct."

An hour after returning to the precinct, Pressley came to their cube. "You won't believe this, but police went to the residence you identified near the stadium, and Tomas wasn't there. In fact, the apartment is vacant, and the landlord has no idea where he went."

Lex was stunned. "Are you serious? Where the hell is he? I'll bet anything he is not coming back to work."

"We'll get an APB out for him, but it's a big city."

"Who says he's still in New York?" Gil commented.

"Great," Lex said. "We let him go when we had him."

CHAPTER 19

Lex walked up the steps leading to her front door and opened the mailbox to find a rolled up annoying flier and an electric bill. Inside, Cassatt seemed to be normal, yawning and lying on the couch. When she set the mailings on the kitchen table, she saw a note from Liz.

I'm at Shannon's. Will have supper there and should be back by seven.

Kicking off her shoes, she tossed the flier into the basket. The $149 utility bill could not be ignored. *It keeps going up.* She tossed it on the counter with the other bills she had yet to pay.

Cassatt finally made her way into the kitchen and mewed. "It sounds like you are hungry." After feeding her pet, Lex went upstairs to change into a pair of sweats. She then came down and opened the refrigerator. A container of half-eaten mango chicken alongside rice in a box spoke to her, so she heated the food and ingested a quick meal.

Intending to relax, Lex made herself comfortable, put on her reading glasses, and opened a Grisham book she'd gotten from Amazon. Having read the first ten pages, she was interrupted by the phone. It was Shannon's mom, Elaine. "Hi," her friend said. "I know Liz said she had to be back by seven, but I was wondering if you wanted to come over for a while."

Lex put down the book and rested her reading glasses on the table. "Sure."

Fifteen minutes later, Lex and Elaine sat in the TV room with teenagers out of sight, both moms with a cup of tea in front of them.

Elaine said, "I haven't seen the Phantom, but I'm glad you had a good time."

"We did. I didn't think I would enjoy it as much as I did."

"I'm happy for you. You two seem to get along well."

"So far. I still intend to keep it going slow."

Elaine smugly looked at her. "How slow? You did spend the night with him."

Lex grinned. "You know what I mean, not that slow. And this weekend, he's taking me to Mastrangelo's."

"The one time I met him he did seem charming, not to mention handsome."

"Thanks."

Elaine drank from her cup. "So, I have some interesting news for you. Remember that doctor I told you about?"

"The radiologist?"

"Yes. Doctor Himmel. Well, he came to have blood drawn, and we chatted. He told me his wife died three years ago, and I told him about my divorce."

Lex grinned. "Are you interested in seeing him?"

"Maybe. What do you think?"

Lex touched her hand. "I think maybe is not an answer. I suspect you are interested in him. It's about time you began dating."

Elaine was silent.

"Hey, go for it."

"I will."

The girls interrupted the women's conversation. "I forgot to feed Cassatt," Liz said.

"I fed her. Are you girls all caught up on your homework?"

"Sure," Liz said.

Lex took the last sip of her tea. "Grab your backpack."

The Stall women walked to the door. Lex gave Elaine a hug and thanked her for the drink and conversation.

"We'll talk," Elaine said.

Chapter 20

Lex tried but couldn't stay away from her old habit, so she stopped and bought a Starbucks latte on her way to the precinct. All the while, the detective knew she would hear about it when Hutch saw her.

Much to her delight, Hutch and Benzinger were not in their workspace, so she only had to fend off Gil and Pressley. "I could smell it a mile away," Gil said.

Placing the drink on her desk, she wondered if they had seen the last of Tomas Costa. Where was he, and how was he involved in the kidnapping?

Pressley stood at the open-doored cube. "At it again? What's with the latte?"

"I think better with it."

"About Tomas Costa…what's new?"

Lex said, "Not a thing. Thanks for putting out the APB for him."

"By the way," the captain continued, "Scalderone called. They tried to track the drone by contacting local airports, but it did not appear. According to them, those devices are hard to detect because they act irrationally, no specific flight patterns. Conditions would have to be ideal, or they would have to be aware of those devices in the sky."

Lex said, "And that's why the kidnappers chose three in the morning. It would be very difficult to see, and we would have to be lucky for someone to have videoed it."

"Right. Unless we get a solid lead, the drone is out of play. We'll never know where it flew to."

Gil said, "It was planned well."

Lex finished her drink. "It certainly was."

▲

Having a gnawing feeling that Tomas was on the run, Lex was stunned when Victor greeted them. "I'm glad Tomas is back. I don't think he had the flu."

"What?" she asked. "Where is he?"

"He's with Mister Fullerton."

Lex's eyes widened in disbelief, and Gil shrugged. "Beats me."

"I'm going to drop in on Fullerton. In the meantime, go see Westbrook." *I can't wait to hear Tomas's story. I was so sure he'd never be back!*

She purposefully entered the manager's office. "Is Tomas here?" she asked Betsy.

Pointing to Fullerton's closed door, she said, "He's in there."

Lex knocked and announced herself. "Mister Fullerton, this is Detective Stall. May I come in?"

"The door is unlocked."

Going inside, she saw the valet seated in a chair next to the manager's desk.

"Good morning, Tomas," she said. "I was waiting for you to return my call."

"Sorry about that. I really slept a lot yesterday. I feel better."

"So where exactly do you live? We mistakenly went to Washington Heights. Obviously, you weren't there, and then we had patrolmen go to your flat by the stadium, but it was vacant."

"Geez, I only lived at Mills for a short time. They only knew me by Toco, but I'm sure they smelled police and clammed up. The Yankee Stadium apartment was a month-to-month, and I left that to move in with my girlfriend, Charlene."

"I need to update my list," Fullerton said.

Tomas gave the location, and the manager updated his file.

Lex was still skeptical about him but decided to take a less hostile approach interrogating the valet this time around. "Did you and Svetlana have any conversations before she disappeared?"

"No. I just saw her walking west."

"Would you mind repeating to me what you had said about the man who gave you the envelope? Sometimes people remember certain things later."

"Now that you say that, I did notice a scar on his hand. I saw it after he handed me the money."

"Can you describe it?"

"It was kind of like a gash between the thumb and index finger."

"Anything else?"

"Not that I can recall."

She was sure he told another untruth. *I watched the video twice and saw no scar.* "Thank you. If you think of anything, let me know. And I do apologize for being rough on you the last time we spoke."

As she wended her way to Westbrook's, she saw Gil walking toward her. "He's not there. I mean he didn't answer. I knocked several times, and I called him. No answer. What's the deal with Tomas?"

"Long story. He lived near the stadium for a little while, and he also resided at the apartment where we unfortunately ran into the basketball court shooting. Apparently, he moved in with his girlfriend, a few blocks away from the Bronx location, but he never told Fullerton."

"You're kidding?"

"No, and I'm positive he lied to me again. He stated there's a scar on the hand of the man who handed him the envelope and the money. Did you spot it?"

Gil said, "No. There was no scar. We don't have time to waste. Westbrook may be in trouble or worse yet—dead. We have to get into the suite now!"

Lex winced. "Fullerton should have a master key. Stay here." She hurried back and nearly bumped into Tomas as he was leaving the office. A polite nod was the only attention she gave him. Then she spoke to the hotel manager. "We have to get into the Westbrooks' suite. Do you have a key?"

"I do. Why are you asking?"

"We need it right now."

Swiveling his chair toward the safe, Fullerton retrieved the master key and handed it to her. She left without answering Fullerton's query, rushing to meet Gil at the elevator.

Exiting the lift, Lex opened Westbrook's door and took a quick look around. "I don't see any notes or signs of a struggle. Nothing looks out of the ordinary."

"I'll check the bedroom," Gil said.

In the office, there was a cell phone lying next to the computer. "His phone is here. That's why he didn't answer it," Lex said.

Gil joined her. "Bedroom is okay. His bed is unmade."

She picked the phone up and browsed recent calls. "The last call was from his agent, Lydell Lawrence. It was last night. I don't see any new texts." She moved to the computer and saw an email. "This came in at ten p.m. last evening from Lawrence, and it was not responded to. Come take a look at this."

We can work things out. Again, sorry about Svetlana.

"I'm calling Lydell Lawrence," she said. When the conversation ended, Lex was disappointed. "He's not there. Lawrence says Westbrook won't return his calls or emails. It's video time again."

They raced downstairs to Fullerton, and he retrieved the outside surveillance feed so the detectives could view it. "That's him exiting the hotel," Lex said. "He's alone, dressed in a suit, carrying a brown canvas briefcase." Her jaw clenched. "Are those suitcases still in the safe?"

"Yes, they are."

Gil pointed at the screen. "He left at eight thirty a.m. Where is he off to?"

"Let's go see Victor and Tomas."

Down to the lobby and outside they went. Fortunately, the valets were at their work stand and Lex faced them. "What time did you both get here?" she asked.

Victor said, "Seven a.m."

Tomas said, "I got here a little while ago."

"Did either of you see Mister Westbrook this morning?"

"I did," Victor said. "He left here a little after eight thirty."

"Did he meet anyone or get into a car?"

"No, I only know that he walked toward Penn Station," Victor informed her.

Lex's brain was active with questions. *Was he instructed to do this? Was he told to leave his phone and wear business attire? Was he going to meet the kidnappers? And was he told not to contact us? But how was he contacted?*

"I don't suppose he told you where he was going?"

"No, ma'am," Victor said.

Tomas shook his head. "I have no idea."

Gil tapped Lex on her shoulder. "This isn't good. What do you want to do?"

"You don't want to know."

"Seriously. What now?"

Lex said, "Back to the precinct as she asked Victor to retrieve their vehicle.

Chapter 21

Essex Westbrook strolled uncomfortably among native New Yorkers and tourists on the way back to his suite, holding the soft brown briefcase. His mind was filled with thoughts of slinging his agent up by his balls.

At the Grand Truman entrance, he ran into Victor. "Hi, Mister Westbrook. Those detectives were looking for you."

"They were here?"

"Yes, sir. They left about an hour ago."

The author entered the building. While in the elevator, he checked his pocket and realized his cell wasn't there. The lift's door opened, and he proceeded into his residence, placing the briefcase on the dining table before hanging his suit jacket over a chair. When he walked into his writing space, he saw his phone. The need for a drink corralled his urge to seek his friend Johnnie. He picked it up and went to the liquor bar. Then he called Lex. "Detective, I heard you were here."

"Yes, we were there. We got the key and feared something bad was happening."

"Nothing like that."

"You scared us, and we had to get a master key from Fullerton. I saw the phone by your computer. I also saw the email from Lydell Lawrence and called him, but he said he hadn't seen or heard from you. So where did you go?"

Managing to pour himself a glass of alcohol, he moved to the living room couch. "How interesting that you spoke with Lawrence. That's exactly who we were talking about, me and Joshua Recker.

We're suing the son of a bitch, and I won't talk to that scumbag."

"I wish you had told us where you were going," Lex said. "I didn't see any messages from him."

"Joshua likes to keep things private, so I always print his emails before deleting them. I forgot my phone."

Lex sighed. "That's all well and good, but have you forgotten about Svetlana?"

Westbrook took a swig, and his face became red. "No!" He downed the rest of the drink and huffed, "So what's our next move?"

"Right now, our hands are tied, and we have to be patient," Lex answered.

"I have been patient," he said as he tossed his glass at fireplace, smashing the empty container to pieces.

"Did something just break? What was that?"

"Nothing," he responded as shards landed on the carpet.

"Are you okay?"

"I'm fine. I need to be alone."

"Call us when you are contacted."

The author set the phone on a table and soon after, he received a string of messages.

If we didn't mention it before, you know she has a hell of a body, but that doesn't matter.

Don't let Svetlana die!

And ditch the cops. Gone for good!

He pondered whether or not to redial Lex's number. Picking her card off the table swayed him to do just that. In a fit of rage, his first words were, "Jesus, I just heard from them. All they said was they want you gone for good with another threat about killing Svetlana. Damn it. They also indicated she was being used. Christ! They are fucking her."

"Let's calm down. I know it's not easy. Listen, regardless of what they say about the police, it's apparent they do not care and have no fear. They are filling you with scare tactics."

"Well, it's working."

"We're still here, and we're with you, waiting for the next move."

"Right."

"We'll get them and rescue Svetlana."

CHAPTER 22

Lex sat at her desk, thinking about the author as well as the hostile conversations between him and Lydell Lawrence. Stepping away from her partner, her familiar prance around the squad room began. *We know he has a beef with his agent. There must be more to it than we know. Could Lydell Lawrence be a suspect? He knew he was about to be fired. Might this be what it's all about?*

Lex approached Gil. "We don't know who the kidnappers are, but we do know Westbrook and Lydell Lawrence are feuding. We should hear the agent's side of the story. Is he vindictive enough to initiate a kidnapping? After all, he is losing a moneymaking client."

"You really think he could have something to do with this?" Gil asked.

"Hey, you played baseball, right?"

"What's that got to do with anything?"

"We need to cover all the bases."

Gil gave his partner a smirky grin. "I'll look him up." He faced his computer and googled Lawrence's name. "He has an office on Lexington Avenue. Here's his number."

Lex picked up her desk phone to call him.

A female answered. "Lydell Lawrence Agency."

Lex identified herself and was put through to the businessman. After a brief conversation, she set the phone down. "He can meet with us now."

▲

The agent's office was located next door to a Borders bookstore. "Figures," Gil commented.

Inside, Lex noted the office was on the first floor, suite 112. Upon entering, his secretary named Hanna greeted the detectives who identified themselves. An open door was to the right. "He's expecting you. Go ahead in," she said.

Lawrence raised his head. "Please close the door and have a seat."

Before Lex or Gil could say anything, Lawrence, while placing his glasses on the desk said, "Look, any differences I have with Essex Westbrook are not related to the situation with Svetlana. I'm praying for her."

"We appreciate that," Lex said. "I'm sure he does too."

Lawrence put his glasses back on and clasped his hands. "I don't know what got into him. He thinks I stole money, royalties. Look around. See my inbox? Do you see how many manuscripts are in there? I have no shortage of clients and prospective authors, and reading those things is a chore. Ninety-nine percent are garbage. Anyhow, if I had stolen from one of my writers, and word got out, they'd all be gone. My door would say 'Vacant.'"

Lex said, We saw an email from last evening that he never responded to."

"That ignorant jerk. Somehow he thinks I took more than my fifteen percent of his royalties. I can assure you that has never happened. You know, his ego made him think he was bigger than life when he was named best author, and he said he wanted a bigger piece of the pie. That's not how it works. He wants to go independent and reap a larger percentage of profits. He has no idea how hard that is to do. And whether he likes it or not, and whether his lawyer likes it or not, the publisher owns the rights to his books. He should understand that."

"He fired you, didn't he?"

"He did over the phone, but I have nothing in writing that severs our relationship. I bet he never follows through. And that sleazeball lawyer, Recker, hasn't got a leg to stand on."

Lex continued, "Mister Westbrook seemed extremely agitated and adamant, and I saw your emails."

"Yeah, well, when he gets a bug up his behind, he can be a

stubborn mule. And Svetlana's disappearance hasn't helped his attitude any. I told him I'd file my own suit, because he would be in violation of his contract." He calmed himself and said, "Amazing how Svetlana ended up with him. Do you know that story?"

Gil said, "Actually, we don't. We know she's several years younger than him."

"Right. She had worked at the bookstore next door, and he met her when I arranged a book launch." Lawrence took a deep breath. "I still don't know why a woman that attractive ended up with him." He sat back. "You know Essex's first wife was killed in the terrorist attack on 9/11, don't you?"

Lex nodded. "We do."

"And Jillian, that was a whole different story."

Lex squinted. "Jillian? Who is she?"

"His mistress. He didn't tell you about her?"

Gil said, "He's never mentioned her."

Lawrence took a deep breath. "Wow. He was having an affair with her, and she went to jail not long after his first wife, Margaret died."

"Jail?" Lex asked.

"Yes. As I heard it, she was selling drugs and got twenty years."

"Are you saying Westbrook was an addict?"

"He won't admit it, but he was and got off the stuff after she was gone."

"And Jillian went to jail."

Lex remembered the names of a couple of authors Westbrook had stated. "What about Chandler Browning or Eldridge Gladstone? Mister Westbrook mentioned their names as authors who don't like him very much."

Lawrence nodded. "I know, but I've never had any problems with them. They were at our table at the awards dinner."

"Westbrook said those two were not happy about the awards," Gil said.

"Yes, but only one author can win it; all the others think they should have won it. It's not unusual for some dissention and jealousy."

"We'll have to speak with them," Lex said.

"Browning lives in Worcester, Massachusetts. Gladstone is in

Seattle. Do you want their addresses and numbers?"

Lex took out a pen. "Yes, that would be helpful."

Lawrence gave her the information, and Lex took a card from her purse, placing it on the desk. "Thank you," she said.

After exiting, Gil pulled the squad car into heavy traffic, and Lex called Westbrook detecting extreme tension in his voice.

"They haven't contacted me. I'm going nuts."

"That's understandable," she said.

"Your voice is fading in and out."

"I'm sorry. We're in the car." Lex didn't want to share where they had been. "We're coming to visit you."

"Okay."

▲

Westbrook seemed disoriented when the detectives walked in. "I just took a pill. It's worse. I'm getting headaches now." When his phone rang, he said, "It's my attorney."

Lex and Gil listened to the author's side of the conversation. When it ended, Westbrook was visibly even more dazed and confused. He took a seat in an uncoordinated way.

Lex said, "You're pale. Are you okay?"

"I feel sick." His breathing appeared to slow, and his eyes closed. His body slouched in the chair as he passed out.

"He's out." Lex checked his pulse. "It's shallow."

Gil called 911 and requested an ambulance.

"It may be his heart," Lex said.

Gil looked around the suite. "There's an open bottle of pills by the table. He may have taken more than he should have."

"What are they?"

"Xanax."

"And that dry glass means he's had a drink or several."

She inspected the contents of the open bottle. "Less than half full." Glancing at her phone, she said "It's been close to seven minutes. They better get here soon."

A few seconds later, medical personnel entered. "He just went out," Lex told them.

An EMT checked his airway, and it was clear. She then took

Westbrook's vitals and said, "I see he's been drinking. How much has he had?"

"We don't know," Gil answered. "He said he took a Xanax before we got here. He may have taken more than one. The bottle is on the table."

"The EMT said, "It seems to be a reaction, like a serious drug overdose. Those two, alcohol and Xanax, don't mix, especially if he's taken more than one dose."

The other EMT wheeled in a stretcher. "Oxygen. Let's get him on some." After they had stabilized Westbrook, they took him out to the elevator.

Lex asked, "Where are you taking him?"

"Mid-Manhattan."

Gil said, "We've certainly been to that hospital before."

As they walked toward the door, a beep sounded, and Lex looked around. "Wait." She spotted Westbrook's phone on a table and picked it up. "It's them." She read the message.

We have another plan and by the way, Svetlana is treating us well."

She showed it to Gil. "What the hell do you suppose that means?"

"I don't know, but I'd better reply." She texted: *You're not scaring me.*

And the police stay!

A harsh reply came: *They don't scare us either.*

Lex responded: *I need to make sure Svetlana is safe. And by the way, I have a new plan as well.*

One more text came: *Smartass. You're playing with Svetlana's life. Don't let her die.*

Lex inserted the phone into her purse. "There it is again. Don't let her die."

Westbrook was taken by ambulance to the hospital. "I hope he is alright," Gil said.

Lex sighed. "I'm hoping that he is more than just alright. This really jeopardizes Svetlana's life."

CHAPTER 23

Lex neared Hutch who was leaving Pressley's quarters. "I hear the author is in the hospital."

"He is. Alcohol and Xanax put him there." She knew Westbrook was an alcoholic and took the controlled substance, but she had not been aware of his once illegal drug addiction.

Grabbing a chair beside Gil, she asked, "Have you contacted Mid-Manhattan?"

"Not yet."

Lex opened her purse and placed Westbrook's phone on her desk. "No messages. If they do send one, I'll have to respond. As far as we know, the kidnappers have no idea about the hospital. I'm calling over there now."

Lex deposited the author's cell back in her purse and used her desk phone to contact the medical facility. After a short conversation, she nudged her partner, "Let's go."

▲

The detectives inquired at the hospital's front desk where they would find Westbrook. After being told he was in room 414, they rode an elevator to the fourth floor to make their way to that room.

Lex knocked on the half-opened door and said, "Mister Westbrook."

"Come in." He was seated on the edge of his bed, wearing a hospital gown. A mostly eaten breakfast, was on a swing-armed tray. "Food isn't great, but they are releasing me. They're getting papers ready. What I had was a bad reaction to the Xanax and alcohol."

"You gave us quite a scare," Lex said.

Gil asked, "Do you remember how many pills you took and how much liquor you drank?"

"I don't remember. It was enough to put me here. Can you close the curtain and step out? I have to get dressed."

The detectives did as Westbrook asked and waited for him to open the curtain. Shortly thereafter, clad in the same clothes he wore yesterday, he slid back the curtain. "I'm won't mix Xanax and liquor anymore. You know, I don't have my phone. They might have left a message."

Lex said, "I have it in my purse." She didn't tell him about the messages that were sent after he'd been taken to the hospital. "Nothing yet. I checked."

A male staffer entered the room with the expected paperwork, and Westbrook inked them. "If you weren't here, I'd have taken a cab," he said to the detectives.

The overnight patient got to his feet, and a green-gowned female hospital staffer said, "Not so fast, sir. Please sit back in the chair. Hospital policy. I have to wheel you down."

Gil said. "I'll bring the car around."

Lex stayed with Westbrook as the orderly moved the chair outside. Minutes later, the author stood and with his chaperones were on their way to the Grand Truman.

Inside the suite, Westbrook sat on the couch and blew out a breath. "I don't like hospitals." His head kept lolling backward as if the bar behind him was calling his name.

"I don't think that would be wise," Lex said.

"I don't care about the liquor. It's Svetlana. May I have my phone?"

Lex hesitated before giving it to him. "Listen, after you were taken out of here yesterday, a message came in, and I had no choice but to respond to it. Take a look at your texts."

He did and scowled. "What the hell does this mean?"

"It means they are up to something, and I replied that we have a new strategy."

"And exactly what are we going to do?"

"I'm not sure."

He furiously rubbed his head. "Bastards are treating her as a sex toy."

Lex said, I told you, that's a scare tactic, and you are falling for it." Before she could say anything else, there was a knock on the door.

Opening it, Westbrook was met by Cedric, who held a small FedEx package. "Sir, this is for you."

The harried man accepted it and reached for his wallet to tip the concierge. "Is this what they mean? A new plan?" he said as he placed the present on the table.

Lex inspected the package and noticed the label. "This is the same false Bronx Zoo return address as before."

Westbrook retrieved a knife from the kitchen and slit open the box. Lex couldn't see what he saw; instead, she watched him drop Svetlana's ring on the floor, take a second look in the box, and turn ghastly white. He let out a primal scream and shouted, "No!" Then he rushed toward the bathroom.

Lex and Gil looked at each other, then peered into the box. "My God," she said. "This is disgusting." Sounds coming from the bathroom indicated Westbrook was sickened by the sight. "He's throwing up."

"My stomach is queasy too," Gil said.

Westbrook returned to the room, a washcloth in hand, and glanced again at the unthinkable body part that had been sent. His face was now blood red, and he sat nearly paralyzed for several minutes.

Lex settled beside him. "I have a feeling it's not what it appears to be. It might not be hers."

"They're going to kill her, torture her, slice her up piece by piece. That finger is just the beginning."

Lex sighed. "We don't know that. It has to be analyzed."

"Are you out of your mind? It is hers."

"If it is, we should be able to tell by the prints. We need to get it to the lab."

"Then what?"

A familiar ping sounded from Westbrook's phone. He immediately grabbed it and read the message aloud. "Svetlana is fine, nine fingers and all. We'll let you know what to do next. Our plan is the one that matters." He took a breath. "They want to drive me crazy."

Lex read the message herself. "They know they can't do that if they ever expect to be paid."

Gil said, "I don't think he should be alone."

Lex said to the beleaguered author, "Are you sure there isn't anyone who could stay with you?"

"I'm okay. I don't need anyone. I need this to be over. Please go." He picked the ring off the carpet, and stepped toward his booze.

Lex pointed at him. "You keep off the liquor!"

"Okay."

Gil collected the new evidence by taking a pair of gloves from his jacket and placing the finger in a plastic bag.

Lex whispered to him, "The pills. I'm going to take the Xanax. We can't stop him from drinking, but at least he won't have the drug."

"Good thinking."

She tucked the bottle into her purse. Westbrook was twitching, and she touched his elbow as he moved past her. "Don't tell them about your attack."

"You think they don't know? They seem to know everything else."

"Maybe not. They don't appear to know about your hospital stay."

"Whatever."

"Remember, no alcohol."

"We'll see about that." The frown on his face created impressive forehead wrinkles.

"Look. We can have someone here to keep you company."

"I said no! I'll be okay. Damn bastards. They could text me anytime. Maybe tonight, Saturday, Sunday, Monday. Who the hell knows?"

"When they do, you know what to do," Lex said.

"Yeah. Shoot myself and end it."

"Do you own a gun?"

"No. If I did, why would I tell you? Leave me now!"

The detectives left the hotel and got into their vehicle. "You know damned well the liquor will be consumed," Lex said.

"I have no doubt."

"It wasn't the right time to bring up Jillian. I'm sure he'll tell us a story soon."

Before going back to the precinct, Gil steered the car toward the laboratory. "What do you think?" he asked.

"Your guess is as good as mine. I hope the finger is not hers, but then again, if it isn't, whose finger is this?"

"Rusty should be able to tell us."

"Him? We'll see. I hope you are right."

"Come on, Lex. He knows his stuff."

"If we're lucky, he will do his job correctly."

Twenty-five minutes later, the detectives entered the forensics building, proceeding to the evidence testing area. Lex espied a white-coated employee standing by Rusty's desk. The lead examiner was seated and dismissed the young lady.

The technician turned and walked out of the office, walking past the detectives. Lex and Gil stepped inside, and Rusty planted his elbows on the desk, "What brings you here?"

Gil waved the bagged evidence in front of the chief examiner. "This."

Rusty studied the contents. "A finger? Where the hell did you get it?"

Lex's edgy side emerged as she considered that to be a dumb question. "Where the hell do you think we got it. Starbucks?"

Rusty huffed. "Okay, okay. Tell me about it."

Gil said, "It was sent to Essex Westbrook. He believes it's his wife Svetlana's. We think not and want you to extract prints."

"Leave it. We'll get to it."

Lex said sarcastically, "Check it fast! We want to know whose it is."

"Yes, ma'am. We'll get back to you in due time."

Not pleased with that reply, Lex rested her hands on the desk. "And just what does that mean?"

He leaned forward. "It means I'll log it in, and we'll do it as soon as we can. For now, it's only a number."

"A number? That's it?" Lex shouted. Her power position allowed her to spear him with eye daggers. "You owe me one, maybe more, and now's the time to cash in."

Rusty stood. "Get out of here. We'll handle this when we get to it. Understand?"

Gil pulled Lex back. "Take a breather. Get into the hall. I'll finish this discussion."

A couple of minutes went by, and Gil joined his partner. "It's his job, and we have to let him do it."

"Okay, I've calmed down. Let's call it a day."

CHAPTER 24

While driving to the village, Lex wondered what to wear to Mastrangelo's tomorrow night. The anticipation of the date left her unprepared for the surprise Liz had in store for her. It wasn't long before Liz suggested having pizza for supper at their favorite Italian restaurant on Bleecker. Obliging her daughter, Lex agreed and changed clothes.

They were soon sitting at a table and waiting for their Margherita pie. Lex stared at Liz, whose hair, eyes, and developing shape were nearly identical to hers. She had a feeling some kind of request was forthcoming.

While they ate, Liz finally spoke up. "Mom, I need to ask you something."

Lex put on her serious mom face. "I knew you were up to something."

"No, I'm not. But there's a school dance coming up in a couple of weeks, and Spencer Comey asked if I would go with him."

Lex anticipated this would be starting sometime soon…boys…and she held back her unsettling emotions. "So, who is Spencer?"

"He's in a few of my classes, and he plays baseball. And I kind of like him. He's popular too. Can I go with him?"

Lex pondered her answer, but knew she had to let her daughter grow up. Boys were a reality. She smiled. "You can, under one condition. I have to meet this young man. Okay?"

Liz smiled back. "Thanks, Mom."

Leaving the restaurant, they walked toward the record store, and

Lex stopped to stare into the vacant window. *Dad, it's happening. Your granddaughter is growing up. I hope she makes good choices with boys.*

It has to happen, dear. I know she is everything to you.

That scares me, Dad. You know how I was.

Yes, but you do have to let her be herself.

Lex sighed. *Thanks, Dad. I know.*

Hand in hand, Lex and her daughter crossed Bleecker and Lex said, "I suppose you want a new dress."

"I was thinking about it. Can I get one?"

Lex looked admiringly at Liz. "Of course."

As soon as they got home, Lex's phone beeped, and she answered. "Hi."

"You sound out of breath," Stefan said.

She sat on the couch. "I just got in. Liz and I were out. Are we dining at Mastrangelo's?"

"I have reservations for eight o'clock. I'll pick you up at around seven thirty."

"I'm looking forward to it."

"Me, too, I won't be late. Have a great night."

Lex remembered she was supposed to call her friend. Elaine answered and asked, "How are you?"

"Good. Are you going out with Stefan tomorrow night?"

"Yes. Is it still okay if Liz stays with you?"

"Absolutely. She can come for dinner. Have her here around five thirty."

"I will. How about me taking you all to breakfast Sunday morning around nine."

"That's a deal."

"Okay. I have to ask you something. Has Shannon talked about a school dance coming up?"

Elaine took a breath. "She did. Shannon was asked by Steven Reilly. I told her she could go. I actually know his parents."

"Liz just asked me if she could go with a boy named Spencer. I said I have to meet him first. I'm taking her to buy a new dress tomorrow."

"Shannon asked for one too. Where are you going?"

"Macy's"

"Mind if we come?"

"That sounds like a plan. How's eleven?"

"We'll come and get you."

"I'll see you then."

▲

Late Saturday morning, the four women went shopping, and Liz and Shannon were excited to have new dresses to wear to the dance. After the purchases were made, they relaxed at Macy's restaurant and ate lunch.

The rest of the day passed quickly. After Liz had gone to Elaine's, Lex took a bath, then debated which dress to wear. She decided upon the red one she wore on their first date to the artist showing at Stefan's gallery.

Stefan arrived a few minutes early wearing a sport jacket and solid tie. He viewed his date, more specifically, the dress. "I love that one," he said.

"I like your blazer," she said.

Lex threw a white sweater over her shoulders, and they left for Mastrangelo's.

Nearly every table inside the expensive dining establishment was occupied, but the one Stefan had reserved was waiting for them. "Lovely restaurant," Lex said as the host pulled back her chair for her to sit. "Thank you."

"A server will be right over with the menu and complimentary glasses of white wine."

Lex raised her brow at Stefan. "Complimentary wine? I've never heard of that."

Stefan stared at his date. "If I haven't told you already, you look amazing."

"Thank you, and you look quite handsome."

The server poured wine into their glasses, left the bottle on the black tablecloth, and handed them menus. "I shall be back."

Stefan lifted his glass. "To a fine dinner with a fine lady."

Lex clinked her glass against his and took a sip. "So, how much is this *complimentary* wine costing you?" she asked with a smile.

Stefan laughed. "You are the detective."

The server, with no pen or pad, listened as they ordered their meals. After finishing the first glass of wine, Stefan poured them each a second one. "I know a gallery owner in Newport, Daniel Vanderbilt. No relation to those Vanderbilts, but he does take advantage of the name. He has a couple of condos there; one he rents out. It's only a three-hour-plus drive." Stefan paused and picked up his glass. "Lex, I'd love to take you away for a long weekend."

She gazed into his adoring eyes. "That sounds very nice. May I think about it?"

"Of course, but I do have to let him know in advance."

Lex gave her date a flirtatious grin. "I've pondered it long enough. I'd love to go."

The server brought the meals and said, "Enjoy."

They slowly ate the delicious food and finished their meals with after dinner coffee.

▲

The only light outside her residence was provided by a nearby streetlamp, and it wasn't very bright. Stefan held her hand as they walked the five steps to her front door. She took out her key and unlocked it.

He started to give her a goodnight kiss. "By the way," she flirtatiously said. "Liz is staying at Shannon's. I told Elaine I would take her and the girls to breakfast in the morning." She kissed him. "Do you want to come in?"

Stefan accepted her surprising invitation. "Only if I can use your bathroom."

They entered the darkened front room. Lex flicked a switch. "Go ahead."

She heard the toilet flush, and he joined her on the couch. They started kissing and between smooches, she whispered, "Wanna see my bedroom?" She took his hand, and they went upstairs where they undressed each other. She rolled down the sheets and the sex starved lovers slid into bed.

Morning came quickly and she felt his warm body against

hers. Seeing that it was a little before eight, even though a second romp was tempting, Lex knew she was having breakfast with Liz, Shannon, and Elaine. She and Stefan showered, and dressed before she kissed him goodbye.

CHAPTER 25

Lex was true to her word about treating Elaine, Shannon and Liz to breakfast.

The aroma of eggs, bacon, and other Village Diner house specials appealed to Lex's growling stomach. After the array of food had been served, she stuck a fork into her omelet and ate the first bite. "Very good," she said as she eyed the bacon. "Just the way I like it, crispy."

Breakfast was interrupted when her phone rang. She peeked at the caller ID and uttered, "Oh no."

Captain Pressley said, "Lex, you aren't going to believe this. There was a killing at the Grand Truman."

"What? Westbrook?"

"The victim is Tomas Costa."

"What happened?"

"I don't have the details. He was apparently shot outside the hotel."

"Is Westbrook okay?"

"As far as I know. Get down there."

"Have you called Gil?"

"He's on his way."

Lex put the phone back into her purse and took a last sip of coffee. "I have to go. Sunday is no day off with this job." She looked at Liz. "You go with Elaine and Shannon. I'll see you later."

The harried detective left her credit card on the table. "Liz, charge the meals and give me my card later."

Lex walked toward home faster than normal to get her badge

and weapon. On the way, she called Westbrook. "Are you alright? What happened?"

"I don't know for sure. All I see are police cars and an ambulance. I went down to the lobby but was told to stay away. I heard someone shot Tomas."

"I'm on my way over, and Gil should be there soon as well."

After retrieving her gear, she grabbed keys for the trusted Corolla sped to the scene where an officer at the base of the Grand Truman driveway allowed her car past him. She parked behind a black and white. Several horrified hotel guests were kept back as they continued watching the horde of police personnel in the area. The news mongers were still swarming around, and Lex made her way past them.

Tomas's bloodied uniform, and body were sprawled five feet from the valet stand. Lex approached medicolegal examiner, Pam Bruckman, who looked up at the detective. "One shot to the heart."

"Any witnesses?"

"Oh yeah, quite a few actually. Some inside and some standing in back of the tape."

Lex approached her frenemy, Rusty Brainerd. "Pam said there are witnesses. What about evidence?"

Rusty smiled smugly. "Got that too."

Lex retorted, "What's the smirk for?"

"You don't know, do you?"

"What's going on?"

"Look up, Lex. What do you see?"

"I see the sky." Lex wanted to pound him. "Okay, smartass. Tell me what's going on."

"A drone carried the weapon, and it was fired remotely. I have a weapon, and it appears to be a ghost gun. It broke when it hit the ground. And the drone smashed into the hotel and splintered."

Dumbfounded, Lex walked toward the tagged drone as well as the shattered weapon. *This is crazy. They shot him, and I think they purposely destroyed the drone rather than letting anyone see which way it was going to fly.*

Gil joined Lex and Rusty. "I just got here."

"You need to hear this," Lex said to her partner.

After revealing what she knew, Gil said, "Unbelievable."

Lex tapped the kneeling Rusty on his shoulder. "We're going to talk to bystanders, but I want to get another look at the weapon before we leave."

Pam drew the detective's attention and handed Lex a set of keys, a wallet, and a cell phone. "I took these from his pockets."

Lex thanked her, and she and Gil neared the spectators, over a dozen, who were still watching the police activity. "Who saw what happened?" Lex asked.

Several people almost simultaneously answered, "We did."

"Okay," she said. "Don't all speak at once, please." She addressed a man and woman who appeared to be middle-aged and together. "Tell me what you saw."

The man wearing a gray jacket said, "We came out, and I handed the other valet my stub so he could go get our car. Suddenly, there was a humming noise, and I saw it. Then the drone quickly hovered a few feet from that valet, and I heard a bang. Next thing I saw was him falling to the ground."

She browsed the crowd. A tall, mustached man waved at her. "I saw that flying thing and heard a shot. Then it crashed."

"Thank you."

The detectives rushed into the lobby, and Lex grunted. "News hounds are here already."

The media people sought comments from witnesses, and Lex couldn't do anything about that now. She forged her way through the crowd but didn't see Fullerton. With Gil beside her, she asked Cedric, "Is Fullerton here?"

"Yes, he showed up about twenty minutes ago. He's in his office with Victor, who is pretty shook-up."

"Thanks," Lex said. "We're going up to see them."

When they entered, Fullerton said, "I had to be here."

"I'm sick," Victor said. "It was crazy. Tomas was shot by that thing."

"We obtained statements from witnesses. What did you see?" she asked Victor.

"I actually didn't see much because I was driving a guest's Accord out of the garage for pickup. Tomas was on the ground. I had no idea what happened except it looked like he'd been shot."

Gil said, "I think you should stay here for a while. The press is downstairs." He took out his cell and phoned Westbrook. "Mister Westbrook, we're here and are coming up to see you." The detective faced Lex. "He says he's okay."

Lex blew out a breath and said to Fullerton and Victor, "We have to go. You two try to relax."

Lex and Gil left the management office. "Before we go to see Westbrook, I want to get another look at the gun and drone."

Outside the hotel, the partners approached the ghost gun and broken drone. "This doesn't look like the other drone. What do you think?" she asked Gil.

"Yeah, it's smaller."

She took photos and caught the still kneeling Rusty's attention. "Hey, Rusty. Take good care of these."

Chapter 26

When Lex and Gil entered the author's residence, the glass of scotch in his hand spoke volumes. His eyes were glassy. "They're killers. They're going to kill Svetlana. Take a look at this."

Tomas had to go. He might not be the last.

"Try to gather yourself." Lex knew what she was about to say may not be true, but she had to be convincing. The first step was to stand in front of him. "Look, they shot Tomas because he was in on the kidnapping, and they were afraid he was a weak link. They still want money, and they know they won't get it if they harm Svetlana."

"I agree," Gil said. "They'll contact you again. We should discuss getting you a guard."

Westbrook shrugged. "I already told you. My friend Johnnie Walker is here with me, and he's all the company I need."

Lex snarled at Westbrook, "If that's what you want, we'll leave you two to tough it out."

"That's what you said the last time, you lied."

"And you know why. Goodbye."

The detectives rode the elevator to the lobby where reporters were still seeking witnesses. The emergency vehicles had left, but a few uniforms were still on the hotel grounds. Lex saw Fullerton at the registration counter. "How is Mister Westbrook?" he asked.

"Okay for now. How is Victor?"

"Better. I sent him home."

Gil started for the revolving doors. "Not yet," she said. "The seating area is vacant. Why don't we sit there and check Tomas's things. I have his wallet, keys, and phone."

"I'll follow you."

Sitting next to each other, Lex said, "I'll look through the wallet." She handed Gil the phone. "Check this."

She sifted through the thin money holder. "Twenty bucks and a few credit cards."

He browsed text messages on the cell phone. "I can tell you one thing: he got laid last night," Gil reported. "They sure don't keep things private these days. Take a look at this."

Lex observed the lewd pictures of him having sex with a woman and turned away.

Gil said, "I didn't get a look at her face."

Lex frowned. "No, you weren't exactly looking at her face."

Tomas's cell rang and identified the call as Charlene. Lex answered, "Charlene?"

"Who is this?" the woman asked.

"My name is Lex Stall, and I am a detective with the NYPD."

"What's wrong?"

"May my partner, Gil Ramos, and I come see you now?"

"Why? Where is Tomas?"

"We'll explain when we get there. What is your address?"

Charlene recited her location to Lex and then said in a high-pitched voice, "Something has happened, hasn't it? Where is Tomas?"

"Please stay put. We will see you in about an hour."

"Is he okay?"

Lex hated that question. "I can't discuss him now. I will when we see you."

Telling Charlene that Tomas was shot and killed was a chore that neither detective looked forward to. They had been through this ordeal several times and she knew it wouldn't be easy.

Lex informed her partner, "Charlene has an apartment on one sixty-seventh."

Gil drove, crossing into the Bronx, and down Charlene's street. Lex saw the address as she peered at every building they passed. "There, that brown tenement on our left is it."

"Lucky me, here's a space," Gil said.

The detectives walked beneath overhead train tracks. Noisy pedestrians were on sidewalks, cars were double-parked, and local businesses lined both sides of the street. They entered the brownstone, Lex said, "This is the worst part of our job."

"You do it better than me."

Gil took hold of the wobbly railing as they hiked up one flight of stairs. The devastating news had to be delivered, and a young, slightly dark-skinned, busty girl opened the door. "Charlene?" Lex asked.

"Come in," she said before closing the door.

Gil stood silently behind Lex. She first introduced themselves, then said, "Charlene, Tomas is dead." Charlene screamed, wept, and sat in a chair with her face between her knees. Lex took her shaking hand. "He was shot and killed at the hotel."

Sobbing, Charlene could barely talk. She looked up and yelled, "No. He can't be dead!"

Lex handed her tissues, and the distraught girlfriend dried the water from her face.

Gil didn't interfere and stood next to Lex.

Gazing directly into her eyes, Lex said, "All we know is that earlier this morning, Tomas was shot and killed while he was at the valet stand."

"Who shot him?"

Lex said, "That's just it. Nobody shot him, at least not directly. The gun was fired remotely from a drone."

"What?"

"I know it sounds crazy, and it is."

Charlene cried again, so it took a couple of minutes before Lex continued. Droplets dripped down the grieving girlfriend's face. Lex tried to comfort her by placing a hand on her shoulder. "Listen, I know this is tough. How long have you and Tomas been together?"

"About six months, but he just moved in a few weeks ago."

Lex asked, "Has he exhibited any strange behavior within the past month or so?"

"No. Why?"

Lex didn't answer the question. "Did he receive any calls or messages within the past couple of days that seemed strange? We checked his phone and didn't see anything conspicuous." The detective omitted the part about the sex pictures.

"He didn't tell me about any calls or messages."

"Did he ever tell you he received a hundred dollars from a man in a limo?"

"No."

"What about friends? Does he have many?"

"Not really. His best friend, Gator, lives a few blocks down."

"Gator?"

"Freddy, actually. He's from Florida."

"What about family?"

"I don't know much. All he said was that he had been in a foster home, and then he was adopted."

"He never mentioned his birth or adoptive parents' names?"

"Not that I remember, but he said he was raised an hour from here in Bridgeport."

Lex asked, "May we take a look around?"

"What are you looking for?"

"It's just routine. Any weapons?"

"No."

Lex noticed a computer. "May we see what is on the laptop?"

Charlene got up and closed the lid. "Um, there are some rather personal things on it. I'd rather not."

Lex realized the cell phone photo of her and Tomas having sex might mean X-rated materials were on the computer and backed off. "That's your choice." The detective also knew if she needed the device, she could get a warrant for it. Curious as to the woman's profession, Lex asked, "Do you work?"

"Yes, at DeMarco's Lounge."

"A server?"

"Sort of."

The detective didn't have to be told that Charlene was used to letting men see her in underwear or wearing nothing at all. "And is that where you met Tomas?"

"Yes." She began to cry again. "I want to tell Gator."

"Don't. We'll do it. Can you give me his number?"

Charlene breathed harder, found it on her phone, and showed it to Lex. "How is it that you have Gator's number?"

Charlene huffed, "Let's just say he frequented the bar, and he gave it to me. That was before I met Tomas."

"Please bear with us," Gil said.

She eased her breathing. "I still don't understand. He didn't harm anyone."

Gil assured her, "We'll find out who did this."

Charlene bowed and sobbed uncontrollably. This time, Lex couldn't comfort her.

Gil whispered to Lex, "She doesn't look okay. I'm calling nine-one-one. She may need sedation." He made the call and ten minutes later, medical aides entered the apartment, examined her, and gave the grieving woman a sedative. An older female neighbor, after being informed of the event, offered to stay with her.

The EMTs exited, and the detectives followed the medical team down and walked toward Gil's vehicle while a train roared above them. Lex said, "Let's see what Gator can tell us."

The sound of the train waned as they entered Gil's car. Lex immediately searched, found Gator's number on Tomas's phone and entered it into her cell. "It's ringing." A few seconds later, she left a message. "I hope he calls me back soon. Nice way to spend a Sunday, isn't it?"

"Yeah, and what do you suppose Charlene meant when she said Gator was a customer?"

"You're kidding aren't you?" We know he frequented the bar, but it sounds like he frequented her, too, and he's probably not the only one. He could be on his laptop, enjoying her services."

"I wonder how many men she has entertained?"

Lex sneered at Gil. "You men. I bet you'd like to see all the porn on that computer. Will you just step on it and drop me off at the Grand Truman?"

Chapter 27

Lex drove back to Greenwich Village. Traffic was heavy and it took longer than usual to arrive home. As soon as she parked her Corolla, her cell rang, and she answered Gator's call.

His voice crackled as he said, "I got your message. Charlene said Tomas was shot."

The detective was annoyed by that statement. *So much for listening to me, she phoned him.* Lex asked, "When was the last time you saw him?"

"A couple of days ago. We went to DeMarco's."

"Has he acted strange or different lately, perhaps stressed?"

Gator was silent. Lex heard him breathing hard, and then he said, "No."

"You hesitated," she said. "What made you do so?"

"It was nothing."

"How about telling me what nothing is?"

"He hasn't been himself around Charlene. Even though he moved in with her, he was a little blind as to other guys."

"You mean taking money to have sex with them?"

"Well, I guess you could say that."

"What about you? Have you ever slept with her?"

"Okay, but that was before Tomas began seeing her."

"Did he ever mention a limo or receiving a hundred-dollar tip?"

"No."

"What about other friends?"

"It was usually me and him, but he became infatuated with her and moved into her flat. I didn't see that coming."

"What about before and even recently? Was there anyone he talked about whom you didn't know?"

"Not that I remember."

"Did he ever talk about his job?"

"He never did. He was a private guy."

"If you think of anything, call me?"

"I will, but I don't get it. Who the hell would have killed him?"

"We're trying to find out. Thank you for getting back to me."

▲

The tired detective hadn't had a chance to finish breakfast, and lunch passed her by as well. She needed a large coffee, so she stopped to get one, and then went to Elaine's.

Lex said, "How was your breakfast? I never got to enjoy mine."

"Not the same without you. I see you have a coffee. "Do you want a sandwich or something? I have cold cuts. Turkey or ham?"

Lex drank from her cup. "Turkey sounds good. Are the girls upstairs?"

"Where else would they be? Probably texting friends."

"You mean like Steven and Spencer?"

Elaine made Lex a sandwich. As the starving detective ate, she saw a questioning look on her friend's face. "What's got you in a quandary?"

"Well, I have a little news for you. My new friend, George Himmel, wants to take me to a play on Broadway. We started talking, and he enjoys shows. So, I guess he felt comfortable enough to bypass the small stuff and take me on a real date."

"That's awesome."

Lex heard footsteps coming down the stairs, and Liz and Shannon approached them. "Did you girls have a good day?" she asked.

"Yes," Liz said. "Spencer said he can come meet you anytime."

"Sounds good. I'm tired, so we'll go when I finish my late lunch."

Fifteen minutes later, Lex sprawled out on her couch, and couldn't stop thinking about Liz. *I hope Spencer is not nerdy or a jock who thinks he's God's gift. I guess I will always worry about her. She knows I was raped at her age, and it can happen to her. I have to hope she makes her own decisions and when she is ready, she is ready. It isn't my decision, only my hope.*

CHAPTER 28

Two days before her disappearance, Svetlana had received a letter from an individual she didn't know but had heard about. Someone with a dark past. Someone she chose not to tell her husband about. A recent picture was included, but she wondered how they knew how to contact her. Svetlana wrote 'The Letter' in her diary and put the document into her purse.

Up at her usual time, the unsuspecting Svetlana showered, dressed in her purple sweats, and left the suite, passing the valet on her way out. When she reached the street, she stopped to read an incoming text. It was eleven minutes past seven. Looking east, she reversed her direction and went west. The curious woman timidly walked seven blocks to Izzy's Bakery. *Why now? Why at all?*

Approaching her destination, she saw people bustling in and out of the popular bakery and breakfast shop. A young man held the door for her to enter. Quickly scanning the seating area, she remembered the photo that was sent and recognized the messenger. Svetlana nervously took a seat at that table. "Who are you? she asked.

"I'm someone who has a story to tell you."

"What kind of story?"

"I keep thinking about you."

"Me?"

"Yes. There are some things you should know, and we want to share them with you."

"We? Who are we?"

"Come with me. We haven't much time. It's a little past seven thirty, and my ride will be here momentarily."

They walked outside, and a black limo pulled up. Seated in the rear of the vehicle was a bearded man wearing a fedora hat. When the door opened, Svetlana was pulled into the back seat. Her new female friend sat beside her and quickly shut the door. Svetlana couldn't move. "What is this?" she asked.

The vehicle drove away with a worried Svetlana seated between two people she had never met. She was unaware that the three people in the vehicle were on their way to a place where she would be held hostage.

She wriggled enough to open her purse and reach for her phone, only to have the secretive man slap it away. He was still silent, but the other abductor said, "You won't do that again. Shut up and we'll be at our destination soon."

Her eyes opened wide. "Where are we going? what's going on?"

When the limo stopped, Svetlana recognized the Sheepshead Bay area, but the house they were about to enter was unknown to her. She was forcefully escorted into the living room where she was pushed to sit on a couch. She frantically yelled, "What are you doing?"

The bearded man was silent. A woman who had driven the limo got close to her and said, "You'll be with us for a while."

"What are you talking about? What are you planning to do?"

"This is about your husband. If he wants you back, he'll pay us deeply. You be good, and you'll be fine. It's called ransom."

GRETA'S GONE

The ransom clock was ticking as daylight crept in. Tucker toyed again with cocaine while thinking about the police. In his mind, he had to act.

The photo of a half-naked Greta angered him. Regardless of what they said, Tucker knew it was time to see Harrison Weiss, Westport's chief of police.

A mid-morning visit to the police station gave him a sense of doing the right thing. His Maserati looked out of place parked next to black and white police cars. He walked up the back steps of the brick building to the first floor, the level below housing three jail cells.

A female sergeant at the front desk asked, "Tucker, what are you doing here?"

The harried man said, "I need to see Weiss."

"He's down the hall."

"I know where it is."

Tucker made his way down the corridor and passed Assistant Chief Anton Williams. He continued to the last room on his left. The door was open, and he entered without knocking.

"Tucker. This is unexpected. How's it going?"

He closed the door. "We have to talk."

"What about? You look like you've seen a ghost."

Tucker unzipped his light jacket. "Greta has been kidnapped, and I have been instructed to drop two-hundred grand into a Swiss bank account."

Weiss's mouth froze open. "What?"

"I thought it was a prank at first." Tucker's eyes were glazed as he held up the indecent photo of Greta.

The curious chief said, "Talk, Tucker. When did this happen?"

"A couple days ago. She went for her morning run by the sound and never returned. I got a text." He showed Weiss the message and then the subsequent texts.

"Any idea who might have done this?"

"Who the hell knows? I realize a lot of people don't like me, but I don't know any who don't like Greta." He paused and uttered, "And I know a lot of guys want a piece of that ass in the photo."

Weiss leaned forward. "Okay, Tucker. Think. Anyone you can think of who has a grudge or score to settle? Anyone you owe?"

"Owe?"

"Drugs, Tucker. Be straight with me."

"Damn it, I'm straight. I kicked the habit a long time ago."

"Are you sure? You're awfully restless."

"You would be, too, if someone kidnapped your wife." Tucker wiped his eyes to try to hide the truth.

"Okay. Again, is there anyone you can think of you owe something to? What about your father?"

"He's dead, remember?"

Weiss raised his voice. " I remember."

Tucker sat back in the chair and thought about the question for a second. "I do know he screwed some investors."

"So, you think one of them may be the kidnapper?"

"Maybe, but I'm supposed to wire the money. They said they would contact me by tomorrow with the Swiss bank account number."

"Don't do it. Let us deal with it. I can get my brother on it too. You know he's a private investigator."

Tucker watched as Weiss phoned the former detective. "Marty, can you get over here? I have to talk to you about something. Tucker Rutledge is here now." There was a break as Weiss listened to Marty. He ended the call and remarked to Tucker, "Marty will be here later. Go."

Tucker stared at Weiss. "I can't sleep. I want this to end well."

"It will. In the meantime, wait for instructions."

"Okay."

"Wait, damn it. If you are lying to me about drugs, you better tell me now."

Tucker Rutledge left after engaging the police. Had he put Greta's life in danger? Only time would tell.

Chapter 29

Lex and Gil were briefing the captain. They now had a homicide to deal with, as well as the kidnapping. She explained, "Tomas and Charlene lived together, and it appears he hid a lot from her."

Gil said, "She works at night at a local club."

"A bartender?" Pressley asked.

"Not quite," Gil said. "It appears she is more than a stripper."

Lex said, "We may need a warrant to seize her computer. Charlene is very protective. I'm sure it's because there is porn on it."

Gil faced his partner. "One question. Why would Tomas give us info about the man in the limo, the scar on his hand?"

"I believe that. Tomas gave a false marker to throw us off. I also think he wanted out and said so."

Benzinger caught his comrades' attention. "Hey, Svetlana's phone records are here. Verizon downloaded them to my computer sometime Saturday. I looked at the past three weeks."

"What about Westbrook's?" Lex asked.

"I was getting to that. His too."

"Show us what we have," Lex said.

"I will. Let me tell you what I've seen."

Pressley said, "Have a seat."

Benzinger continued, "I'll start with his. There are calls and messages with about a dozen people including Lydell Lawrence, Joshua Recker, Svetlana, and a few other people. The only ones suspicious are the ones to Lydell Lawrence."

"We know those two have a feud going," Lex said. "We.ve

spoken to them both. What about Svetlana's?"

"She responded to a text the morning she disappeared. It told her to go to Izzy's."

"What time?" Lex asked.

"Seven ten a.m., and her phone has been silent since then."

"I've heard of the place," Gil said. "Best bagels in town."

"Thank you," Lex said.

"Print the data," Pressley said to Benzinger."

Neil Gerstein burst into the room. "He's back," Lex whispered to Gil as she stood.

He softly said, "Yup. Since the FBI got involved, we have Mister Agent to deal with too." The detectives attempted to make a break for their cube.

Pressley said, "Come back here!"

Gerstein faced the detectives and irately asked, "What the hell is going on? You should have contacted me. A second drone and, as I understand it, there is evidence…some sort of ghost gun."

"There is," Lex said. "It's being examined by the lab. And that drone was a different model than the last one. I took photos of it."

"Let me see." After seeing them, he said, "Do me a favor and send the pictures to me. Has Mister Westbrook heard from the kidnappers?"

"They want the money," Lex said. "Westbrook will not turn over any cash unless there is a face-to-face, and he is satisfied that Svetlana is unharmed."

"And just how are you and he going to insure her safety?"

"I'm hoping we can convince them to meet him and arrange the swap."

Gerstein smirked. "You have to be kidding. They won't go for that. Got a plan B?"

Lex added a little sarcasm to her reply. "And you know that for a fact?"

"I'm serious here," Gerstein said.

"Then act like it," Lex replied. "You're the experts with this type of crime. You come up with something."

Gerstein grimaced and then lashed out. "If you would bother to keep us informed, we'd be better suited to help. Damn it." He rose to leave and directed a darting comment at Lex. "And remember to keep me informed."

The hostile Lex saw the look on Pressley's face as he jumped in. "Here we go again. You two knock it off!"

The FBI agent left, and Pressley wiped his brow. "Lex, could it be any clearer that you and he don't exactly enjoy each other's company?"

Lex smiled at her boss. "And if I didn't have to go to the ladies' room before, I do now. I think he breathed on me."

As she was leaving, she heard Pressley say to Gil, "Can you keep her in tow?"

"I heard that. I'll be back." Walking away, her mind was running. *Idiots, I hate idiots. First Rusty and now Gerstein. Give me a break.*

As she came out of the bathroom, her desk phone rang, and Gil answered it. "It's Rusty," he yelled to Lex.

"Put him on speaker." She joined her partner. "Rusty, what have you got?" she asked the examiner.

"It's the finger. We can't tell whose it is. The skin has been compromised by acid, and fingerprints aren't unattainable."

"You're kidding."

"Jesus, Lex. Would I kid you about this?"

"No, but it has made our job harder. Thanks though."

Gil and Lex set out on a mission. They had to visit Izzy's "We'll park at the hotel and make the same walk she did, but I intend to see Westbrook first," Lex said. "I want him to open up about Jillian."

⚔

An unsmiling Westbrook opened the door and was pacing the living room like a hungry caged animal. "This wait is killing me." He shoved the latest message under Gil's nose. Then Lex read it.

Remember. Tomas was a warning. Don't be stupid!

Lex said, "That doesn't scare me." she observed the author's empty hand and was glad to not see a glass of booze. "We talked with Tomas's girlfriend as well as his pal, Gator. Neither one claims to know about the valet's involvement in this case."

"What are you telling me?" Westbrook asked.

"At this point, we know Tomas was involved but that's all."

129

Lex paused to change the direction of the discussion. "We also know that apparently, on the morning she disappeared, she received a message to go to Izzy's. That's why she walked west, and that's where she went. We're going there as soon as we leave here."

"The bagel shop by the train station?"

"Yes. Why do you think someone would want to meet her at a busy eatery like that and then force her to go somewhere with them?"

"How do I know?"

"We are hoping there is a camera that can give us a lead."

"I'll come with you."

Gil said, "That's not necessary. We can handle this."

Westbrook's phone rang, and he looked at the screen. "Hold on. It's my attorney."

Lex and Gil listened to the author's side of the conversation. When it ended, Westbrook said, "The lawsuit will be filed soon. A couple of loose ends still but we're moving forward. Lawrence will pay."

Lex thought that to be a perfect transition. "So, interestingly enough, we did talk to Mister Lawrence, and he told us a few things we didn't know."

"I can imagine."

Lex pursued the topic. "Well, first off, he swears he is legit and doesn't scam anyone. But the most interesting revelations were how you met Svetlana and the part about Jillian."

Westbrook filled his glass with scotch before taking a healthy chug. "Jillian? Just what the hell did he tell you?"

"He said you were involved with her, and after Margaret died, Jillian went to jail for drug trafficking."

"That bitch was doing drugs alright and was sent away for twenty years. What exactly did Lawrence say?"

"We know what he said. What is it that you can tell us?"

Westbrook frowned. "Hell, she was selling drugs and damn it, I admit I did cocaine for a while before quitting cold turkey."

"What is her full name?"

"Jillian Stemple."

Lex continued to probe. "And you had an affair with her?"

"Affair, my ass. She was a sex toy, a real slut. Can we get back to Svetlana?"

Lex knew she must have hit a nerve. "In a minute. Why the affair? What are you hiding?"

He frowned. "What business is that of yours? I told you; she was an easy lay and got me hooked on drugs until she was arrested."

Lex realized she wasn't getting all the information she was after and switched gears. "Okay. We understand Svetlana worked at the bookstore next to Lydall Lawrence's office, and then quit."

"Here we go again. He told you she quit?" The author shook his head and huffed. "Lawrence always had a hard on for her and he never could handle the fact that she married me."

"So why did you stay with him?" Lex asked.

"Ever hear of a contract? Are you saying Lawrence could be involved?"

"Every person in your life needs to be scrutinized," she replied. "We're going to Izzy's and will let you know if we find out anything."

The detectives entered the hallway, and Lex pressed the elevator button. The door opened. "Wait," a raspy voice said, "hold it." Gil extended his hand to stall the closing door.

"Thanks," Benton Kimball said as he and his wife stepped into the car.

"Poor Svetlana and Essex," Claudia uttered.

The lift proceeded down. "We're still trying to get to the bottom of it," Lex said.

When the door opened, Lex asked the Kimballs, "Do you mind if we chat for a few minutes? We can sit in the upper lobby area. You're not in a hurry, are you?"

The old man shrugged. "Not really."

They walked to the seating area. Lex waited for the couple to get comfortable. "How well do you know the Westbrooks?"

Claudia said, "I can't say we socialize, but we are neighbors. You know, he pretty much stays to himself, and he likes to drink."

Gil asked, "When was the last time you saw Svetlana?"

Benton said, "I saw her the day before she disappeared. We rode up together."

"Did you talk?"

"Briefly. She told me a little about their recent cruise. That's about it."

Lex said, "We haven't met or seen your other neighbor."

"Him? Anderson Flanagan? You have to get up pretty early to catch him and stay up pretty late to even see him because he spends all day on Wall Street. He's pretty private and when we do see him, he usually has some woman with him. He's what they call a player."

"Thank you," Lex said. "We'll follow you out."

Chapter 30

Lex walked with Gil toward Penn Station. The never-ending Manhattan noise began to assault the detective's ears. Joining pedestrians, they crossed busy intersections and zigzagged through scaffolded sidewalks.

Finally arriving at Izzy's, Gil said, "Look at this." The detectives took their place at the rear of the line. A patron said, "It's always like this."

Lex decided to exercise her police privilege by proceeding to the front of the line with Gil and displaying her badge. "Forgive us for cutting. We're police officers."

As a woman carrying a brown bag exited, Gil held the door for her and entered the establishment behind Lex. All the tables were occupied, and the counter had customers standing three deep.

"We'll never get to talk to Izzy," Gil said.

Lex approached a server, who had a pen and pad in her hand, and she again displayed her identification. "I'm sorry for interrupting, but my partner and I would like to speak with Izzy."

"Izzy's not here."

"Who's in in charge today?"

"His daughter, Janet. I'll get her."

The staffer walked through a set of café doors. A few seconds later, a slender woman, appearing to be in her mid-thirties and wearing a white apron, came out. "You want to see me?" she asked.

"Yes," Lex said. "Can we go somewhere a little quieter?"

"Follow me." She led them to the back of the store into a small room. "What did you want to talk about?"

"Svetlana Westbrook," Lex said.

"Her? I heard about that. She was kidnapped. What's that got to do with me?"

"We have reason to believe she was here the morning she disappeared. We think she met someone. Do you have cameras?"

"We have an alarm system but never had a need for cameras."

"Might you have seen her?"

"That's not possible. I've been in Florida vacationing with my boys. We visited my mother in Orlando. I also took the kids to Disney World and Daytona. Today is my first day back."

Lex knew she was getting nowhere fast. "We hoped you might have seen her and possibly had a video."

"Sorry, I couldn't help."

"When will your father be back?"

"Next week. He's taking a few days off."

"What about the other employees?" Gil asked. "Could they have seen something?"

"Do you see how busy it is? Sometimes it's like a zoo. I can ask, but don't get your hopes up."

Lex said. "I'm leaving my card. If anyone knows anything, call me."

"How about a bagel with a schmear?" Janet asked.

Gil looked at Lex. "I'm in. You?"

Lex said, "Sure. We understand you have the best in the city."

"Stay here. I'll be back. I'll have them wrapped to go because you'll never find a seat out there."

Sure enough, a few minutes later, the detectives were back on the street. In their hands were fresh egg bagels smothered with cream cheese. Anxious to eat the food, they sat on a bench that was on the way back to the hotel. Gil took a bite. "Great bagel. I tried one with lox once and hated it. I guess you have to be Jewish to have a taste for that."

"I am sort of Jewish, but I agree. I don't like lox."

Gil said, "Come on, you're nowhere near Jewish."

"That's not true. I do have some Jewish blood in me. My Ancestry DNA shows relatives from Austria who migrated here in the late 1880s. They settled in Brooklyn, but names were likely changed. However, I was raised Catholic."

"So, your true name might not be Maitland?"

"That's the name my father grew up with. It appears that whoever logged my ancestors in at Ellis Island may have written Mainland instead of their real names. They didn't speak English and may have been so happy to be here they may have said mainland, or the worker just wrote it as their names. That's what the immigration records say. Census records from 1910 show Maitland." She got up. "We have to see Westbrook."

While walking, Lex noticed a Starbucks. "I want to have one." She winked at Gil. "I'll tell you what: since I treated for the bagels, you can buy us coffee."

Gil sneered at her. "That's rich, Lex. Real rich." He did as she suggested, and with drinks in hand, they continued to the Grand Truman. Near the hotel Lex tossed her empty cup into a recyclables bin and Gil followed suit.

Lex said, "Jillian. I intend to make Westbrook go deeper into his story about her."

As they approached the valet, Victor said, "Hi again."

Gil replied, "We're going to see Mister Westbrook."

"He's not here. I saw him leave about a half hour ago."

"Was he alone?" Lex asked.

"No. He was with Mister Recker."

Gil asked, "Do you know where they went?"

"No."

Lex decided to try Westbrook's cell. The author answered after one ring. "How'd you make out at Izzy's?"

"Great, they gave us free bagels," She said. "Where are you?"

"At Recker's office. He's taking me to lunch."

"Where are you eating?"

"I'm not sure yet."

"Thanks for letting me know." She said to her partner, "He's with Recker, and they're going to lunch." Speaking again to Westbrook, she said, "Have a fine meal."

▲

The determined author anticipated suing his agent, but Recker was not about to submit a court filing of the legal matter.

Jennifer Recker, Joshua's wife and law partner greeted him when he entered their office.

"Joshua is waiting for you."

"Hi. Nice to see you again," he said to her.

Recker sat behind his desk and opened the file that was in front of him.

"When are we serving him Josh?"

The lawyer swung the file toward his client. "Take a look at these papers."

The author leafed through the documents. "What about them?"

"Is this everything you have?"

"Yes. Isn't this enough?"

Recker leaned forward and rested his elbows on the desk. "This is pretty standard stuff. Jennifer dug into the financials, but I'm not confident we have enough to go after him."

"But you said we were suing him."

"I said we will pursue suing him."

"What? He's milked me. I know he has."

"If so, then he's done it with precision. We can't find the discrepancies you claim are there. And the contract you signed is valid. However, you can still fire him without consequences if we can prove your allegations."

"Son of a bitch. I could kill the bastard."

"I suggest you patch things up with him. You have more important matters to worry about. What's happening with the kidnappers?"

The unhappy author hit the desk with his hand. "Nothing. We're in a waiting game." He then blurted out, "And Lawrence...the detectives went to see him, and he told the detectives about Jillian."

Recker slouched back in his chair. "Really. What did he say?"

"He told them she was in jail. I had to admit to doing drugs back then."

"That's all true, but I had to cut a plea deal for her. And do you see that yacht?" He pointed at a framed picture on one of the bookshelves.

"I see it."

"Yeah, that cost me. I had to sell it to the judge for a lousy hundred bucks. Jillian could have gone away for life after those two addicts died from the shit she sold them. We couldn't let her go to trial."

"I know."

Recker stared at his client. "I've been thinking a lot about what you said back then…and again more recently."

"What did I say?"

"You were drinking, and after you had downed a few, you said you were having a hard time with Margaret's death. Remember what you also said?"

"Damn it. Bringing her up and how she was killed still makes me cringe."

"I bet!" Recker focused on his client-friend. "I'm hungry, let's have lunch. Come on, I'm treating."

They walked two blocks to Wyoming Steak and Ale House. Sitting at a table near the bar, The alcoholic looked over his left shoulder. "I can use a drink."

"I cut that stuff out a while ago. Order one with your meal."

Westbrook faced the server and said, "I'll have a scotch on the rocks, make it Jack Daniels and a medium-rare filet mignon." Recker was up for a T-bone. They made small talk while waiting for their meals to arrive.

Once the drink came, Westbrook had a few sips of alcohol, and needed to have one thing clarified. "I just want to understand one thing, Josh. I still want to sue Lawrence. If I threaten and he's served papers, he may fess up."

"Look, I can do anything you want…for a cost, but in this case, I don't think it would be worth it."

They were interrupted when their meals were placed in front of them. Recker dropped his fork on his plate when he received a call and abruptly stood. "I have to get back. A client unexpectedly showed up and has to see me. I'll pay on the way out. Call me later."

▲

Recker stormed into his office to see his uninvited guest. "What are you doing here?" he barked.

"That's a hell of a way to welcome me."

"Who said you are welcome? Get the hell out of here."

"I want to talk."

"Make it fast."

"Okay. You know what I am going to tell you."

As soon as the intruder left, Recker said to Jennifer, "We have a problem."

▲

Westbrook finished his drink and most of the meal before returning to his residence. Stewing over Recker's words about the lawsuit being a bad idea, the author thought about it while pacing back and forth for twenty minutes. Then he settled into his sanctuary and continued editing his manuscript. At page fifty-five, he scratched his head. *This is crap and needs work. Rewriting is a bitch.*

A beep from his cell stopped him, and he held his breath.

We hope you enjoyed lunch. You're beginning to play with fire. Will forward an account number for wire transfer. Last chance to send money. AND NO COPS!

Although no one could hear him, the author shouted, "Bastards!" He responded: *I need to see Svetlana and talk to her. No Svetlana, no money!*

A new photo was sent. This one showed Svetlana sitting in a chair, her hands tied behind it. A sign appearing to have been written in red crayon read, "PAY THEM. I WANT TO COME HOME. I'M TIRED."

He was mesmerized by the photo and called Lex. Barely able to keep his voice from shaking, he said, "They're torturing her. There's a new photo, and they want me to wire the money to an account. They also reiterated you have to be gone."

Lex asked, "Did they say when you will receive the account number?"

He spoke louder. "No. It will be coming. I am going to pay them, or I'll never see Svetlana again. Did I mention the photo?"

"Yes, you did. Tell me something: can you see her hands?"

"No, they're behind her."

"So, you can't see her fingers?"

He walked to the dining room table and stared at her ring. His hands shook. "No, she just looks tired. I need to pay them."

"Under no circumstances will you wire money to them. We will counter their demand and try to set up an in-person trade…Svetlana for the cash."

Westbrook was reeling. First, Recker tells him he can't sue his agent. Then the kidnappers send that awful picture of Svetlana that burned a hole in his heart. And now the police want to do the opposite of what the kidnappers are asking. It was all too much. With the drink he had at the restaurant down, he was determined to have a few more. "I need to get blind drunk."

"Don't you do that. We will get her."

Chapter 31

Lex heard her cell and viewed the message.

I'm at Shannon's. Spencer is here.

With trepidation, she answered her daughter's message: *I'm on my way. I should be at Elaine's in about twenty minutes.*

Lex sighed, but also smiled. *I know it's happening right before my eyes. Liz is advancing to her next stage in life. So many things are quickly changing. She's really a smart, loving daughter. I have to back off and let her grow up. I am looking forward to meeting Spencer.*

A half hour later, Elaine met Lex at the door. "Spencer seems nice. Steven is here too."

Lex tugged at her glasses. "I'm sure you're right." They entered the den where the teenagers were talking. "Hi," Lex said.

Liz got up, as did Spencer. "Mom, this is Spencer."

"Nice to meet you, Misses Stall," the polite boy said.

Shannon introduced Steven.

"It's nice to meet you young men. Please sit." Lex glanced at the red-haired Steven and then drew a bead on the neatly combed, dark-haired Spencer, who was about the same height as Liz. He had a clear complexion, brown eyes, and a nice smile. "I understand you play baseball."

"Center field."

Lex caught herself and cut short her instinctive interrogation. "That's great. You guys continue your conversation. Elaine and I are going to have some tea."

The adult women sat at the kitchen table, sipping their hot

drinks. Elaine said, "Guess what? George asked me to come with him to see *Jersey Boys* Saturday night. The only thing is he wants to book a room at the Marquis."

"Hold it. He brought up sex already?"

"He didn't exactly say that."

Lex sighed. "Really. If he did that with me, he would be kicked to the curb. I kept Stefan waiting. I know he wanted to dive into bed right away, but I wasn't ready to have sex until after our fifth date."

"I have to think about it."

"Elaine, what's to think about? You know men. They all want to get laid."

"Yeah, you are right." Elaine got up. "I think it's time for the boys to go home." She and Lex reentered the den. "I hate to break up the party."

Spencer and Steven grabbed their backpacks. "See you in school," Spencer said to Liz and Shannon. Steven offered a shy wave goodbye.

As soon as the young men had left, Lex looked at Liz. "Thanks for letting me meet Spencer and Steven. And I'm glad you brought them here when Elaine was around. You understand that boys are not allowed in our house unless I'm there, right?"

"Mom," Liz huffed. "I know. That's why they were here. Did you really like Spencer?"

Smiling at her daughter, Lex said. "Yes, dear."

GRETA'S GONE

Nothing had happened since he went to see Weiss, no contact from him or the chief's brother, and no messages from the kidnappers, but Tucker wasn't prepared for what he found this morning. Opening the front door, a small box was on his doorstep. He picked up the lightweight package and set it on the foyer table. After ripping it open, he gasped. Inside was an earring, an expensive diamond earring. He recognized it as part of a pair he'd purchased for Greta. Next to the jewelry was a note written with a red marker pen.

The earring is yours. Tomorrow you will forward the money or Greta and Van Gogh may have something in common, a need for only one earring.

Look in the garage. The car is a down payment.

He ran outside toward the open garage and didn't see Greta's red Porsche Boxster. Not wanting to believe the surreal mess his life had become, he rushed inside the estate, quickly retrieved his cocaine and put it to use. The effects washed over him, putting him in a better frame of mind. He phoned Weiss and spoke faster than usual. "I need you to come out here."

"What's wrong, Tucker?"

"Shit, that's what. They stole her car and left me a present."

"What kind of present?"

"Get the fuck out here."

Less than fifteen minutes later, the police chief's car was in Tucker's driveway. Weiss rang the bell and yelled for him. There was no answer, so Weiss opened the door and found Tucker unconscious on the floor. He quickly knelt to check for a pulse, and he found one but also spotted white powder under Tucker's nose. Without hesitating, he began to shake the passed-out addict. "Tucker, wake up."

He groggily sat up. "What happened?"

"You tell me. I knew you weren't clean." Weiss gave him a caustic stare. "Damn it, Tucker. Where is it? I'm going to flush the stuff down the toilet."

Glassy-eyed, he said, "Okay, okay. I'm done."

Weiss saw the note, then he noticed the box containing an earring. "Is this it?"

"It's Greta's. I bought it. Did you read the note?" Tucker was speaking rapidly.

"I did."

"What should I do?"

"What you shouldn't do is send the money. They'll be pissed, but they can't harm her if they really want the money. We can buy time."

"Find her car and get those bastards. They have to be nearby."

"We'll get out a BOLO, and I'll make sure Marty knows about it. In the meantime, you snap out of it and keep me informed."

Chapter 32

Fixated on the recent photo of Liz that was on her desk, Lex held it for a few moments.

"You look perplexed," Gil said.

She held the picture. "I had an interesting meeting last night. I met Liz's friend, I guess boyfriend, Spencer. He seems like a respectful young man."

Gil ran his hand across his face. "Don't they all. I know the boys, and I'd probably slap the you-know-what out of any boy hitting on my daughter...if I had one. I'm glad I don't have girls."

Lex nodded. "That was spoken like a true parent of a teenaged girl."

"She's a good kid, Lex, and she is as pretty as her mother...maybe prettier."

"Thanks, that's just what I needed to hear." A call on her cell phone interrupted their discussion, and she put the framed photo back down.

"That could be Westbrook," Gil said.

To Lex's surprise, it wasn't the author. It was Stefan. "Hi," she said, "To what do I owe the honor of this call?"

"That's a hell of a question. Lex, you won't believe this. A few minutes after I got here, a couple of men questioned me. They were special agents, from Boston, named Murdock and Gaines."

"What? They were the ones investigating the Gardner heist."

"They asked me all kinds of questions. I think they think I was somehow involved."

"How?"

"I told them I didn't know much. They asked about Adrienne Chandelle. I had to tell them I knew her, and she fled the country. I haven't heard from her since."

"It's obvious they haven't found the stolen paintings."

"No, but they also can't find Altman."

"What? Are you serious?"

"Yes. I haven't seen or heard from him in months."

"Oh my God. Do they suspect him?"

"It sure sounds like it."

"Did they mention you and me?" Lex felt a knot forming in her stomach.

"No. I'm sure they don't know about us."

Lex sighed. "I won't be surprised if they show up here. We'll talk later." She disconnected the call and set her phone back on the desk.

A puzzled Gil asked, "What was that all about?"

"The stolen artwork from the Gardner. I'll tell you in a minute. We have to see Pressley." They walked to the captain's quarters. "You need to hear this," Lex said.

Sitting forward, the captain said, "You look frazzled. What's going on?"

"It's the Gardner theft. Even though we solved the Cambourd murder and tied it to the Metropolitan Museum of Art, the connection with the Gardner theft is still unsolved." Taking a breath, she then said, "Stefan called me. Those agents from Boston, Murdock and Gaines, were at his gallery earlier this morning and asked a lot of questions about it. I suspect they'll be coming here."

"Holy cow." Pressley's eyes shifted up. "Don't look behind you, but they just came in."

"Greetings," Murdock said. He spoke to the detectives. "I'd like you two to join us in the captain's office."

"What brings you back here?" Pressley asked.

Murdock said, "A few loose ends." Both agents wore serious faces.

The captain motioned across his body. "Why don't we go to the meeting room." Once there, they all sat around the rectangular table. "I take it you haven't found the paintings," Pressley said.

Gaines never said much. He was kind of like Teller of Penn and

Teller, the magicians.

Murdock said, "We spoke with Stefan Martine this morning."

Gil nonchalantly took a gander at Lex, and she gave him a quick nod as if to say *keep quiet*.

Murdock continued, "We don't believe Martine is involved with the Gardner heist, but we are sure about Adrienne Chandelle and Heinrich Altman. Supposedly, she's in France, but Altman has disappeared." He looked at Lex. "Tell us everything you know about them." He paused. "We know what you said last time, but I'd like to hear it again."

Lex reiterated that Adrienne Chandelle was a gallery owner who had planned to merge with Martine, but she had gone back to France. As for Heinrich Altman, she told them he was another gallery owner with high-priced goods who had bought the stolen Ku and relinquished it to the Met before they got involved.

Gil interjected, "Altman wasn't just there." He looked at Lex. "You're still alive because of him."

"We know," Murdock said. "We know he had a gun and shot one of the confessed thieves who aimed his gun at you. It's all very interesting. One thing I didn't tell you is that the brains behind the heist, the Boston Museum Director Maxine Simmons, was found dead in her cell a few days ago. So that source is gone."

This news surprised Lex. "Oh, my goodness."

"We are attempting to locate Altman, but so far, we have no leads. We inspected his shop, and artwork is still on the walls. We spoke with his employee, Laura Inglesby, and she told us that a month ago, out of the blue, Altman said he was closing up shop and told her not to come back. He then handed her a check for three thousand dollars. She was shocked, had no idea, and couldn't come up with a reason for his actions. We can't find any evidence of an airline ticket purchase, at least not under the name Heinrich Altman. We've checked cruises and buses. We can't find his car or evidence of rentals. Also, we can't find any purchases made on credit cards, and he cleared out his bank accounts three weeks ago."

"That's very strange," Lex said.

"Any ideas?" Murdock asked. "Did he ever mention any places to you or any names he might be using?"

Lex said, "We did interrupt a cruise to the Bahamas."

"We are aware."

"Did you look into his enlistment in the military?"

"We checked that too. He's disappeared into thin air."

The two men got up, and Pressley opened the door. "Good luck," he said.

Murdock replied, "If you think of anything, let us know." He and Gaines walked toward the front exit.

"Looks like Stefan is in the clear," Gil said.

He and Lex went inside their cube. "Phew," she said to Gil. "They didn't say anything about me and Stefan dating each other."

"And what if they do find out about you lovers?"

"Friends. And your guess is as good as mine."

Gil grinned. "With benefits?"

Ignoring the snide remark, Lex said, "One thing we haven't done is to ask shops near Izzy's for videos, nor have we tried to obtain footage from street cameras. I'll call Gerstein to tell him about Izzy's and to inform him we are going to attempt to obtain videos from neighboring businesses as well as the street cameras." Lex contacted her adversarial FBI man, put him on speaker, and told him about their visit to Izzy's.

Gerstein said, "You don't have to seek out footage. We already did and have three different videos. Unfortunately, one is fuzzy, while the others don't tell us much. We do see her entering alone and leaving with an unknown woman. They were picked up by a black limo, and the unknown woman is seen forcefully pushing Svetlana into the back seat. The vehicle drove off. Cameras lost track of them."

"How did you know about Izzy's."

"Let's just say a little birdie told me."

"Let's play fair here."

"Fair? You went behind our backs." Not giving Lex time to retort, Gerstein said, "We tracked her phone too. I was there when Izzy was working."

"He wasn't there when we went, but his daughter Janet was. Apparently, he never told her about you. Gil and I want to see the videos."

Lex said goodbye and faced Gil. "I still think he's an idiot." She made one more call. "Stefan, those two agents who came to see you were here. They never asked and didn't seem to have any idea about us seeing each other, but they did say you are not on their suspect list."

Lex heard him sigh. "That's a relief. What do they think happened to Altman?"

"It's a mystery. He just up and left."

"I never would have believed it."

"Me neither."

"Thanks. I'll see you soon, Lex."

CHAPTER 33

More than two weeks had passed since Svetlana was abducted, and Westbrook was conflicted. He felt like disregarding the detectives again by wiring the money. He also kept hearing what the detectives told him. *Do not give in to their demands*. His main concern was having Svetlana back, but even if he sent the cash, there was no guarantee that he would ever see her again.

Voices in his head bounced around making him a wreck. He called his only friend, besides Johnnie Walker, Josh Recker.

A half hour later, the lawyer was at the author's residence. Wearing a black business suit, he asked, "What's going on?"

"I'm scared, Josh."

"I can see that, but don't do anything until you get more instructions."

"I'm sick of hearing that. I want this to be over."

Recker said, "We all do." Have a cup of black coffee."

"You know what I'd rather drink."

"Yeah, and that will make you even crazier. Look, I rushed over here, but I have to be in court to handle a case. We'll talk later."

▲

It was still morning when the detectives approached Westbrook's door. In the hallway was the cleaning cart, and Lex saw Addie coming out of the Kimballs' residence. "Addie," she called, "May I speak with you?" Lex turned to Gil. "Go check in with Westbrook."

The housekeeper stood by her cart as Lex joined her. "Have you already been to Mister Westbrook's?"

"Yes."

"Can you think back a month or so when the Westbrooks were on their cruise?"

She handheld a vacuum handle, and her face wore a frown. "Why are you asking?"

Lex said, "I'm just curious. You cleaned their suite that week, didn't you?"

"Yes."

"Was anyone else inside?"

"You mean the Tuesday I cleaned?"

"Then or anytime else."

"That day I forgot to get the keys before I came up here, so I called Mister Fullerton on my cell phone and told him. He sent Tomas to give me the keys to the residences on this floor."

"Did you see Tomas go into the unoccupied Westbrook unit?"

"I didn't see him. But he told me he was there a few days ago and left something of his inside, so he borrowed the keys and returned them to me maybe fifteen later."

"Did you see him lock the door?"

"I assume he did."

Lex knew that Fullerton had given Tomas the elevator code a while ago.

"Thank you. I appreciate you speaking with me."

The author was talking on his cell when Lex entered, and Gil shrugged. "He's been on it since I walked in."

She heard Westbrook say, "I know it's a big misunderstanding. Look, Recker isn't proceeding, and I want to make things right." There was silence as Westbrook listened. "Okay," he said before ending the conversation.

Lex asked, "Who was that?"

"Lydell Lawrence. I have to see him. Recker advised me to drop the lawsuit and patch things up."

The aroma of scotch on the author's breath prompted Lex to seek out the bottle of liquor, and she found it on the dining room table. It had very little liquid in it. He blurted out, "I'm doing it as soon as they get me the account number. I already spoke with the bank manager, and she said she'd help me with the wire transfer."

"Maybe that's one way to do it," Lex said, "But we want to make them back off."

"Back off?"

"Tell them you need more time because the bank needs to authorize the transfer."

He raised his arms. "But that's a lie. I got the suitcases from Fullerton, and they are in my bedroom."

Gil said, "They don't know that."

"Play along with us," Lex said.

"What the hell will that do?"

Lex blew out a breath. "It will buy us time."

He lifted his glass. "I need some more,"

"You need to stop drinking," Lex said. "You haven't purchased more Xanax, have you?"

"Hell no. I gave that up. Alcohol is the lesser of two evils."

"Please put that glass down and walk away."

He sneered and held his ground, filling his glass with the remainder of the hard stuff.

Lex knew she was fighting a losing battle. "Call when the next message arrives."

The detectives waited for the elevator door to open.. When it did, a man stepped out. "Excuse me," Lex said. "Are you Anderson Flanagan?"

"Yes."

The detectives let him know who they were. "May we chat with you?" Lex asked.

Flanagan's unit appeared to be the same size as his neighbors. Her first though about the interior was that this room could use a woman's touch. *Typically, male bachelor, leather chairs and sofa.*

Gil spotted a large TV and a work area with a computer and three monitors. "Quite a setup," he said.

"Yeah, I have to keep up with the market."

"Have a seat," the host said. "I still can't believe it about Svetlana. She is so nice."

Gil asked, "What exactly do you mean?"

"Nice. I've been in the gym when she has, and we've talked."

"She is quite attractive, don't you think?" Lex asked.

"Wait a second. I do think she's a good-looking woman, but I can assure you there is nothing going on between us."

"What about other men in the gym?"

"I couldn't tell you. Guests use it all the time."

Gil said, "We have spoken with Benton and Claudia Kimball. She indicated you have a lot of female friends."

"I have a lot of friends who like money. Some are women. Wall Street has been very good to me. I spend ten, twelve, sometimes sixteen hours a day there. You know, a lot goes on after the bell rings."

"I'm sure it does," Gil said.

Lex ended the brief interrogation satisfied that the Wall Street fanatic knew nothing about Svetlana's kidnapping.

The detectives walked back to the elevator and rode down to the lobby. "He seems genuine," Gil said.

"I detected nothing abnormal. Now we must wait until Westbrook receives the next text. If it comes soon, he may just blindly wire the money. Let's hope that doesn't occur."

Chapter 34

Lex remembered Easter was fast approaching, and Liz would be with her father and stepbrother. Interestingly, she and Stefan hadn't discussed the holiday.

Lex opened her front door and saw Liz putting her phone away. "I just spoke with Dad. I am looking forward to spending the weekend with him and Adam. "I'm taking Adam egg hunting on Saturday. Dad said he wants to talk with you."

"I'll talk to him later."

Early that evening, she entered her ex's number into her cell. "Hi. How are you doing?" she asked.

"I'm mostly fine. Looking forward to having Liz join me and Adam. I ordered a ham and other things. What about you?"

"I really hadn't thought about it. I don't have any plans."

"Look, Lex, I know we will be forever bonded because of Liz. She's terrific, and I'm thankful you're a great mother. I wish all the grief I gave you in the past could go away. Is there any chance you would come here for Easter dinner? I know Liz would love it if you did."

Having no idea that ask was coming, she paused before speaking. "I don't know, Jon. I'm not sure that would be wise. Liz could develop a false hope that we might get back together."

"That's not my motive. I know it's over. Julie is gone, and I said I was okay, but I am still grieving and could use the company."

"I can understand that. It's easy for me to say time heals all wounds. I appreciate you asking, but I really don't think it would be wise for me to be there."

"Maybe you're right. Liz told me about Stefan."

Lex was a little surprised he mentioned her love interest. "You know, it took me a long time to start seeing anyone, and it may take me a while to trust any man again. Let's not go there."

"I'm sorry."

"Liz loves you very much, and Jon, I do have a piece of you in my heart. I wish you well. Enjoy the weekend with the kids."

"Thanks, Lex."

When the conversation ended, Lex sat Liz down. "Did he tell you what he wanted to talk to me about?"

"Yes." Liz dropped her head ever so slightly.

"Listen, I understand that he is still hurting. You are a bright light that he needs very much, as well as Adam. He asked me to join you. I hope you understand I can't be at your Easter dinner."

Liz hugged her mom. "I do. I know you can't get back together." She began crying. "But sometimes it hurts me too."

Lex was drawn to tears as she hugged Liz tightly. "You know, all marriages start out in bliss, but somehow along the way, things can go off track. That's why I am so protective of you and pray that when your day comes, your bliss will last a lifetime."

The hug was reassuring, and they dried their eyes. "I love you, Mom."

"I love you too. And so does your dad. Enjoy your time together."

"I will."

Lex realized she had not discussed the subject with Stefan, picked up her cell and called him. "How are you?" she asked.

"I'm good. What about you?"

"Still alive. No wounds."

"That's good, I guess."

"Ha ha. I need to ask you something. We never discussed Easter. Liz will be at her dad's, and I'm sure you have plans."

"Not really. I don't have anything on my schedule. I thought you may be doing dinner with Liz or your friends, and I didn't want to be a third wheel."

"No. I was afraid of stepping on your toes. So, what do you think about having an early Sunday dinner at one of the village restaurants?"

"That sounds great. What about Saturday night? I'll be at the gallery during the day, and later I'm free."

"How about a movie? I make a great bowl of popcorn."

"Got any root beer?"

"I'll get some."

"Great. It's a date."

Soon after hanging up Lex received a call from Westbrook who spoke twice as fast as ever. "Damn it. It's happening. They will kill her."

"Hold on. Take a breath."

"They texted a warning that if I don't send the money, consider Svetlana dead. You're playing with fire. Don't let that boat sail."

"I still do not believe they are killers. Tell them the bank has yet to approve the impending transfer. That will keep them at bay."

"You are nuts. I will send the money as soon as I am told to."

"I understand how upset you are but trust me. They are not going to murder her."

Shouting into the phone, he said, "Easy for you to say. Svetlana is my wife, not yours or your partners."

"Alright, please stay put and don't jump the gun." Lex changed the subject. "What is going on with Lydell Lawrence?"

His voice became less tense. "We will settle things. I'm going to visit him."

"When?"

"Soon."

Lex heard the swishing of liquid and assumed Westbrook was pouring a glass of alcohol. The clanging of ice cubes and a moment of silence did more than convince her she was right.

"I feel calmer now," he said."

"I'm sure you do."

"Yes," he said as another Johnnie Walker filled his glass. I will talk to you later."

"Gil and I will see you soon."

155

GRETA'S GONE

Another day passed with no message. Odd, Tucker thought, because yesterday was the day the kidnappers said they'd give instructions along with the Swiss bank account number. His nerves frayed, he espied the friendly white powder that Weiss didn't find and destroy.

Then his cell phone rang. "Tucker, it's Sal."

"Hey, man, I fucked up. I took a bad hit a couple of days ago. I overdosed, but I'm okay now."

"I heard Chief Weiss was there. You should have called me. Should have told me about Greta when I saw you at the barbershop. She's the best thing that ever happened to you."

"I know, but Jesus, Sal, you saw her. She was always flirting with you and every other guy in town."

"Christ's sake. You have to give her some slack. She never meant anything by it."

"Maybe not."

"Tell me what happened."

It took a half hour to tell Sal everything about the entire event. "Holy moly," Sal said. "And they had the balls to take her car and drop off an earring. That should tell us something. Whoever has her, they aren't far away."

"I know. Someone had to have seen her car, and Weiss has one of those be-on-the-lookout things going."

"I'm coming over. And stay off the shit."

"Okay, Sal. But when I get the Swiss bank account number, I'll have to call Weiss. He says not to send the cash."

Sal was the only person, other than Weiss and the chief's brother, Marty, who could be trusted, which is why Tucker decided to sit with Sal in the man cave and thoroughly examine everything. The TV was tuned to ESPN, and bottles of Budweiser were in the oversized chairs cupholders. "I've been looking at my father's client list, and at least a half-dozen shitheads who lost a lot of money are on it. One is in California, one in Hawaii, one in Florida, two in New York. The only one I could find around here is a guy named Cochran, Frances in Greenwich."

Tucker looked at his phone as it dinged. "It's them." He read the message silently.

You have 2 days.

Wire the money to this bank account number: US45 9977 4000 6728 5555 1.

He replied: You don't scare me.

The next text terrified him.

REALLY? Here's a photo.

Tucker clicked on the photo and kicked the leather chair nearest him, almost toppling it.

Startled, Sal said, "What the hell?"

Tucker stared at the picture of Greta, naked with duct tape across her mouth, sprawled on a bed. With a look that could kill, he angrily shouted, "Motherfuckers!"

Sal observed the picture. "Oh no."

Tucker slammed his fist on a table. "Damn it, damn it. How many times has she been raped?"

Sal put his arms around Tucker's shoulder. "Calm down. Let's go see Weiss."

Tucker's face was flushed when he walked out with Sal, who drove to the police station. They marched in to see Weiss. The chief stood and looked at Sal. "He just got a message and a photo."

Weiss asked, "What happened?" Tucker showed him the message. The chief wiped his hand across his face. "This isn't good. What about the picture?"

"I can't," Tucker said.

"Damn it," Sal said, "show him!"

Reluctant to reveal it, Tucker allowed the police chief to see the lewd photo. "Jesus. That is very upsetting."

"I need to send the money," Tucker said.

Weiss said, "Don't wire it. Tell them you have the cash and will only give it to them when you are sure Greta will be set free. Arrange to meet where you can see her and turn over the cash, but not before Greta is let go."

"I can't stand them treating her as a sex toy," the irate Tucker said.

Weiss addressed Sal. "Can you stay with him? I don't want him back on cocaine. I have to call Marty."

Chapter 35

There was a dark cloud hanging over Manhattan and the squad room was quiet, Hutch and Benzinger were not there.

Westbrook was quiet too, "It has to come to a head soon," Lex said.

"And I hope we are right that Svetlana is alive and will be freed."

"I don't want to even breath the thought that they will kill her."

"He's irrational as it is."

Suddenly, Lex heard thumping footsteps and Hutch's voice fill the air. "In there," he said as he directed two captives into an interrogation room. Benzinger escorted the cuffed men and sat them at a table. Hutch stood at the door and shouted to Pressley, "We have them, but they haven't confessed yet. They will though. I'd bet on it."

Benzinger stayed in the room with one suspect, while Hutch escorted the other male into the meeting room.

Lex watched and approached her boss. Before she asked, Pressley said, "They got a tip about Gwyneth Lancaster's murder. Pictures and a positive ID."

From her cube, fifteen minutes later, she heard a door open and saw the husky sleuth walking out of the meeting room. He tapped the door of the interview room, and Benzinger stepped out. The two detectives talked and then switched positions.

"They're playing the suspects against each other," Lex commented to Gil.

"Nice. Good cop, bad cop routine."

"Maybe. I know Hutch, he's a hardball player."

Ten more minutes passed before Hutch came out of the interview room, leaving one suspect behind. Lex decided to walk up to him. "It looks like you are frying them."

"One of them is going to crack soon. I want them to think about what they did for a while. I have to check in on Benzinger."

It was no surprise to her when Hutch, Benzinger, and the tall suspect, his hands cuffed behind his back, emerged from the interview room. Hutch gave Lex a thumbs-up. Benzinger collected the other cuffed suspect. "We're taking them down to be booked," Hutch said.

Pressley stood and nodded his approval.

The clamor settled down. Lex and Gil began discussing the forthcoming Easter. "Are the boys coming in from Florida."

"No. They aren't on break. We'll be going to Ray-Ann's sister's house in Scarborough. There should be eight of us with her husband's brother and their kids."

"Liz will be with Jon, and I invited Stefan down."

Their cordial conversation was rudely interrupted. "Lex, Gil. Get in here. Now!" Pressley yelled.

Rushing to him, Lex asked, "What is it?"

"Don't sit. You have to get over to Lexington Avenue. Lydell Lawrence was stabbed to death. His secretary came in this morning and found him."

"No," Lex said. "You can't be serious. He couldn't have killed him."

"Really? You know how crazy he was about stringing up Lawrence," Gil said. "Not to mention the agonizing stress the kidnapping adds. He may well have gone off the deep end."

Lex was silent for a moment. "But he said he was going there to resolve matters."

Gil shrugged. "It appears he sure did."

"Something went wrong, but I can't believe Westbrook would kill him." She paused. "Then again, we've seen stranger things. I'm calling him."

Lex was relieved when he answered. Without saying hello, in a derogatory tone, he said, "I hope you have good news."

Lex disregarded the pointed comment and asked, "Did you go

see your agent yesterday afternoon?"

"Yes, why?"

"What time?"

"Sometime after three. We had a good meeting, and we're not fighting anymore."

"When did you leave?"

"About an hour later. I stopped at a liquor store on the way back. What the hell is this? What happened?"

Lex thought it was unusual for him to go to Lawrence's and then, as if nothing happened, stop at a liquor store. She didn't detect anything other than innocence in his voice. "Did you see anyone coming or going from the office?"

"I didn't see anyone."

Without testing him further, she said, "I'll be right over. I'm leaving now."

"What's wrong?" he pleaded.

"Twenty minutes, I'll be there in twenty minutes."

Gil said, "You go there, I'm heading to Lawrence's office."

Lex drove to the hotel and even with the siren blaring, traffic delayed her arrival.

Thirty minutes later, she stood at Westbrooks' front door, and he opened it. Lex's opinion was the author looked as pale as he had when he previously passed out. An uncapped bottle of scotch sat on the wet bar.

"You've been drinking. Sit up and have some water, better yet, black coffee."

"I'm fine," he said with a smile."

"Stay put, I'll make it."

Minutes later, Lex handed him a cup of brew. "Drink this."

He blew on the hot liquid before ingesting some. Setting the cup down, he said, "I tried to call Recker, and all I got was his answering machine. He may be in court."

His eyes were hazy, but he appeared to be coherent. As the author began to rise, Lex said, "Explain to me what happened with Lawrence."

"I told you. We had a good meeting and settled our differences."

The untrusting detective stared into his eyes. "How?"

"What do you mean how? Are you going to tell me what is

going on?"

"He's dead. Lydell Lawrence is dead."

"What? I was just there."

Lex was direct with her response. "Yes, you were. Did you kill him?"

"What?" he yelled. "I don't even own a gun." His tone emphasized his innocence.

It was apparent Westbrook's impression was that agent had been shot. But Lex wondered if he was being coy. She cataloged his answer as interesting. "What makes you think he was shot?"

"I thought you said he was shot."

"No, you said that. He was stabbed."

Westbrook jumped off the couch. "A knife?"

Hearing her cell, Lex answered Gil's call. "It's a bloody mess. He was stabbed in the back. He's face down on the floor beside his desk."

"How many times?"

"It looks like twice. The knife was on the floor. Rusty has it, and it appears to be a regular steak knife. One other item is beside the body. A comb, a thin handled black comb."

"Take pictures and make sure Rusty bags the evidence."

Gil snapped at her, "Lex!"

"Okay! What about a phone, computer?"

"One of the last calls was from Westbrook at a little after two yesterday afternoon. It lasted twelve minutes. The computer is on the floor, smashed. Interestingly, papers on his desk are linked with Westbrook. His contract is in plain sight. Hannah came in this morning and saw her boss. She called 9-1-1 and she is being examined by the EMT's."

"Do you know what time she left the office yesterday?"

"About two-thirty."

"So, she never saw Westbrook."

"What about cameras?"

Gil paused. "Well, that's just it. Remember when we came here to talk with him?"

"Yes, but what has that got to do with anything?"

"A lot. There were no renovations going on. There are now. Scaffolding was erected outside this building. Cameras are gone and a street view won't capture anything but the scaffolding."

"Are you serious?"

"Would I joke about anything like that?"

"What about his wife?"

"He was divorced and lived alone. There are appointments jotted down on a calendar. We may be able to get the visitor's phone numbers from his cell. Looks like fourteen within the past few days."

"How about Pam? Is she able to estimate time of death?"

"Not yet. His body is cold. She might be able to give us a window later. What's happening with Westbrook?"

"He's very strung out and drinking coffee." Lex looked over at the author, and the sight of him rang true with her assessment.

"Call me later."

"Will do."

Lex told Westbrook, "Hannah discovered him this morning."

"Who would have killed him?"

Again, Lex quickly took note of Westbrook's statement about Lawrence being surprised that his agent was stabbed in the back. She was sure she hadn't said that, and Westbrook appeared genuinely surprised.

"There are no suspects yet. Have another cup of coffee. I'll go get it."

Lex entered the kitchen to pour more dark liquid caffeine. She opened a drawer of forks, spoons, and knives. The utensils drawer contained six spoons, five forks and six steak knives. She also noticed silverware and dishes in the sink. Lex checked the dishwasher and found three forks, two spoons, and one knife. She'd accounted for a set of eight of each pieces of silverware, except for the knives. With her phone, she took pictures of the utensils and then brought the coffee to the author.

He took a sip and set the cup on the table. "It's hot."

She sat beside him. "Let's start again. I want to make sure of your timeline."

He protested the inquiry. "You think I killed him!"

"I'm not thinking anything," she said. "I'm trying to establish that you did not do it."

"I didn't."

"Okay. Then let's go over it again. How did you get there?"

"I left here around two thirty and took a cab."

"What time did you get there?"

"I'm not sure. Wait, the clock on the wall said five before three. I set my attaché on his desk to remove my—our contract, and we rehashed our differences. He read every line and made sure we agreed. I was satisfied. About an hour later, we shook hands, and then I left, went into a package store before stopping at Greeley Square Park to sit on a bench. It was a nice afternoon.

Lex again mused. *For a homebody, that seems like very unusual behavior.* She asked, Do you remember the name of the liquor shop?"

"Hell no. It was across the street from the park."

"Did anyone see you returning here?"

"There were people in the lobby, and I said hello to Victor."

Her phone beeped again with another call from Gil. "I'm done here, and I'm on my way to the precinct."

"Don't go there, come here instead."

"Okay."

Lex watched the author drink his coffee and saw him nodding off despite the caffeine. Twenty-five minutes later, Gil joined them. "He dozed off," Lex said. "Do you have a photo of the knife?"

"I do." He showed it to her.

"Except for the blood, it looks similar to the knives in the kitchen. I made coffee and checked the silverware. One steak knife appears to be missing."

Lex noticed the brown briefcase that was resting on a corner chair. As Westbrook was waking, she nudged her partner and whispered, "The chair."

"I see you were sleeping," Gil said when the author opened his eyes. "That's a nice tote you have."

"It's a briefcase."

"May I hold it, take a look inside?"

"Sure. You'll find my contract in there."

Gil did what Lex had wanted him to do and placed the briefcase back on the chair. "There is nothing in it."

Westbrook rubbed his forehead. "I must have left it on his desk." The author's mood became sullen. "This is all crazy."

"It is," Gil said. "Homicide is one thing, but Svetlana and the money are another thing."

"Waiting. That's all we do is wait," Westbrook said. He raised the cup of tepid coffee and gulped most of it down. The last of the liquid dribbled from his mouth and he grabbed a napkin from the box on the table. Wiping the moisture from his lips, he said. "That's what I get for drinking too fast." He then tossed the crumpled tissue on the table.

"May I use the bathroom?" Lex asked.

She walked down the hall and re-entered the kitchen to examine the knives again. To her eyes they appeared to be identical to the one Gil had taken a picture of. Taking a closer look at the blades, she noticed something she hadn't seen before. *Serial numbers. These are expensive.* After sticking one in her purse, she snuck across to the bathroom, relieved herself and flushed the toilet before rejoining the two males.

"You better now?" Gil remarked.

She gave him a mock smile and said nothing.

Essex said, "I can't believe he's dead. He slammed his fist on the couch. And damn it, Svetlana may be dead too."

Lex stared at the pretty woman's picture on the credenza. Westbrook turned and uttered, "She's all I have, save her."

"That's exactly what we will do. Stay here." Lex nudged Gil. "Let's go."

As they reached the lobby, Lex said, "I took a knife from the utensil drawer. It looks just like the one you photo'd."

"Let me see it."

Lex opened her purse and showed him. "It does appear to be the same kind as the picture in my phone."

Studying the photo, Lex said, "Rusty has that knife, and he should see this one."

"He has the comb too."

⋏

After they arrived at the precinct in separate cars, Lex removed the knife from her purse and placed it on her desk for Gil to take a closer look. She pointed to what she had observed. "See that serial number? If it matches the one on the murder weapon, then that ties Westbrook directly to the killing. I'm guessing there will not be any prints on the knife that Lawrence was stabbed with. Westbrook is a mystery writer, and he would know to wipe the handle clean, but he never spotted the serial number."

Pressley approached them. "What have you got?"

Lex explained everything and the captain said, "Nice catch." She then wandered off to the ladies' room. When she returned, the captain re-entered the detective's cube and spouted words that irked her. "I just spoke with Gerstein and told him what we know. He and his agents are taking over the kidnapping."

"No!" she protested.

"You heard me."

Infuriated, Lex said, "I heard you, but it is our case, and that jackass needs to back off." Pressley stared at her and forcefully said, "Gerstein is in charge and that's that. Go home."

"Let me talk to him," Lex said.

"And start another battle between you two! I said get out of here."

Chapter 36

Svetlana sensed the kidnappers' plans were changing as they gathered at the Sheepshead Bay house. She surmised there was at least one other kidnapper who may be the mastermind. She had overheard phone conversations, but that person had yet to show up at the house. While her caretakers managed to keep her in the dark about their plans, she now feared for her life. They told her Tomas Costa had been killed and so had Lydell Lawrence.

As darkness set in, an unknown to her male entered the residence. A female, the mastermind's wife whom Svetlana had never met before she was taken, was in the living area with the other conspirators. The male began speaking to them. Svetlana, who was in the bedroom, tied to the bedpost and blindfolded, was sure she recognized his voice. *It can't be. How is it that he is behind all of this? That bastard!*

Shutting the bedroom door didn't keep her from listening as the familiar sounding man addressed his co-conspirators. "I'm not confident we'll get any money. The cops, especially those two detectives, are not going away. The game has changed, and Westbrook may be arrested for the murder of Lydell Lawrence."

A distraught female conspirator lashed out, "You didn't have to shoot Tomas."

The speaker became hostile. "You're right, but Tomas was talking to the police. He was never any good, and you know it. He would have caved. There was no other way to keep him quiet."

Svetlana anchored her chin on her shoulder and cringed.

"And as for you, I'm not the one who made you do what you

did. Blame yourself. It was your idea, and it was working."

"What are you thinking?" the other male conspirator asked. "Svetlana can identify us."

"I'm not sure what to do with her."

Svetlana yelled, "Let me go! I'll get you the money. Don't kill me."

The concerned leader opened the bedroom door, and said, "I haven't decided anything yet, but you will be coming with us when we end this, and whether you are dead or alive will be determined later."

Again, Svetlana shouted, "Let me go!"

He left the bedroom door open, and his wife asked, "Now what?" He addressed her and the other three people in the room. "I need to think about it."

Svetlana wondered what he was considering. She told him she would get him the money, so what was there to think about?

A few seconds later, he whispered to his wife, "We need to talk." She followed him into the kitchen. "One thing is for sure. You know who has to go, right?"

"I agree."

"Tonight. I'll do it tonight."

Frightened more than ever, Svetlana's mind was spinning. *He is going to kill me.*

CHAPTER 37

The detectives had to bring the knife Lex had taken to Rusty Brainerd, a task that always made her uncomfortable. "I hope he's in a good mood," she said.

Gil asked, "Are you? Lex, he's not that bad. Besides, it seems to me you two have been less hostile lately."

"That's the Julia Roberts in me."

"Don't hand me that acting crap."

"Okay, but he still gets under my skin. I'll be fine as long as he doesn't say something stupid."

Gil laughed. "According to you, everything he says is stupid."

"Trust me. I'll be nice as long as he is."

"This I have to see."

Once they were inside the forensics building, the detectives entered the testing facility. Lex glanced at Rusty's unoccupied desk. "He better be here."

Pointing to his right, Gil nudged his partner. "Rusty is over there."

Lex couldn't resist. "We're looking for you."

The chief examiner acknowledged the detectives, and he went back to his desk. "What brings you two here?" he asked.

Lex smiled. "Essex Westbrook."

"Look," Rusty said. "I know he's your priority, but we are understaffed here because of budget cuts, so step back and let us do our jobs. You're not the only cops in town."

Lex began to get agitated, huffed, and hastily said, "Will you let me finish my statement?"

"And will you sit down?" He straightened his lab coat. "Okay, what do you want?"

She took the knife from her purse and placed it on the examiner's desk.

"It's a knife. It appears to be clean."

"It is, except for my prints. Do you have the knife Lydell Lawrence was stabbed with?"

"It's with the comb."

"Has any analysis been done?"

Rusty snarled. "We'll get to it."

Lex bristled at the remark. "How the hell long does it take your employees to analyze a knife?"

Rusty glared at her. "Hold it, Miss Detective. Do you have any idea how many cases we have going here? I have three staffers, down from five. That's what budget cuts have done to me. You may be in charge at the crime scene, but we're in my house now, and I call the shots."

As hard-pressed as it was to not bite her tongue, she did so. That lasted a few seconds, and she glared at the examiner. Frustrated and smirking, she demanded, "Just get the damned knife."

Gil said, "Hold it, you two." He addressed Rusty. "We want to see if the knife you have matches this one."

"Judging by the looks of it, it appears to be the same kind."

Lex sneered at him. "Will you get the knife already?"

Rusty reluctantly heeded Lex's demand and walked into the lab.

Lex felt Gil's hand on her shoulder as he whispered, "I thought you two were going to come to blows. Keep your hat on."

Lex softly said, "I'm not wearing a hat."

"Then keep your panties on straight."

"Nice."

He returned with the bagged blood-stained murder weapon and set it down next to the other knife. Lex pointed to the serial number below the blade handle. "See this number? She asked Rusty. "It's the same one as on the clean knife. Fingerprints or not, the bloodied knife is his. That's enough to arrest him. And the comb. Even if the hairs match his, it can be explained. He was at the agent's office and admits it. DNA testing will prove nothing."

Rusty said, "It might. What if they are not his?"

"Then that will shed a new light on things."

Gil said, "What a kick that would be."

"Don't count on it," Lex said as she rose from her chair. Staring at Rusty, she said, "We're leaving now."

The detectives made their way out of the facility. Before reaching the car, Gil stopped and faced Lex. "You two need to knock it off."

"Right." She began laughing. "And for your information, I'm not wearing panties."

Gil softly said, "Um, I think that's a little too much information."

Still giggling. Lex said, "You idiot, of course, I have underwear on."

He joined the laughter and smiled wryly at her. "Lex, what am I going to do with you?"

Chapter 38

The next morning as Lex walked toward Hutch, she smiled while pointing to her shoes. "Don't worry. These really are Jimmy Choo."

Hutch laughed. "Mine are Skechers."

She noticed the captain was gone. "Where is Pressley?"

"Captains meeting downtown," Hutch replied.

Lex continued over to her desk. "How is it going, partner?"

"Fine and dandy. Hutch has been a little tamer lately."

"I don't think he'll forget my TB's too soon."

Gil again cringed. "Nor will I."

Lex's desk phone was ringing, so she picked up the receiver and listened to Captain Pressley. "Didn't you say Westbrook received a message about a boat sailing?"

"Yes."

"There was a boat fire at Pier sixty-three."

"Really," she said. "We'll get right on it."

"What now?" Gil asked.

"Pressley got word of a boat fire at Pier sixty-three. There was a victim who was taken to Mid-Manhattan. The fire is out, and he wants us to go to the hospital. Get up, lazy."

"Hey, be nice. My hand still bothers me."

"And the kidnappers bother me."

After leaving the precinct, Lex phoned the author from their unmarked vehicle while Gil drove. "Good morning," she said.

Immediately, he growled, "Good? I got another message."

"What did it say?"

"The text said, Warned you, that ship has sailed."

Lex didn't detect that he was aware of what had happened. "Something came up and we have to take care of it. We'll be at your suite a little later. Sit tight."

Mid-Manhattan Hospital was beginning to haunt the detectives. Several of their injured or even dead suspects ended up there, but none had been taken to the burn unit. Entering the hospital and proceeding to the front information desk attendant, Lex asked, "Can you tell us where the burn unit is?"

"Second floor. Take a left."

"Thank you."

When they got there, Lex tracked down a white-coated doctor. She stopped him and identified herself and Gil. "We understand a boat fire victim was brought here."

He pointed to a closed door. "She's in there. The burn team is with her."

"A woman," Gil said. "Have you identified her?"

Before he could answer, another doctor came out of the room. Lex said, "We're detectives. What can you tell us about the patient?"

"She's got burns over ninety percent of her body. She may not make it."

"Have you been able to identify her?"

Grimly, this doctor answered, "Not yet. The only thing I can tell you is her left hand is missing a finger."

Lex sighed. "Oh no."

Gil suggested, "Svetlana?"

"Please, as soon as you are able to identify her, call me." Lex handed him her card.

"I will," the doctor said. "We are hoping to save her."

Lex tapped her partner. "Let's go to Westbrook's."

⬥

Inside the Grand Truman lobby, Lex saw Fullerton who was on his way out. "Good morning," Lex said.

"I'm on my way to a meeting. Have a good day."

It was another visit to Westbrooks and Gil knocked on the door. When they entered, the frustrated author said, "I'm doing it. I'm wiring the money. And who the hell killed my agent?"

Knowing Westbrook was a suspect, and an arrest was coming, Lex wasn't ready to play that card. She said, "We don't know who stabbed Lydell Lawrence. What about the money? Did you receive an address to send it to?"

"No, but I know they will text it. Once I have the account number, it's going to happen."

"Don't be foolish," Gil said. "You can't be sure Svetlana is going to be set free."

Lex said, "Mister Westbrook, the truth about this morning is that there was a boat fire sometime last night or this morning, and a female victim was transported to the hospital. We were just there. She's badly burned and can't be identified at this point."

Westbrook stared at Lex. "No, not Svetlana!"

"We don't know," Gil said. "The only thing known is that she's missing a finger."

Westbrook plopped down on the couch. "I know it's her. Christ's sake, they killed her."

Lex tried to comfort the antsy author. "We're not concluding that yet."

Westbrook jumped up. "Holy Jesus! How can you say it's not Svetlana?"

Lex said, "Listen, that finger was never identified, and we're quite sure it wasn't Svetlana's. The finger was tampered with. Think about it. Why would they alter the prints?"

Westbrook wore a glazed look. "I guess that makes sense. So, where is she, and what's happening with her?"

Gil said, "We're still trying to unravel this whole thing."

Westbrook looked to Svetlana's picture on the credenza, and he pleaded, "Please be alive. Please come back."

"I know this is all extremely difficult," Lex said.

"Goddamn right," Westbrook huffed.

"I'm still concerned about you being alone."

"Don't be. It's me and Johnnie. Remember? Besides, Recker will be coming here."

"At least you will have company."

Gil asked, "Will he be staying too?"

"Not if I can help it."

Moments later, the attorney entered the room. "Hi," he said to the detectives.

Lex said, "We were just leaving."

Recker said, "Adios."

CHAPTER 39

The lawyer had been long gone and sweat poured off Essex Westbrook's forehead. *You son of a bitch, Tucker. I wish I'd never created you.*

He assumed the police hadn't read his failed book. He also knew it wasn't all false, but he couldn't let the cops delve into it. The author relived Lex's grilling about the killing of Lawrence and worried about his own future.

The concierge had deposited the morning newspaper outside his door as well as those of his neighbors. Westbrook retrieved his morning edition and laid it on the table. Already there were a bowl of Wheaties, and coffee. A photo of Lydell Lawrence was on page two, and Westbrook studied what the press had written. Fortunately, there was nothing said that accused him of the murder. The only mention of him was as a client of the agent.

He picked up the empty bowl and his phone rang so he answered. "Joshua, I read the news, and I don't care what they say. Those detectives believe I killed my agent."

"Are you sure?"

"I can tell."

"If they start talking to you again about the killing, call me. Don't answer any questions without me being there."

"Okay."

"Listen, before the detectives come back, I'm advising you to delete all the emails that went back and forth between you and Lawrence. From what you told me, the tone was hostile and could be seen as a motive if they ever got to court. If any of these are still there, get rid of them, and delete any of mine."

"Okay. I didn't kill him."

"I know that. Listen again and listen good. Innocent people go to prison all the time, and you want to eliminate as much as you can in order to make it hard to prosecute, if they go that route."

"Okay, I'll do it right now."

The informed author went to his computer and did as his attorney advised. He deleted eighteen emails.

▲

Lex, armed with a latte, proceeded to the stable where Butterscotch was munching on a bale of hay. She knew the horse sensed her presence when the animal shifted away from her morning meal to move toward the friendly detective. "Hey, how's breakfast?" She stroked the horse's head, and Butterscotch neighed her approval. "I hope your day is going to be great. Time for me to go to work."

Upon settling in beside her partner, latte still in her hand, he commented, "Hard to break that habit, isn't it?"

"It's my only vice." She saw Gil's eyes staring into hers. "Get off it. How about getting to work?"

Before she sat, Pressley joined them in their cube. "A guy named Grayson Dufour went to the pier and saw his boat was missing. The remains appear to be his stolen craft."

"He's sure it was taken?" Lex asked.

"Gerstein's talking to him now."

Lex drank her coffee. "I wonder if the burn victim has been identified?"

"For all we know, it could have been a homeless person."

"We'll see." She called Mid-Manhattan and contacted the doctor she had seen at the burn center. "This is Detective Stall."

"Hello, Detective, this is Doctor Wyman. I'm sorry to tell you, the burn victim is deceased. However, we were able to make a positive identification on the woman. Her name was Jillian Stemple, age 49."

Lex's eyes opened wide when she heard that name. "Thank you, sir." Stunned, she said to Gil, "The victim wasn't Svetlana. The woman was identified as Jillian Stemple."

"Whoa," Gil said. "Westbrook's girlfriend?"

"His mistress. How the hell is she tied into the kidnapping? I want to check the criminal database." Lex accessed the file. "There it is. Drug dealing and second-degree manslaughter. She was sentenced for twenty years, and in my opinion should have been sentenced to life."

"Where did she do time?"

"It happened in Connecticut, and she was sent to the York Correctional Institution in Niantic. Jillian must have gotten out early and was likely on probation." Lex turned away from the computer. "But the question is why was she here, and what is Westbrook not telling us?" She rose from her chair. "We have to ask Westbrook a few more questions, and I don't want him to know what we know."

▲

The detectives, without notifying the author, were outside his door and Lex knocked on it. Hearing him approach, she could tell he had looked into the peephole before letting them in.

"You should have called me."

Lex and Gil stepped inside. "I'm sorry about that," she said. "Have a seat. I'd like to tell you about the boat fire and then ask you a few more questions."

Westbrook clenched his jaw. "Svetlana, it was her."

Gil said, "No, it wasn't. I'm sure you are relieved to hear that."

Westbrook breathed a sigh of relief. "Thank God. Who was it?"

Lex said, "That's the interesting thing. Her name was Jillian Stemple. Tell us about her again."

"What? I thought she was in jail."

"It appears that she received an early parole." Lex said. "I don't think you've told us everything about her and you."

He appeared to struggle while attempting to answer the question. Hesitatingly, he began to talk. "Okay, she sold bad stuff to a couple of addicts who died. Actually, two others survived only because EMTs got to them with Narcan."

"Where and when did that happen?"

"A long time ago in Westport, Connecticut. I was living there at the time, and she had several customers in the area."

"If I recall correctly, you said you got hooked on drugs too."

"That's true. Jillian was at a bar in town, and I went there for a drink. We sat side by side, she came on to me, and we left together. Need I tell you more? We started seeing each other and before long, I was on cocaine."

"What about your wife? Did she know?"

"She found out and was going to leave me. But before that happened, nine-eleven ended Margaret's life. I guess her death, for lack of a better term, sobered me up. I got into rehab and after Jillian got busted, I never saw her again."

"So why would she be part of a scheme to kidnap Svetlana?"

"How the hell do I know?"

"Did she have any friends?"

"Yeah, addicts, all of them." He got up and peered toward the kitchen. "I need some coffee. I'm trying to get off the booze."

Gil leaned toward Lex. "What do you think?"

"It's a good story, but something is missing, and I don't think he will tell us."

"I sense that too."

The author returned from the kitchen, set his mug on a table, and Lex decided to test the waters. "Would you mind if I browsed your computer?"

It was obvious to Lex that Westbrook tensed up and he protested, "What are you looking for? I can't let you use my laptop."

"Why is that?" Lex asked. "Are there items there you don't want us to see?"

The author picked up his cell. "I'm calling Recker." He phoned the attorney and said, "Josh, the detectives are here, and they're asking to browse my computer."

Westbrook glanced at the detectives and said, "Excuse me. I need to take this conversation into my office." He stormed off into his workplace where the detectives couldn't hear him.

Lex said, "Recker must have said to speak with him in private."

"That's what we call attorney-client privilege," Gil said.

Entering the main living space again, Westbrook said to the detectives, "My attorney said not to answer any more questions and no, you cannot browse my computer."

"Fair enough," Lex said. "We'll let you think about things between now and Monday. It should be an interesting Easter. Lydell Lawrence won't be celebrating."

Lex's cutting remark didn't set well with Westbrook. "Get out!"

She and Gil left his residence. "That was a sharp hit on him," Gil said.

"It was. We have enough to arrest him, and I want that computer. I'm asking Pressley to get us those warrants."

Chapter 40

The detectives met with Pressley upon returning to the precinct and he agreed with Lex, assuring her the appropriate paperwork would be signed by a judge and an arrest would be forthcoming.

Leaving for the day, Lex and Gil headed in opposite directions. She was stalled in traffic and used the car's Bluetooth to phone Gil. The background chatter told her that he was either on a train or waiting for one.

"Hey, what's up?" he asked. I'm still at the subway station, my train is late."

"It's a little noisy," she complained.

"There are a lot of people on the platform. Talk louder. Why the call?"

"It's Westbrook."

Gil stepped toward a less crowded spot. "I can hear you better now."

"What is it that he won't reveal about Jillian?"

"Lex, forget it for now. Have a good weekend. Get back into it Monday unless we get called out again. My train is coming."

"That's one thing I admire about you. You can let it go and not let it bother you."

"I have to think of it as a job, just a job. And it's not true. I do have a hard time with the nasty ones. I have to go."

Trying to heed her partner's words, she continued toward the village and arrived in time to wait with Liz until the teenager's father picked her up. Five minutes later, Jon idled his SUV next to a parked vehicle. While Liz squeezed her bag next to Adam in the back seat,

Jon got out and walked toward Lex, handing her an envelope.

She opened it and found a check for back child support. "Thank you. I wasn't expecting it so soon."

"Nice to see you, Lex."

After Jon drove off, Lex went inside and sat on the den couch for a few minutes. *I'd love a good long bath.* She had a small dinner and then went to change into a robe before filling the tub with water and bubble bath. The enjoyable soak took her mind off business, and she relaxed in the water for nearly forty minutes.

Drying herself and putting on comfortable sweats, she settled in the den with a cup of tea when Elaine called. "Hi," she said to Lex. Shannon just left. Is Liz with Jon?"

"She is. I took a bath and am kind of vegging out."

"Do you want company?"

"Sure."

"I'll be over in a few minutes."

Lex greeted her friend, and they sat on opposite ends of the couch. Elaine said, "I knew you were right. I turned down my date with George."

"That was a wise decision."

"I know, Lex."

"Listen, at least you are interested in dating again. You'll find someone."

Elaine wryly smiled. "Yeah, like the night I had to leave you at that bar, and you wound up sleeping with a guy half your age, barely out of college."

"Stop. You know it was a huge mistake; I was also a little inebriated."

"A little?"

"Hey, I'm certainly not proud of that night."

Elaine got off that subject. "How is Stefan?"

"He's well, thanks. I invited him over tomorrow evening, and we'll watch a movie. Sunday, I'm taking him to Donovan's for late lunch."

The women chatted for an hour before Elaine said, "I'm going now. Have a good weekend."

As soon as she was gone, Lex called her boyfriend. "Hey, what are you doing?" she asked.

"Believe it or not, I'm doing laundry."

"How exciting."

"Yeah. What about you?"

"I took a nice bath, and I'm relaxing. I'll probably pick up a book and then go to bed. I can use a good night's sleep."

"So could I, but I have to iron a few shirts first."

"You iron too? Impressive. What else is there that I don't know about you? Do you do windows?"

"I'll never tell. Have you chosen a movie to watch?"

"We'll decide when you get here. Sunday, I'll take you to Donovan's. You'll like it."

"I'm sure I will. Anywhere you go is anywhere I like."

▲

Lex had a good night's sleep and did her household chores before making sure she was ready to see Stefan. The only thing that could spoil this evening was being called to a crime scene, and she was well aware that it had happened before. *It just can't happen, not tonight.*

At 7:15 p.m. he rang the bell, and she opened the front door. "It was a long week," Stefan said. "I smell popcorn."

"Really? That's a sweet way to greet me."

"Sorry," he said as he put down his duffle bag and placed his Eddie Bauer light zip jacket on a chair. "I couldn't wait to see you."

Lex eyed the sports tote. "What's in there?"

"Just a few overnight things."

She laughed. "Mighty presumptuous, don't you think?"

"Do you have a movie in mind?"

"Sit down. *Steel Magnolias.*"

"I haven't seen it, but isn't your sister, Julia Roberts in it?"

"Very funny. I have been told that I resemble her."

"Nah, you're better looking than she is."

"Thank you."

"Got any root beer?"

"Yes."

She brought him a glassful and they settled on the couch with Lex snuggled against him as they watched Netflix. When the picture ended, Stefan gently woke her. "You fell asleep."

She held back a yawn. "I guess I really was exhausted."

"Yeah, you missed the end."

"And you finished the popcorn."

"Guilty."

"I'm going upstairs to brush my teeth and get ready for bed."

"You mean sleep?"

She took his hand. "Did I say that?"

"Wait, I have something in my bag, I need."

"Pajamas?"

"Close. A box of condoms."

She gaped, and quizzically remarked, "A whole box?"

He grabbed it, shrugged, and smugly said, "I can dream, can't I?"

After her bathroom visit that included a spray of Chanel, Lex sauntered into the dimly lit bedroom while wearing nothing but a smile, slid into bed, and they began passionately kissing. "I think number one waiting," she whispered.

Twenty minutes later, their pleasurable sexual encounter climaxed. They rested for a few minutes, and then both showered. Afterward, Lex and Stefan fell asleep with him snuggly nestled up to her.

Waking a few minutes before eight, Lex unmistakably felt his erection against her buttocks. "And just what is that?" she said with a grin. "Let me go to the bathroom while you hold that thought." When she rejoined her bedmate, she playfully said, "Now, what was that you were saying?"

⋏

Freshened, the lovers were downstairs where Lex prepared a small breakfast with coffee. She sipped her brew and said, "About Newport. I was there a long time ago and look forward to visiting again. Have you spoken to your friend yet?"

"No, but I will. Thanks for the reminder."

She put her nearly empty cup down. The morning was quickly passing, and Lex placed their dishes into the dishwasher, wiped the table, and said, "How about taking a walk. We can end up at

Donovan's."

"Sure, show me around."

They strolled hand in hand down Bleecker to her father's old record store. "I know that I told you about it, but I still can't pass by without saying hello." She took a few moments to speak with her Dad and then moved on with Stefan. Continuing their walk, Lex saw a vacant bench at the edge of Washington Square, and they stopped to sit.

Glancing at the arch, Lex couldn't help thinking about Westbrook and the drone fiasco. Sitting there wasn't an option. She rose. "Let's keep walking."

They continued meandering, until arriving at the restaurant where they were escorted to a table. A server filled their glasses with water, and they browsed the menu. Hot plates were soon sitting in front of them, and they concentrated on eating. When they finished, Lex picked up the check. "I promised, my treat."

"No, I'll pay." Stefan reached for his wallet.

"Not this time." She placed her credit card on the table. "The next one is on you."

He nodded his approval. "I guess that means we'll have another date."

"I'll have to think about it." She was silent and then smiled. "I suppose, if you ask nicely."

Stefan admiringly said, "I swear I've never met anyone like you."

Lex coyly responded, "Is that a good thing or a bad thing?"

"I'm not sure yet." He laughed.

Exiting the eatery, they approached a bakery. "Come on. I want to get a few things. Liz loves this place." The smell of freshly baked unhealthy food wafted through the air. "They have the best cupcakes, and apple tarts."

With a tied box in her hand, she and Stefan made it back to her residence where they relaxed and talked for a while. "You never told me what your parents died from," Lex said.

"Well. My father was a heavy smoker, cigars mostly and they kind of did him in. My mother had liver cancer."

"I'm so sorry."

He rubbed his forehead. "I never told you about my sister. She's two years older than me and is still in Brisbane. It's not like we never got along. She had a different calling in life. At eighteen, she went into a seminary and several years later became a Nun. Her given name is Amelia, but she is known as Sister Cecilia."

"Wow." Lex uttered.

"We love each other but have gone in different directions. The last time I saw her was four years ago, when I traveled back home. Don't get me wrong, I admire her conviction, but I was never very religious."

"That makes two of us."

Lex glanced at the time on her cell. "Liz should be back soon."

"Would you mind if I see her before I go?"

"You know, she would like that."

It wasn't long before Lex heard footsteps on the stairs and Liz opened the door. Carrying her overnight bag, she was greeted by her mother and Stefan. "I hope you had a great weekend," Lex said while giving her daughter a hug.

"I did, but it's good to be back here."

Stefan said, "Hi, Liz. I was hoping to see you before I left."

"Oh. I saw your Jaguar and thought you were here for dinner."

"Not this time. Your mother and I had a late lunch at Donovan's. By the way, there's a present for you on the kitchen table."

"From you?"

"Not exactly." Referring to the bakery box, he added, "Mom said you would enjoy it." With his jacket in his hand, he picked up his duffle bag and walked toward the door. "Bye ladies."

Call me," Lex said. "Have a safe trip."

Lex saw her daughter's face and was sure Liz knew Stefan had been an overnight guest, but neither one said anything.

Later that night, Lex said to herself. *I must be crazy. Why can't I have a nine to five job and get away from this life of chasing down dangerous criminals?* She paused for a few seconds. *Someday, but right now I have a job to do, and unless I get that annoying call sometime tonight, tomorrow reality will set in again.*

GRETA'S GONE

Tucker waited for another message. "I can't get that fucking picture out of my head."

Sal was beside him and agreed. "I know it's killing you, and so is the waiting."

Two days had passed without any word, then there it was…a text.

Tucker, Don't fuck around. Today's the day.

Wire the money at exactly 1:00 p.m.

Tucker messaged back: Not so fast. I can't wire the money. We have to meet and exchange the cash for Greta.

Back came: That's not the deal. Wire the money and you'll get her back.

Boldly, Tucker replied: Bullshit! This game has changed! I need to see Greta in person, and you need to let her go when I give you the cash.

A hostile response came: So that's what you want? Okay, we'll play it your way.

We'll get back to you with a location and time. Besides, it will give us another day or two to enjoy Greta's company.

Chapter 41

Lex's distinct fragrance followed her into the squad room, and it didn't escape Hutch. "Good morning, Ms. Stall," he said without even looking her way.

She was sure the recent comments about her ball-busting shoes kept Hutch on good behavior. Smiling at the older detective, she said, "Thank you. I hope you had a good holiday weekend."

Benzinger caught her attention. "Morning, Lex."

As she walked to his cube, Lex saw Gil approaching. "Hi. How did it go at your sister-in-law's?"

"Good."

"Good? That's it? Good?"

"Yeah. We ate a lot, and I watched a game. How about you?"

Lex knew she shouldn't have expected more of a story from her male partner. "It was nice. Liz was at Jon's, so Stefan came down and we spent the day together."

"Have you been thinking about Westbrook?"

"Of course, I have, and the evidence is the evidence."

Captain Pressley interrupted them and handed Lex two warrants.

"Thanks," she said.

Pressley moved to Hutch and Benzinger's cube, and Lex heard the captain say, "You two need to go to Bryant Park. There was a shooting. Two victims. "All we have is a gunman attacked a couple. Uniforms are at the scene, and the shooter was seen running toward the nearest subway station and dropped the gun. They recovered it."

"On our way," Hutch said.

Pressley moved toward his workspace, and Lex held her cell. "I don't want to simply drop in on Westbrook again. I'm calling and telling him we are on our way over."

▲

Arriving at Westbrook's residence, Lex was surprised to see Joshua Recker. "Morning, Detectives," he said.

"Good morning," Lex replied.

"What brings you here?" The attorney had an expansive stance, arms crossed at chest level. His eyes were dark and intense.

Gil said, "A few questions that have to be answered."

Westbrook stared at Recker when Lex asked, "Have you heard from the kidnappers?"

The author slammed his fist on a nearby table. "No."

Recker tugged at his client. "You don't have to answer any more questions."

Gil pulled the legal papers from his jacket. "Maybe not. With all due respect, Mister Recker, these are warrants for the author's computer, as well as his arrest."

"May I see them?" Studying the documents, the lawyer asked, "What evidence is there?"

"I think we'd better sit," Lex said. When everyone was comfortable, she continued. "We have identified the murder weapon. There is no doubt it belonged to Mister Westbrook. She held up the now bagged knife she had taken."

"What the hell does that prove?" Recker inquired.

Lex pointed to the serial number. "These numbers prove that this knife matches the one Lawrence was stabbed with."

"He could have misplaced it, or it could have been stolen."

"Stolen?" Lex inquired. "He and Svetlana are alone most of the time."

"What about fingerprints?"

"Glad you asked," Gil said. "There were none on the murder weapon. We're sure the knife handle was wiped clean. Gloves may have been worn."

"May have, and a matching knife. That's all?"

Although she knew the DNA on the hair was immaterial, she

said, "And the comb that was left at the crime scene… DNA analysis confirms it was your clients."

"We'll see you in court."

"What's happening?" Westbrook yelled.

"Be calm," Recker said. "You're under arrest. I'll be at the arraignment."

Gil read Westbrook his Miranda rights and commanded him to sit on the couch while Lex walked toward the office.

"Where are you going?" Recker asked.

"As the warrant says, we're seizing his computer."

"This is bull." Westbrook sat and huffed a few times.

Lex pivoted to face Westbrook. "I believe I heard you say this was bull. Is it? Would you care to tell us what else you know about Lydell Lawrence and Jillian Stemple?"

Recker said, "You don't have to answer her." He swung his head toward Lex. "Detective, you can address your questions to me. For the last time, he's not talking to you anymore."

"Have it your way," she said as she continued and seized the laptop.

Gil removed a pair of handcuffs from his belt.

"Must you?" Recker raged.

"I believe we do," Gil said. "It is our job."

"Fine. Put them on him."

Gil escorted the suspect toward the door as Lex carried the computer.

The author looked at his lawyer. "Help me."

"Go with them. After booking, you'll spend the night in jail. I'll be at your arraignment. It should be tomorrow."

Lex said, "We don't control that, but you and I both know it has to be done within seventy-two hours of arrest. Remember the sixth amendment?"

"What about Svetlana, the kidnappers?" Westbrook asked his attorney.

"Give me your phone. I'll pretend to be you when they send the next text."

The detectives and the cuffed suspect waited for the elevator. Lex saw the Kimballs coming down the hall. "Oh my," Claudia said.

"You're arresting him?" Benton uttered.

"We are," Gil said. "Why don't you wait for the elevator to come back up."

The door opened and the detectives, along with Westbrook, descended to the lobby. Lex saw several people watching as they took their suspect outside. "Get the car," Gil said to the valet.

▲

Pressley met the detectives in the precinct's booking area. "His lawyer plans to be at the arraignment," Gil said.

Westbrook glared at the captain and snarled, "They have it all wrong. I didn't kill anyone. This is a travesty. My lawyer warned me that innocent people are imprisoned all the time."

"Straight ahead, Mister Westbrook," Lex said.

Gil released him to the sergeant. "He's all yours."

"Have a good day," Lex said. They left the author to mull over his predicament.

Upstairs, Lex set the computer on her desk and then joined her partner, who was with Pressley. Gil said, "Maybe this time he will talk about what he has been keeping secret."

"Certainly not without his attorney present," Lex said. "But we may be able to get him alone in the morning before he is arraigned."

"Make sure he waives his rights first," Pressley reminded his detectives. "I'll let you know when I find out about the arraignment. It's been running about forty-eight hours. He may have more time to think about his situation than he wants."

Gil flexed his hand, and Lex noticed. "Does that still bother you?"

"Not really," he said. "Every now and then I get a twinge. Apparently, the bite came close to a nerve, but it's okay."

The squad room's silence was suddenly broken. Hutch's voice echoed as he stormed into the captain's already occupied space. Benzinger settled in at his desk with an evidence bag.

"What's the story?" Pressley asked.

Hutch said, "Two people were shot. Male and female. According to the first responders, the male, Jerry Trager, was dead at the scene. The female, Bee Rodriguez, is alive and was transported to Mid-Manhattan. Witnesses said they saw a man wearing tan pants and a black hoodie with a dragon embroidered into it approach the couple as they left the park. He pulled out a gun and just shot them. Then the shooter took off toward the subway but dropped the gun along the way. We obtained a couple of cell phone videos and should be able to get a good look."

"Stay on it," Pressley said.

Chapter 42

The incarcerated Westbrook awaited his arraignment, which wouldn't be until Wednesday morning. Pressley had informed Lex and Gil of the author's court appearance date, and Lex anticipated a call from Recker. Right on cue, five minutes later, the hostile lawyer phoned. "I called the courthouse. They told me my client's arraignment is tomorrow morning, and we're not happy about that."

"I can't say I'm sorry. You know we don't control those proceedings."

"I know that, but you know he is innocent."

"Do we? I think that's for you to argue and for us to prove."

"It is, and I'll make you look incompetent."

Lex had heard enough. "We'll see about that. Thank you for calling."

Gil said, "That was Recker, wasn't it?"

"It was. He's not happy about the delay in the arraignment, and he's hot that we arrested his client." Lex set her glasses on her desk. "It's interesting that neither one of them has said a word about Svetlana."

"It is."

Rethinking what she thought might be a good idea, she said, "Going down to attempt to have Westbrook waive his rights and speak with us is unrealistic. Would you do it?"

"No."

Lex then remembered they had overlooked someone. She got up and began pacing the squad room. *We know Tomas was involved, but there is one other person who had access to*

Westbrook's suite all the while. He also could be the on-site spy. How could we have missed him? She sidled up to her interested partner.

"What are you thinking?"

She picked up her glasses and put them on. "We might have missed someone very obvious. Who else had access to Westbrook's suite, as well as every other unit in the hotel?"

Gil furrowed his brows. "Fullerton?"

"Right. It would have been easy for him to get in and plant the listening devices. Maybe it wasn't Tomas who did that. Think about it. If Tomas delivered the key to Addie and went inside, he might have just been observing the suite, or he may truly have left something behind. How could he have had the devices on him?"

"But what happened to the theory that he came back later to install the listeners?"

"Remember, the video doesn't exist," Lex said. "At this point anything is possible."

"That is true. Fullerton could have done it."

"And I can't help thinking about how he led us on a wild goose chase by giving us the wrong address for Tomas Costa. They may have been in cahoots, and he sure covered for Tomas when the valet was supposedly sick. He really didn't appear sick to me. Fullerton also told us there were no videos of when the Westbrooks were on their cruise. Did he destroy them on purpose. Or is it a hotel policy to keep footage for only a month?"

"That's deep. What about Betsy?"

"I don't get the sense she knows anything."

⋏

Heavy traffic slowed their vehicle, while honking of horns seemed to be louder than ever as the detectives were in route to the Grand Truman.

Finally, after arriving, they marched into the lobby and proceeded to the manager's office. Betsy greeted them. "Good morning. What happened yesterday? Mister Westbrook was taken out of here in handcuffs."

"That's true. We can't discuss it," Lex said. She peeked into

Fullerton's quarters and didn't see him. "Is he here?"

"No, he's at our sister hotel, the Rembrandt, today."

"When will he be back?"

"Probably in the morning. Can I help you?"

"Maybe." Lex mentally organized questions for the secretary. "Do you have access to all the residences?"

"Yes, but only in an emergency. The pass key is here."

"Have you ever had to go to Westbrooks'?"

"No."

"Do you know if Mister Fullerton has?"

"No. Well, I guess he has with you two."

"Anytime else?"

"Not that I can think of."

"Is it true that camera videos are destroyed or taped over after thirty days?"

"I think that's right."

Lex said, "Then, you don't know for sure?"

"I never thought about it."

Gil didn't say anything while his partner continued her interrogation.

"Can you think of a reason your boss would give us an old address for Tomas?"

"I guess that was a mistake."

"Maybe so. Why would he read from a hard file when the information is on the computer. The address file online must be current?"

"I don't know. And that data was wrong too. We were not aware that Tomas had moved again and was living with his girlfriend."

"Did Tomas appear sick to you when he came back?"

"Not to me, but he might have been ill the previous day."

Lex took a step toward the door. "Thank you. Please tell your boss we will be coming back."

The detectives went into the hallway, and Gil said, "I think she's truthful."

"I agree. Wouldn't it be interesting if Fullerton somehow didn't show up tomorrow?"

"It would. Betsy said he's at the other hotel, but is she

correct? How do we know he is at the Rembrandt right now?"

Gil stared at his partner. "I know you. We're going to the Rembrandt, aren't we?"

"You bet, It's the only way to verify he is there."

CHAPTER 43

Located on Broadway near Lincoln Center, Gil pulled into the Rembrandt hotel's circular driveway, and he stopped at the valet stand where an orange clad male said, "Welcome. Would you like me to park your vehicle?"

Gil presented his badge. "We're here on business. Is there self-parking?"

"Yes, sir. If you want to self-park, you can go into the garage."

"Thank you."

The squad car entered the underground parking facility and Gil steered it into a parking space on level 1.

Walking into the lobby, Lex said, "Nice." She noticed a water fountain in a sunken sitting area. "That looks relaxing. I like the falling water."

As the detectives walked to the registration desk, Lex noticed the employee's orange uniforms. "Interesting, the dress code here apparently is orange, while the Grand Truman is red."

Two guests were checking out, and Gil asked the third clerk, "Have you seen Clark Fullerton today?"

"I haven't," she said.

"Wait," another employee said. "I saw him earlier, walking toward the board room. There is a meeting. Would you like me to page him?"

"That's not necessary," Lex said. "We'll see him later."

They were almost in the garage Gil said, "Are you satisfied?"

"Do I look happy?"

He hesitated. "Should I have asked that question?"

They approached the car and Lex stood at the passenger door. "I'm a lady, you know. How about opening my door?"

Gil snickered. "Really? It's not like we're on a date."

Lex stared at him. "Heaven forbid." She got in and poked him in the ribs, just above his holster. "Typical male!"

On the way back to the precinct, Lex's cell phone rang. "Hi, Charlene. How are you today?"

"Fine. I'm calling because I was clearing data on my laptop, and I found something you should know about."

"What did you find?"

"They are files containing information about drones and bugs."

"May we come over now?"

"Yes."

Lex ended the call. "Change of plans. We are going to Charlene's. She found things on the laptop that we have to take a look at."

Forty minutes later they were at Charlene's apartment, the laptop was on the kitchen table. She said, "I'm so confused. I don't understand. I don't know what this all means."

"Why don't you show us?" Lex asked.

"I opened a folder that he had named UFO. I have no idea what it is." She accessed the file. Gil and Lex studied it.

"Drones, several different types." Gil said.

"Look," Lex said. "Amazon orders for drones." The file titled 'Bugs' also intrigued Lex. "I want to see what's in here." Instantly she said, "Listening devices."

She asked Charlene, "Did he ever discuss these with you?"

"No."

Gil asked, "Have you seen any credit cards or credit card statements?"

"He always kept them private."

Wanting to peer at other data, especially emails, Lex asked, "May I browse the rest of computer?"

Charlene hesitated. "I'd rather you didn't."

"Why is that?"

The young woman blushed, "There are still some personal things on it, and I'm not done cleaning it out."

Lex was determined to have her turn it over. Even though the detective knew it would take time to obtain a warrant, she removed her glasses and espied the girlfriend's sad face. "Listen. I don't want to sound disrespectful. You have to understand that you may let us take it now, or we can obtain a warrant and be back here in no time."

Not speaking, Charlene gritted her teeth. Lex continued, "I know it's hard to part with, but we will only have it for a little while and will return it as soon as possible."

Still mulling the idea, Charlene asked, "Do I have to?"

Lex calmly said, "Look, we have already seen pictures of you and Tomas having sex. They are on his phone, and I suspect there are still videos on the computer that you would rather we not see."

Charlene trembled and began to cry.

Lex handed her a tissue from a box on the kitchen table and once more asked for the computer. "Honestly, would you rather we left with it, or would you like us to come back with that warrant and forcefully take it? It's one or the other. Why don't you make it easy on yourself?"

Charlene breathed in and then said, "Okay, but please give it back as soon as you can."

Gil closed the lid, picked it up, and asked her to sign for it.

"Thank you," Lex said.

"Oh wait." Charlene got up and opened a desk drawer, took out a receipt, and handed it to Lex. "I found this too."

She read the receipt. "Walmart, prepaid phones…two dozen. "Did you see any phones here?"

"Only a couple. He said they were going to be Christmas gifts."

"May we have the receipt?" Lex asked.

"I guess so."

"Thank you again," Lex said. "If you think of anything else, you have my number. Please call."

The detectives exited the apartment. "This certainly ties Tomas directly to the kidnapping. Now all we have to do is figure out who he gave the drones and phones to and who he was working with."

Gil carefully set the computer in the back seat, and Lex called Gator. Street noise interfered with their ability to hear each other. "We were just with Charlene, and I wanted to touch base with you again."

"I'm on my way to work."

The street noise grew louder, and Lex heard horns. She raised her voice. "I'll make it quick. Did Tomas ever talk to you about drones, listening devices, or phones?"

Gil pointed. "Speaker." Lex hit the button.

Gator said, "Yes, he told me he was thinking of buying a drone."

"Did he say why?"

"No."

"What about listening devices or prepaid phones?"

"Say that again?"

"Did you ever see listening devices or phones?"

"Phones. I was with him when he bought a bunch of prepaid phones at Walmart. He said he was going to give them away as gifts for Christmas, and I was to get one. Hold it. I'm ducking into a shop."

"Did he ever mention any names of people you were unfamiliar with?"

"That's better. Not really."

"What about the name Jillian or Jill?"

"Wait...I did hear him talking to someone and heard the name Jillian."

"Do you remember when, and do you know who he talked with?"

"No. We were at the club. I gotta go."

"Thank you."

"That wasn't much help," Gil said.

"He did say he'd heard the name, Jillian. I'm going to see if our good old techie pal, Foley will examine the computers."

Chapter 44

The jolt Lex got when she walked into her living room sent a message she didn't like. She heard music, and she saw Spencer and Steven seated along with the girls on the couch. Lex held back her viewpoint and smiled. "Well, this is a surprise. What are you all doing?" *I must remain calm.*

"Just talking," Liz said.

"Oh, I see. How about turning down the music."

Liz did, and Lex said to her daughter, "May I see you in the kitchen for a minute?"

Liz followed behind her mother. Standing face-to-face with her daughter, the upset mother sternly said, "You know the rules. Why are the boys here?"

"I thought we could hang out."

"Liz, you know I said you are not to be here alone with boys. I made that perfectly clear."

Liz huffed. "We weren't doing anything, and I'm not alone."

"I see that, but that's not the point. Liz, don't try to bend the rules. They can stay a little longer but not again unless I am here."

"Gosh, it's not like we were having sex or something."

Lex seethed and asked, "What did you say, young lady?"

"Nothing."

Lex was upset by that empty answer. "Nothing is right. Go back out there. We'll discuss this further after they leave."

Liz sulked and walked back to her friends. Fifteen minutes later, they were gone. The young girl slowly entered the kitchen. "Mom, I'm sorry."

Lex shook her finger at her daughter. Still agitated, she asked, "And just what did you mean when you said you weren't having sex?"

"I told you. Nothing."

Lex made direct eye contact. "Tell me the truth. Are you engaging in sex?"

Liz emphatically answered, "No, but you and Stefan certainly are."

Not happy with Liz's attitude, Lex said, "Hold it, young lady, that's a little off base. We're adults."

"And you were once my age, weren't you?"

Lex sighed. "I was, and you know the mistakes I made."

Irked, Liz loudly commented. "I know. And we've had the talk, Mom."

"Calm down. I know you are growing up fast, but I worry about you because I love you."

Liz took a breath. "I love you too. And you need to not be so protective."

Lex sighed, "Okay. Go feed Cassatt and let me change before dinner."

"Are you going to tell Shannon's mom?"

"I should. Don't you think?"

"Please don't. I don't want to get Shannon in trouble."

Lex didn't give her an immediate answer. A few seconds later, she said. "Promise you will not do it again, here or at Elaine's."

"I promise. Mom, are you still going to chaperone us to the school dance?"

"Yes. Elaine and I will."

Chapter 45

Lex had Liz on her mind while she drove to work. Even Fleetwood Mac couldn't keep her from thinking about the young lady she was raising. *She is me. A lot smarter, but she is me. I can't protect her forever. If she's going to do it, she's going to do it.* Lex was so focused on Liz that she passed Starbucks and came to work empty-handed.

"You on the wagon again?" Gil asked.

"No, I'm preoccupied and somehow drove right by Starbucks. May I ask you something?"

"Since when do you ask permission to ask me anything? What's up?"

"Do you think I'm overprotective of Liz?"

Gil sat back. "What's going on?"

"Boys are in the picture now. She's going to a school dance with a classmate named Spencer. I met him. Actually, it's a foursome: Liz, Spencer, Shannon, and Steven. Elaine and I are chaperoning."

"And your problem is what?"

"I think you know. It's boys and dating."

Gil nodded. "I get it. They all grow up and then leave. You don't own them, and they somehow end up being adults. Liz is smart, and she'll be fine. Let her be herself."

Lex appreciated her partner's comments and relaxed. "You know what? I've never heard you make so much sense. Thank you for the lecture."

"Wow," Gil said. "Are you okay?"

"Yes. Do you want to go downstairs and buy me a coffee?"

"Are you asking, or is that an order?"

"Take your pick. Cream and sugar."

Gil glared at his partner. "I'll be right back." He muttered, "Sometimes I wish that new cafe wasn't here."

With two cups of coffee in his hands, he set one on Lex's desk. She removed the lid to take a sip. "That's hot."

"Hey, you asked for it. Drink up."

"I will, and then we will visit Fullerton."

"What about Foley?"

"I contacted him while you were gone. He'll be here this afternoon."

Pressley appeared at their cube. "I just got word from the courthouse. The arraignment was this morning, and a hearing date was set for May sixteenth. Recker will bond him out."

"Great," Gil said. "We're about to drop in on Fullerton."

▲

The hotel manager's door was closed when the detectives entered the waiting area. Betsy said, "Hi, I told Clark to be expecting you today. Addie is with him. I don't think it will be long. She's retiring."

Lex and Gil waited, and Gil picked up a sports magazine from a table. "Mets are off to a good start," he said.

Clark Fullerton's door opened, and Addie walked out. "We understand you are retiring," Lex said.

"I am in thirty days, and then I'm taking a Mediterranean cruise."

"How about taking me?" Gil kidded. "Wish I could come. Have a great time."

Fullerton faced the detectives. "Come in. Betsy said you would be back. Sorry I missed you yesterday. I was at the Rembrandt."

"We've driven by it, but we've never been there." Lex decided to hide the truth.

"It's about the same size, and it's just as nice."

Lex asked, "Is there anything else you can tell us about Tomas? Did you know his girlfriend, Charlene?"

"No. He didn't mention her until we found out he was living

204

with her."

"Did he ever mention the name Jillian or Jill?"

He asked, "Wasn't that the name of the woman who died in that boat fire?"

"Yes."

"Why do you ask?"

Lex ignored the ask. "May we go back to the cruise Essex and Svetlana were on a couple of months ago? As we understand it, the cleaning crew, Addie specifically, had access to the Westbrooks' suite."

"That's right."

Lex stated, "She told me she forgot keys that day, and Tomas was sent to deliver her a set."

"I remember that."

"Addie said he had to go into Westbrook's suite to retrieve something he had left there. He never told her what."

Fullerton furrowed his brow. "I didn't know that. He shouldn't have entered."

Lex said, "Tomas might have been scoping out the suite and later came back with the listening devices."

Fullerton thought for a second. "If Addie locked the door as she should have, then how did Tomas get in a second time?"

Gil spoke, "Tomas gave her back the keys and she never saw him lock the door."

"Can you have Addie join us?" Lex asked.

"She just left so she should be nearby. I'll get her."

He returned with Addie by his side and Lex said. "Addie, we spoke with you about that day Tomas brought you the keys. After Tomas gave you back the keys. Did you by chance lock the Westbrook's door ?"

"I assumed he did."

Lex now had a plausible answer as to how Tomas may have entered the unit again. He was there either later that day or soon after. "Thank you, Addie. You may leave."

Gil said, "Mister Fullerton, it's a shame those videos do not exist."

Even though she and Gil knew Tomas was one of the abductors, she had to probe the hotel manager. "Mister Fullerton, do you safeguard all the keys that access the suites?"

"I do, and the housekeepers have to obtain them from me."

Lex said, "So, you also had access to the Westbrook suite."

Fullerton's composure rapidly changed, and he raised his voice. "What are you insinuating? Are you thinking I'm involved because I have access?"

"I'm not saying that, but I am curious. How is it that you gave a wrong address for Tomas Costa? You have the same database as Betsy."

"I told you, I looked at an old file." Fullerton grimaced and leaned forward, casting an evil glare at Lex. "You are accusing me!"

"Calm down," Gil said. "We're not accusing you. We know Tomas was part of the kidnapping. We also know he knew the man in the limo who handed him the letter to deliver. And we know Tomas bought the drones, the listening devices, as well as a number of prepaid phones. We don't know who he gave them to."

"Well, I had nothing to do with it!"

"We never said you did," Lex assured him. Although she wasn't ready to eliminate him as someone potentially connected, she knew everyone was still in play until they solved the case. "Thank you for your time."

Fullerton's shoulders dropped significantly. "I can't exactly say it was a pleasure. Have a good day."

Lex and Gil proceeded to the lobby and bumped into two familiar faces at the front door. Recker and Westbrook were entering the hotel. "I should have known you two would be here," the attorney said. "He's off-limits to you. Don't call us."

⚜

The detectives waited at the precinct for the techie. "The last time we saw him, he'd lost over one hundred pounds," Lex said. "We used to call him Roly-Poly Foley."

Gil laughed. "We did, and now he's married."

Lex heard whistling as Foley walked in. "Hi, guys, it's been a while," he said.

Lex smiled when she greeted him. "You look good."

"I'm jealous," Gil said. "You do look good."

Foley said, "Here's some news: we're expecting."

"How nice," Lex said. "When?"

"September."

"Congratulations," Gil said.

"What have you got for me?"

Lex grabbed Westbrook's computer. "This. It belongs to Essex Westbrook. We arrested him on a murder charge. We know he deleted a bunch of emails. Do you think you can recover them? They could be vital. Specifically, emails between him and Lydell Lawrence."

"Move over." Foley sat beside Lex and opened the laptop. He put on a pair of glasses to browse the files. After clicking the keyboard a few times, he said, "Here we go. I see where they went." Two more clicks and he sat back. "There they are."

"Damn, you're good," Gil said.

"And you guys call me a nerd."

Lex grinned. "Yes, but always affectionately. Thank you."

They viewed Westbrook's data and Lex said, "There are incriminating emails here. Print them all."

Foley did so. "Am I done?" he asked.

"Not so fast." Lex set the laptop they took from Charlene on her desk. "This belongs to Tomas Costa's girlfriend, Charlene. He is the dead valet who was involved in the kidnapping. I know there are deleted files on it as well."

"What am I looking for?"

"I'm not sure," Lex said. "A clue to who Tomas Costa might have been working for would be helpful."

Foley began his search. "Here's an interesting file labeled XXX." Is this what I think it is and is this what you are searching for?"

Lex curled her lips knowing the videos had existed. "No. It's not what we are seeking."

"Run one," Gil said.

Foley turned to see Lex, and then glanced at Gil. "It's up to you guys."

Gil placed his hands on the nerd's shoulders. "Play one," he said.

Before the lewd video started, Lex spun away. "I'll be looking out the window while you two boys enjoy yourselves."

After viewing less than three minutes of a sexual encounter, Foley stopped the video and exited the file. "You can come back now, Lex."

She huffed. "Are you sure?   Did you get your fill of pornography?"

Lex moved away from the window. "I'm interested in deletions that may be related to listening devices, drones, Jillian, or anything that we can hang our hats on."

Foley did his magic and retrieved what he could. "I take it you are interested in bugs and UFOs."

Lex sat beside Foley as he dug into the UFO and bug files. "This is interesting. He bought four drones, each one different."

"Open the 'bugs.'"

Foley did. "I see he ordered those listening devices."

"We knew he did," Gil said.

The computer expert continued searching.

Lex said, "I don't see anything indicating who the other abductors. He must have communicated with the leader of the kidnapping by way of the phones he purchased, but we still have no idea who the boss is. Please print those files."

Foley sent the emails to the printer. "Now am I done here?" he asked.

Lex said, "For now. Thanks, and let us know if you have a boy or a girl."

"Have a nice day," Foley said.

Digesting what they saw on the computers, Lex said, "I told her we would get the computer back to her as soon as possible. We'd better do it."

Lex carried the laptop to the car Gil had the keys for, and they did as promised by returning the computer to Charlene.

Chapter 46

Gil was seated in their cubicle and Lex said, "I've been thinking about Tomas and Jillian. What do we know about him? We know Jillian did time in Niantic. Could Tomas have been there too?"

"I suppose it's possible. But you know, she was forty-nine. Tomas was what, twenty-two? She's old enough to be his mother."

Lex was stunned. "What did you say?"

"I said she's old enough to be his mother."

"And what if she was? That would tie him to her."

"If that's the link, holy cow!"

Lex twisted to her computer. "First things first: we never checked the database to see if Tomas was incarcerated at any time." She entered his name, and nothing came up. "He has no record. We can't prove it yet, but what if Jillian Stemple was indeed Tomas Costa's birth mother? I have a funny feeling about that. We were told he was from Bridgeport. If he was born there, we may be able to obtain birth records, and it may be possible to find the couple who adopted him."

Pressley stepped into their cube, and Lex was quick to react. "Jillian Stemple. She may be Tomas's mother, and he might have been born in Bridgeport. I want to see if we can obtain the birth record."

"Ever been to Bridgeport?"

"Not yet."

"I have." Gil said. "My boys played a baseball tournament there."

"Go," Pressley said.

▲

Gil retrieved a squad car and drove it up to Lex. "Get in."

She pointed at him. "I thought you agreed to open my door."

"And next you'll want me to take you to dinner. Get in."

Gil drove east toward Connecticut. An hour and twenty minutes later, they were on Broad Street in Bridgeport at the Bureau of Vital Records. Inside the room were several people waiting for their number to be called. "This is like the DMV," Gil said. "Do we have to take a number?"

"I don't think so. Morticians don't."

"Well, we're not funeral directors."

"I believe we have that privilege too."

A person walked away from the service window farthest to the left, and the detectives went up to it. Gil displayed his badge.

The clerk said, "New York Police Department. How can I help you?"

He answered, "We need a birth certificate."

From Tomas's driver's license, Lex had written down his birth date, February 27, 1997. She informed the clerk. "His first name is Tomas, and the parents' names may be Stemple and/or Westbrook."

Eying Lex, the female clerk, who appeared to project the sense that she didn't exactly enjoy her job asked, "Have you completed a form?"

"I'm sorry. We haven't."

She handed Lex one. "Fill this out."

Completing the paperwork with a borrowed pencil, Lex submitted it to the woman. "Wait here."

Moseying toward the records room. She returned several minutes later with the form in hand and a book. She had marked a page and went to a photocopier. Taking a copy of the birth certificate, she then handed the copied document to Lex. "Here it is. No charge."

Lex read the document. "Oh my God. As we suspected, he was born Thomas Stemple. Mother, Jillian Stemple. Father unknown. Par for the course. Interesting that his name was spelled traditionally, T-H-O-M-A-S."

"It is. Westbrook knew Jillian had given birth to his child and gave it up. He might even have known the name Thomas, but he never connected it with Tomas sans the H. Hopefully we can find a Costa family at the tax collector registry."

Entering the records room, Gil retrieved his ID again and presented it to the clerk. The man asked, "What do you want?"

Lex noticed a cane leaning against the side of the counter where he stood.

Gil said, "We're trying to find out if there are any taxpayers with the last name Costa. That's C-O-S-T-A."

"Why are you asking?" The tax clerk had a deadpan tone as if he didn't want to be bothered.

"It has to do with a missing person with that name," Lex said.

The clerk clicked on his computer. "There are eight families with that name. Any one in particular?"

"Is it possible to print all the names and addresses?" she asked.

"I'll be right back." The employee grabbed his walking stick and ran off copies before handing a sheet of paper to Lex. "No charge."

"Thank you," Lex said.

Before they left the building, Lex veered away from the front door. "I see the restrooms in the corner."

"Yeah, I better use the men's room. I'll meet you back here."

After their bathroom visits, Gil drove west to Manhattan, and with heavier traffic, it took them almost two hours to get to the precinct. It was late in the day, and the detectives trudged into the squad room with information that linked Tomas and Jillian.

Pressley approached them as they entered their cube. "Any luck?"

Lex showed the captain the legal record of birth. "It's true. Jillian is Tomas's mother. There is no father listed, but Westbrook knows the child was his, but he isn't aware of the spelling. Thomas, minus the h. I knew he was hiding something all along. And we obtained a list of taxpayers in the area named Costa. If we are lucky," she said as she nudged Gil, "we may hit a home run."

▲

Westbrook was back from his torturous nights in jail. His relationship with the detectives had grown cold, and he felt betrayed. He relied on his lawyer, who bailed him out.

Later that afternoon, the author sought to use his computer but forgot it wasn't there. He instead studied his bookcase, spotting the unpopular book he'd wished he'd never written. *Greta's Gone* was in his hands as he sat in his chair. Startled by a knock on his door, the author put the book on his desk, walked to the door, and peered through the peephole. He saw the concierge and let him in. "Cedric."

"Yes, sir, this package came for you a little while ago."

Hesitating to accept it, he did and said thanks to Cedric. He slammed the door shut. His hands shook as he feared what might be inside. Suddenly, a tingling paralysis mixed with tension struck him, and he wondered what he was going to find this time. He breathed hard, tore off the tape, and removed the bubble-wrapped package. Upon seeing the contents, he froze and became queasy. Then he saw a note hanging from the object's handle.

You'll receive another delivery later with instructions.

He held the sent gun in his hand, flipping it and turning it. *Jesus, I need to call Recker*. The attorney answered, but before he could speak, Westbrook uttered, "Josh, they sent me a gun."

"A what?"

There was tension in his voice. "A fucking gun with a note. It's not loaded, but there will be another package coming. What the hell is this for?"

"How the hell do I know?"

"What does the note say?"

"It says there will be one more package."

"When?"

"It doesn't say."

"Should I call the cops?" The author was crippled with anxiety.

"Not yet. Wait for the instructions."

"Jesus, Josh. I think I've aged twenty years."

That queasy feeling became an urge to throw up, so he rushed to the bathroom and emptied his guts. Afterward, he fell asleep on his couch.

CHAPTER 47

Lex had no idea how this day would end. She and Gil were armed with new information about the kidnapping, but solving the case was still not on the table. The detectives were piecing together what they had learned, yet they remained at the mercy of the money mongers. In addition to their investigation was Lydell Lawrence's murder. Without the full cooperation of Westbrook, Lex and Gil geared up for a court case that could put the author in prison.

Movement in her peripheral vision drew Lex's attention to the entrance of the squad room. Agents Murdock and Gaines's heavy-footed steps continued into Pressley's quarters, and she heard Murdock say, "Hello again. We have more to discuss. I want Lex and Gil to join us."

"Let me get them, and we'll go to the conference room."

They proceeded to the designated area. The captain turned on the light and then closed the door. Taking a seat at the table with the rest of the law enforcers, Gaines remained silent as Murdock said, "We found Heinrich Altman. He's dead."

"Dead?" The news surprised Lex.

"That's right. We kept up the search for him, and we were sure he'd left the country. He wound up in San Diego where he was shot to death in a car outside a motel."

"When?" Lex asked.

"A couple of days ago. We think he was eventually going to Mexico. Detective Stall, does the name Daniel Vanderbilt mean anything to you?"

"I've never met him. I know he lives in Newport."

Murdock continued, "We know he's friends with Stefan Martine. What else can you tell us about Vanderbilt?"

"I heard he rents out condos in Newport."

Murdock paused and faced Lex. "You and Stefan Martine are, shall we say, close friends."

It was difficult to keep her composure with the hint of redness burning her face. She replied, "Okay, so you know."

"I mentioned Altman was dead. Vanderbilt was a second victim of that shooting."

Lex wasn't sure where the agent was heading, and nervously said, "You're not suggesting Stefan Martine is connected, are you?"

Murdock glared at her. "Is he?"

"Hardly, he's a gallery owner who is an honest man," she asserted.

"Maybe he is."

"Oh my God," Lex said. "That's why Stefan hasn't been able to reach him. He was planning to rent one of Vanderbilt's condos, and we were going to spend a weekend in Newport."

"We don't know how Vanderbilt and Altman were linked. The whole Gardner heist is still a jigsaw puzzle with more pieces than we know. We want to talk to Stefan Martine again. I want to know his ties to Vanderbilt."

Lex sighed. "I can get him down here."

"Excellent," Murdock said. "Please do."

Lex was trembling as she went to her cube to call Stefan. She wondered if she could be wrong about him. Was he the nice guy he seemed to be, or was he going to break her heart? She spoke to him, and he agreed to come to the precinct, while leaving his assistant in charge of the gallery.

The sharply dressed gallery owner appeared in the squad room forty-five minutes later, and Lex met him outside the conference room. "You sounded frazzled. What's going on?" he asked.

"Just be calm. Those FBI agents know about us and much more. They're waiting for you." Lex led the way.

As soon as the door opened, Murdock took charge. "Hello, Mister Martine. Have a seat. We have a few more questions for you."

Lex pointed to a seat for Stefan to take next to Gil. She sat next to the captain and positioned herself to see everyone's facial expressions. Murdock and Gaines were at the other corner of the table.

"What's going on?" Stefan asked.

"It's your friends, Altman and Vanderbilt," Murdock said.

"What about them? I've already told you what I know."

"Have you?"

Lex saw the confused and frustrated look on her suitor's face. "What are you trying to say?" he asked.

Murdock said, "First, let me tell you that Heinrich Altman and Daniel Vanderbilt were both in San Diego, and they were shot to death."

"Are you kidding me?"

"No, this is no joke. We have what you said about Altman. Tell us about your ties to Vanderbilt."

"You know he was in the art business, don't you?"

"We're quite aware of that," Murdock said. "When was the last time you saw him?"

"It's been a while, but we talked about business as recently as three months ago."

Murdock asked, "Where and when did you last see him?"

Stefan breathed hard and wiped his brow. "A little over a year ago in Newport."

"And who were you with?"

Reluctantly, he said, "Adrienne Chandelle."

That answer hit Lex hard. *They all lie, don't they?*

"And you had a relationship with her."

Stefan shifting uncomfortably in his seat said, "It wasn't like that. She was going to be my partner, but we were never serious."

Lex looked away from Stefan. *He should have told me.*

Murdock continued questioning Stefan. "And Vanderbilt and Altman?"

"I don't know about their relationship, and as I stated before, I only knew them as contemporaries."

"Have you told us everything you know?"

"Yes. I don't know anything else."

Murdock tapped Gaines on the leg, and they stepped out of the room. Lex kept her head down, focused on her lap. The rest of the room remained silent. A few minutes later, Murdock leaned into the room and said, "Thank you all for your time and cooperation."

Pressley rose, as did Gil, to exit the room while the distraught detective and her lover stayed. "Please, close the door. I want to talk with Stefan," Lex said. Hiding her sadness was not possible. With a grimace, she glared at Stefan. "You told me you never slept with her. That was a lie."

Stefan raised his hand to his face. "Lex, please, I know I did. The truth is Adrienne, and I were having sex, and it was just that."

Beginning to cry, she harshly uttered, "So she was your sex toy? Am I one too? I asked you about her, and you denied ever having sex with her. Why did you lie to me?"

Stefan reached for her hand, and she pulled it away. "You know how special you are to me. The first time you came to the gallery, I was smitten. I never wanted to hurt you. I thought about telling you but feared losing you."

She wiped the tears from her dour face, and angrily said, "I just can't stand lying. I've been hurt before, and now it's happened again."

"Damn it, Lex. I never wanted to hurt you. My feelings are real. Look, Adrienne and I had a little fling, but it was never serious."

"And you want me to trust you?" Her tone reflected the disappointment she was feeling.

Stefan reached for her hand again and grabbed it. "Please stop. You're the best thing that has ever happened to me. I can't let you get away. Please. I'm sorry, and I haven't lied about anything else."

Lex freed herself from his grasp. Frowning, she said, "So now I'm a thing? You've said enough. Please go."

Stefan pleaded, "Lex."

"I have to get back to work."

She walked out of the room and didn't watch Stefan leave the precinct. When she was sure he was gone, Lex freshened up in the lavatory before returning to her partner. She knew Gil was going to ask, but he looked hesitant. Then he broke the silence. "It looked like something Stefan said bothered you."

With a mock smile, she said, "I don't want to talk about it. We have work to do. I intend to find out what it is that Westbrook is still not telling us."

"How? Westbrook is off-limits."

"But Recker isn't. If I reach him and convince him we have to speak with his client, we may have a chance."

Chapter 48

Lex was determined to speak with Recker, and hoped he would listen. The attorney answered her call. "Detective Stall, I wasn't expecting to hear from you."

"I'm sure you were not. I'm aware of attorney and client privilege. I called to say we have information that Mister Westbrook can shed light on, and we'd like to talk with him."

"I think not."

"It's not about Lydell Lawrence. It's about the kidnapping. Help us out. Sit with him and advise him what he can and can't answer. Your rules."

"How important is this?"

"Meet with us. I promise there will be no Lydell Lawrence talk."

"I don't think that would be a good idea."

Lex changed her tone to be more insistent. "Look, you're an attorney. We both know he can take the Fifth to any question I ask. It won't hurt to let me speak with him."

"This better be good. Let me call him."

A short while later, Recker informed Lex they could meet in two hours at the suite.

▲

When the detectives arrived at the author's residence, it was Recker who opened the door. "I can't wait to hear what you have."

"I bet," Lex said.

Westbrook was sitting in a chair, and Lex noticed a weapon on the dining table.

Recker said, "It came yesterday afternoon with a note. The gun is absent of bullets. The note indicates another package will be delivered soon. My guess is it will contain ammunition."

Gil asked, "Why didn't you call us?"

Ignoring the question, Recker asked Lex, "Now, what is it you want to discuss?"

Westbrook uttered, "Let's get this over with. What the hell do you want?"

Lex rolled out her soft voice with the intent of breaking the ice. She calmly said, "I don't believe you have told us everything about Jilian Stemple."

The author looked at Recker, who nodded his approval to answer her, and he said, "I already told you about her."

"You did tell us a few things, and we discovered that she was in prison in Niantic for approximately eighteen years. What about her past? You said you met her at a club and began having an affair before your wife died, and we suspect it was about the same time Jillian got pregnant."

"That's all true."

"Did you know Jillian had to put the baby boy up for adoption?"

That question appeared to make Westbrook uncomfortable. "I was aware of that, but I never knew him."

"Yes, but did she ever mention his name?"

"No, like I said, I never saw him."

"I'm curious about this baby." Lex treaded carefully as to not anger the author.

"What are you getting at?"

"Could you have fathered the baby?"

Westbrook again looked at his attorney. "You can answer her," Recker said.

"She was sleeping with several guys," Westbrook answered.

"What about you? You slept with her too."

"Yes."

Lex continued, "So, you could have fathered the child."

With his face turning red, he loudly asked, "What are you trying to say?"

"I'm saying we went to Bridgeport and have the birth record for that baby. His mother was Jillian Stemple. There was no father listed on the document, but it was you, wasn't it?"

Westbrook got up and shouted, "Are you crazy? She was a drug dealing whore."

"We are sure your DNA from hair on the comb left at Lydell Lawrence's office will match that child's."

"You are nuts," Westbrook yelled.

Recker told his client to calm himself. "Detective, we've had enough."

"Not quite. That baby was adopted by a family named Costa, who at this point remain unknown. And interestingly, the baby's name on the birth certificate is T-H-O-M-A-S. Apparently, somewhere along the line, the H was removed, and he became T-O-M-A-S."

Westbrook began to sweat. "What are you saying?"

"Tomas Costa was your son."

Looking at his attorney, Westbrook didn't have to say a word.

"Now, it's time to go." Recker moved toward the door.

Lex had no intention of ending the conversation. "We'll leave in a few minutes, but I want to disclose something else. We have evidence to prove Tomas purchased drones and listening devices, as well as prepaid phones. He must have been communicating with the rest of the kidnappers with prepaid phones. We also know Tomas planted the listening devices."

Westbrook wiped his forehead. "You know I am being framed. I did not kill Lawrence."

Recker pointed at the author. "Stop. Lawrence is off-limits."

"He is," Lex said as she looked into Westbrook's eyes. "Why would your mistress and son want to kidnap Svetlana, and who else is involved?"

Recker pointed to the door. "We are done."

Lex said, "If you say so."

As Gil drove to the precinct, Lex asked, "What do you think?"

"He obviously didn't know who Tomas Costa really was."

"He did not, but there is still something else we do not know."

⚑

Westbrook remained in his suite along with Recker. "This is a mess. You know I'm innocent. He quickly went to his liquor stash and filled a glass, taking a big swallow before turning to Recker. "That bitch, she was a whore, a no-good drug dealing free fuck. That Tomas could be anybody's."

"Maybe, except for me."

The alcoholic walked unsteadily and leaned against the credenza, staring at a photo of the Twin Towers and another one of Margaret next to it. "Those buildings are buried just like Margaret is."

"And you know all about what happened that day. And that's what's so ironic. You're being framed for murder. It's early yet, but if we go to trial, a jury may not believe us. There's no way I'll let you testify. I'll have to poke holes through the prosecutor's story and the evidence. If we have to plea-bargain to keep it from going to trial, we may have to do it."

"Yeah, you're good at that. That day has never left my mind."

"I know and it has come close to leaving. You're drinking has made you say many things you don't remember. I have to go."

Later that evening came another message.

The end is near.

You'll get the last delivery Monday.

And there it was again.

You didn't believe the message about that boat sailing, Now you have to. Next time it will be Svetlana on that boat.

Chapter 49

The dance on Saturday reminded Lex of when she was a student at Stuyvesant High School. Thinking about her junior prom brought back bad memories. That was the night she was raped.

Tonight, would not be like that for her daughter.

Liz wore her new mauve dress. As Lex helped her zip up, she said, "You look beautiful."

"Thank you. I'm excited! Spencer and his mom will be here soon."

A few minutes later, the doorbell rang, and Lex greeted their guests. "Come in," she said. "You look very handsome, Spencer."

"I'm Sarah," the boy's mother said.

"I'm Lex. It's nice to meet you. Elaine will be here with Shannon and Steven soon."

"Liz looks lovely," Sarah said.

"Thank you," Liz replied.

At ten fifteen p.m., all the flashing lights and loud music Lex could not identify with ended. Not a minute too soon as far as she was concerned. It certainly was not Fleetwood Mac or anything of that ilk. "We better get the boys home," she said to Elaine.

They did so and before going to bed, Liz smiled. "Thanks, Mom. I had a good time."

"Good night." Lex stared at her daughter. "If you're texting Shannon, tell her I like Steven too."

Liz laughed. "Mom! Go to bed."

▲

Sunday, Lex slept late. She was still simmering about Stefan, but really liked him. *Maybe he is that good person I have been intimate with, and if he is sincere, he might have learned a painful lesson.* In her heart, she wanted him to call. Had she seen the last of him?

That evening, it was ten past seven when she heard her cell. Seeing the caller ID, she nervously answered. "Stefan."

"Lex, I'm sorry. I'm really sorry. Please accept my apology."

She took a moment to breathe. "You really hurt me."

"I realize that, and I ask you to listen. I don't want to let you go."

She sighed because, she had hoped he would phone her. "I appreciate that. I wasn't sure you'd call."

"I've thought about it all weekend, but I just didn't know when the right time was. You really tore into me."

"I did, and you deserved every word."

"You're right. I hope you truly understand. Believe me, I'd never intentionally hurt you. I want to see you and make it up to you."

Lex smiled to herself, knowing she wanted to see him.

"Lex, listen to me." In a desperate tone, he said, "I learned a lesson that I will never forget. Believe me. Please."

She hesitated, making him wait a few seconds. "Stefan, I really hope you are true to your word." He started to apologize again, but Lex cut him off. "Stop. Does that mean we can still go to Newport?" She heard his sigh of relief.

"Thank God, Lex. I miss you."

"Enough said."

"There are plenty of hotels in Newport. We'll have a good time."

"I'm sure we will. Call me soon. I'm going to get a good night's rest."

"Have pleasant dreams, my love."

Lex was silent for a second. "What did you say?"

" Uhm, it just slipped out."

"What slipped out?" she teased.

"You know."

"I do know. You sleep tight too, my love."

GRETA'S GONE

Another twenty-four hours elapsed. Tucker and Sal waited for the kidnappers to name the location and time for the exchange of money and hostage. Then it came.

Okay, pal. Remember your father's airplane?

That's where we'll meet. Be at the airport at 10:45 p.m. tonight. Drive up to the hangar and you will see a white and red Piper M350. Get out of your car with the money packed in a large suitcase. Wait there. Greta will be escorted to you, and we'll take the money. BE ALONE or we will fly away with her, and you will never see her again. GOT IT?

Tucker answered: I'll be there.

Immediately afterward, Tucker pulled his friend's arm. "Come on. We're going to see Weiss."

Harrison Weiss was on the phone when Tucker and Sal arrived. He waved for his visitors to sit. "That's correct. I'll take care of that." He hung up and faced the two gentlemen.

Tucker held up his hand. "It's on. Tonight, at the airport. They have a plane."

Weiss sat back. "A plane? Like your father's?"

"No, a Piper. They will bring Greta to me, and I'll hand them the money."

"Wait," Weiss said. "About your father's accident...that mechanic, Eddie Franco? What happened to him?"

Sal said, "I think he's still working at the airport."

Weiss asked Tucker, "What time?"

"Ten forty-five p.m. They reiterated that I need to be alone."

Weiss blew out a breath. "Do you have the money?"

"I'll get it when we leave here."

"I'm going to have a perimeter set up, so there is nothing to fear.

The Special Operations Unit will be out of sight."

"But what if they are spotted?"

"The kidnappers won't see a damn thing because it will be dark. The squad will have infrared and can be on them in seconds."

Sal asked, "What if they have guns?"

"That's why the team will be there. Call me, Tucker, when you're heading to the airport."

After obtaining the ransom amount, the demanded money was stuffed into a blue suitcase that sat on the man cave floor. Tucker paced anxiously while Sal kept him away from drugs. Time slowly passed, and darkness set in. Finally, at 10:00 p.m., he called Weiss. "I'm all set," Tucker said. "I'll take my father's Mercedes."

"Good. The airport is about twenty minutes from you. My guys are there, and you won't see them even if you have Superman vision. You should leave soon."

"I will."

Sal said, "I think I should come."

"You can't. I have to be alone," Tucker reminded him.

"Yeah, but I can lie low in the back seat, and no one will know. And I do have my Smith and Wesson with me. They'll never see me back there."

Tucker thought about Sal's request. "You know, that's not a bad idea."

Not wanting to be late, Tucker and Sal got into the sedan at 10:15 with Tucker driving and Sal lying low in the back seat.

The open airstrip, unattended tower, and lonely hangar rarely saw activity at this time of night. The only light was provided by a couple of beams from the tower, and the moon. The light that usually shined from the tower was out.

As the Mercedes traveled down the dirt road, its headlights enabled Tucker to see the plane. He looked around and saw no one. "Where are they? Stay down," he said to Sal as the vehicle stopped fifty feet from the aircraft.

Except for crickets chirping, there was silence. Then Tucker heard a car coming toward the plane, and it came into view. When it stopped, a couple of shadowy figures exited.

Tucker opened his door, retrieved the suitcase from the passenger seat, and walked a few feet on the tarmac. As the two men got closer to him, Tucker was stunned. "What the hell?"

Chief Weiss said, "Hand it over, Tucker."

"You?" He looked over at Marty. "You bastards. I'm not giving you this money."

"Whoa," Chief Weiss said. "Let's not play games. I'll take the suitcase."

"Let her go, you liar. There's no one else out here, is there? That stuff about being surrounded with armed police was bullshit."

"Good observation, Tucker. Now let's go. The money."

"Not yet. When Greta gets into my car, I'll drop the case and get the hell out of here."

Chief Weiss pulled out his gun and pointed it at Tucker. "Not quite, you killer. You think we don't know it was you who reset the ailerons on your father's plane? I knew from the get-go it was you. Admit it."

"So what? My greedy father, he was no dad."

Keeping his gun aimed at Tucker, the chief sternly said, "And you decided to kill him, then attempted to blame it on Eddie Franco."

Looking squarely into the nose of the firearm, Tucker began to shake. "I had to. It was the only way I could get my hands on his money." He pleaded, "Greta, where is she?"

"Keep begging, but it won't do you any good. She could have identified us. And so can you. You're not leaving here alive."

While Marty counted the money, Tucker, on his knees and praying, looked up. "Greta, what's happened to her?"

"Let me put it to you this way. Your father is dead, you will be soon, and Greta? I think they'll find her eventually at the bottom of Long Island Sound."

A loud bang sounded while a bullet entered Chief Weiss. He fell to the ground. Tucker saw Sal approaching and another shot rang out. This one pierced Marty in the chest.

Tucker stepped over the two dead bodies as Marty's sobbing wife walked slowly down the plane's ramp. Sal ordered her to get on the ground, face down.

Tucker said, "I'm calling the police station."

"Ask for Captain Anton Williams and get him out here with a crew of officers," Sal said.

Tucker spotted Eddie Franco, who was standing at the Piper's door. "I heard it all, Tucker. You tried to fry me, and it was you all along."

"What are you doing here?"

"I'm a pilot. Did you forget? I was paid to fly the Weisses to Costa Rica."

Tucker asked, "So, you had nothing to do with kidnapping Greta?"

"Of course not. Didn't you hear me?"

Tucker blew out a breath. "Okay, I did. Look, I apologize for trying to implicate you in my father's death. You can come down here."

Three police vehicles arrived. Their sirens were turned off, but the flashing blue and red lights continued to pulsate. Officers rushed to take charge. A minute later, two ambulances were on the scene. Assistant Chief Anton Williams walked past the bodies to talk with Tucker.

Tucker told Williams everything, and then picked up the luggage and carried it toward the Mercedes.

Sal shouted, "Tucker, come back here. You forgot to tell him one thing." Tucker spun around as Sal said, "You admitted to killing your father."

The Smith & Wesson kept Tucker from trying to get away. "Sal, what are you doing?"

"I'm doing what's right, turning you over to the police."

Williams cuffed Tucker, read him his rights, and shoved him into a cruiser.

Sal asked the captain, "What about the suitcase and the money?"

Williams replied, "We'll take that and put it into custody."

Chapter 50

It was the start of a new week, and it began on a high note. Hutch and Benzinger were leaving the precinct as Lex came in. "Where are you going?" she asked.

Hutch said, "Downtown. Last night, the Bryant Park killer was arrested, and we are going to interview him. We also learned that Bee Rodriguez was released from the hospital yesterday."

"I'm glad to hear it."

Lex settled in at her desk, thinking about Tomas Costa's adoptive parents, and almost didn't hear Gil arrive. "You look lost in space," he said.

The birth certificate and list of Costa taxpayers in Bridgeport were on Lex's desk. "These have been sitting here since we got back from Bridgeport. I know it's been hectic, but we have to attempt to locate the Costas who adopted Tomas."

"I agree. There are eight families with that name. If we are lucky, we'll get a hit."

"You realize they might have left Bridgeport, or they may be dead."

"In that case, we may never find them."

Gil made two calls with no success, while Lex connected with one other party and had to leave a message with another. "Nothing yet," she said. She kept phoning and on the next call, she had success, speaking with a female named Juanita Costa. "Misses Costa, I'm Lex Stall with the Manhattan Police Department. You haven't done anything wrong. I'm seeking information about a Tomas Costa."

"Tomas? What about him?"

"You know him?"

"I haven't seen him in six years. I think he's in San Juan, Puerto Rico with Miguel and Carmine."

"Miguel and Carmine? Are they his parents?"

"Yes. They adopted him in Bridgeport when he was two."

Assuming Juanita hadn't heard about Tomas's death, Lex held back the news that he'd been killed and was involved in a kidnapping. "Are you in touch with your husband's family?"

She sighed. "No. My husband died two years ago, and he and Miguel were never close anyhow. I haven't talked to them in a long time."

So, you don't know if they are in San Juan?"

"No."

"What kind of jobs do they have?"

"Carmine cleaned houses. And Miguel used to hop around from job to job. The last I knew he was landscaping."

"What about Tomas?"

"I have no idea.'

Lex's optimism was turning into frustration. "Are there any other relatives in the area?"

"Just me."

Disappointed that she was not receiving information about the parent's whereabouts, Lex tapped her foot. "Thank you," she said. Lex read her number to Juanita. "Please call me if think of anything you have not told me."

Lex put her phone down and Gil commented, "I'm not having any luck, but it sounds as if you have."

"I don't know about that, but it's a start. Juanita Costa is related by marriage but hasn't been in touch with Tomas's parents, Miguel and Carmine. As far as Juanita knows, they are all still in San Juan."

Gil noted. "You didn't mention Tomas was killed New York."

"No. We've got more work to do."

⋏

The leader of the hostage takers knew the end was near, and he had to plan an exit strategy. Showing up at Sheepshead Bay was risky because without blindfolding Svetlana again, she would recognize him. The call to his wife insured that Svetlana would be able to see him when he got there.

With Svetlana again locked in a bedroom, he gathered his co-conspirators in the nearby seating area. "We have our lives to consider, and leaving town is what we need to do."

The male co-conspirator asked, "Where will we go?"

"I have a timeshare in Costa Rica."

He pointed to Svetlana's room. "What about her?"

"At this point, she's excess baggage. I'll think about what to do with her."

"And when are we going to get rid of the limo?"

"Tonight. We'll do it tonight after dark. We can set it on fire."

"And she will be in it."

"I'll rig it and use the remote to light it."

His voice resonated and sweat began to pour off Svetlana, and she yelled, "You're going to kill me?"

"Shut up," the female accomplice said.

The ringleader said to his wife, "I have to talk to you." They went from the living room into the kitchen and huddled. "Those two, Miguel and Carmine, are just low-income pawns, and it didn't take much to get them involved."

"Are you saying what I think you're saying?"

"Damn right. I'm going to have Miguel and Carmine drive the limo somewhere to get rid of it. I will tell them we are going to be behind them, and they can join us so that we can all get out of here."

"What about her?"

"Svetlana? Let me think hard about her."

Chapter 51

Westbrook awoke in anticipation of receiving another delivery, perhaps the final message from Svetlana's abductors. The absence of her warm body in bed overwhelmed him, and he went to the kitchen dressed in his pajamas. A loud rap on the front door brought him to the entryway. Looking through the peephole, he opened the door and was presented with a small box.

The author held the container and shuddered, assuming it was from the kidnappers. He slammed the door shut, almost in the concierge's face. His fingers shook as he ripped open the package and saw a box of bullets. The nearby gun silently screamed to not be surprised.

What the hell do they want?

Recker needed to know about this, and Westbrook could barely punch the cell phone numbers to make the call. "Josh, I just got that second package, and it contains bullets."

"Wait for me. I have an important client to see, and then I'll come over. It could be a while, but I'll be there."

Westbrook held onto his phone despite hanging up. Minutes later, a text came in.

This is it. You are to load the gun. Then wait for final instructions.

He plunged himself onto his couch and sat speechless. Tucker Rutledge flashed through his mind. Westbrook rushed to his book rack and picked up *Greta's Gone*. Opening it to the last chapter, he skimmed the last few pages. He stopped, closed it, threw it on the floor, and realized that Browning and or Gladstone must have read it. "Son of a bitch," he uttered. "It's one of them, Chandler Browning or Eldridge Gladstone. It had to be one, or both authors who probably killed Lawrence."

Recker had said he was going to be with a client, but the author called the attorney anyway. At first, there was no answer, but then Recker spoke. "I told you I'm busy. Hold on while I excuse myself for a minute."

"Josh, I know who the kidnappers are."

"What? Are you sure?"

"I know it's either Chandler Browning or Eldridge Gladstone. Who else would try to frame me? Both of them would like nothing better than to put me away."

"Didn't you say one of them called you a plagiarizer?"

"Browning, that bastard." Changing subjects he asked, "What about the detectives?"

"I don't want the police asking you questions without me there. Do you have contact information for Browning and Gladstone?"

"Yes."

"Give them to me. I'll call Detective Stall," Recker said.

"Shit. What the hell do I do with the gun and bullets?"

"Nothing right now."

He had hidden a bottle of Xanax and ran to the medicine cabinet to take one, before falling asleep on the couch.

▲

Lex hadn't anticipated a call from Recker, and when her desk phone rang, she raised her brows and answered. She alerted Gil and hit the speaker button. "Mister Recker."

"Detective, Essex Westbrook received a small package this morning that contained bullets, as well as another message."

"What did the text say?"

"It said, 'A final instruction will be forthcoming. Listen, he may be onto something. He is positive that either Chandler Browning or Eldridge Gladstone or both kidnapped Svetlana."

"Why does he think that?"

"Because he is sure they read his book, *Greta's Gone*, and they talked about it at the award presentation last month. Apparently, it's about a woman being held hostage."

"Why the heck hasn't he ever mentioned that?"

"I couldn't tell you, but Browning has accused him of plagiarism in the past and has a reason to go after him."

"What about Gladstone?"

"I know they never got along with each other."

Lex wondered if this information has ties to the stabbing of the literary agent. "He is implicating either author in the murder of Lawrence."

"I'm not going that far, but he is."

"Thanks for the information," Lex said. She looked at her partner, her eyebrows raised.

Gil said, "Do you believe there is any validity to what Recker claims?"

"That's hard to say, but we can't rule out his theory."

"To validate or invalidate the involvement of either author, we have to talk to them." Without a word being said, Lex strutted into the squad room and began pacing. *One thing doesn't make sense. If Browning or Gladstone were involved, how do they know Tomas or Jillian?*

She returned and Gil said, "That was a short one."

"Yes. We have to find out if either author knows Tomas or Jillian. She picked up her desk phone. "I'll start with Browning. You can listen."

Browning picked up quickly. "Good morning."

"Sir, I'm Detective Lex Stall from the Manhattan Police Department."

"Is this about Lydell Lawrence? I can't believe he's dead."

"I'm sorry to confirm that," Lex said. "Would you mind if I asked you a few questions?"

"Okay."

"When was the last time you saw your agent?"

"Gosh, it was about two months ago."

"We're you at the awards dinner last month?"

"Oh. I was. I sat with him, Eldridge Gladstone, and Essex Westbrook."

"What about Westbrook? His wife, Svetlana?"

"She was with him at the dinner."

"We understand you and Westbrook had some sort of argument."

"Argument? I know he copied from one of my books. We discussed it and didn't resolve the issue, but I still say he did."

"Would you say that you aren't exactly friends?"

"You could say that."

"Where were you on April first?"

"I was here in Worcester. Actually, I bought a new grill at Home Depot and put it together on my deck. Not as easy as it looks. Then I had to go get a propane tank. It took all day, but we finally barbecued steak at five thirty."

"We?"

"My kids and wife."

"What about April sixteenth and seventeenth? Those were a Tuesday and Wednesday."

"I was at Barnes and Nobles, each of those days. Tuesday, I was in Providence, Wednesday. I was in Springfield, and Thursday was Pittsfield. I'll be promoting my new book in New Hampshire later this week."

"One more question. Do you know Tomas Costa or Jillian Stemple?"

"I never heard of them. Who are they?"

"That's not important. Good luck. It sounds like a busy schedule."

"It is, but it comes with the territory."

Lex was satisfied with his responses. "Thank you for speaking with me. Have a good day."

Gil said, "He's out."

With the receiver in her hand, she said, "I want to try Eldridge Gladstone."

"Now? It's early in Seattle."

"I can leave a message if I have to."

She keyed in his phone number and heard three rings. To her surprise, he answered. When she identified herself, he asked, "What's going on out there? My agent is dead."

Lex asked, "Can you tell me where you were the morning of April first?"

"I was here working on my next novel. Of all the days, though, my rottweiler was sick, and I took him to the vet."

"I hope he is better."

"He is."

"How about April sixteenth and seventeenth. Where were you?"

"Why are you asking me that?"

"It's routine, sir. Please answer the question."

"I was in England, first in London, then traveled to Manchester. I got back here to Seattle on the twentieth."

"As I understand it, you, Browning, Lawrence, and Westbrook were all together at the Awards presentation dinner."

"True and in retrospect, I guess Westbrook was worthy of the prize."

"I'm sorry about Lydell Lawrence. I hope I didn't wake you. Thank you for chatting with me."

"I get up at five when I'm in writing mode. I think better in the morning."

"Do the names Tomas Costa or Jillian Stemple mean anything to you?"

"I've never heard of them."

"Thanks again, and good luck with your new book."

When Lex hung up, Gil said, "That shoots holes in Westbrook's theory. Browning and Gladstone have solid alibis. What are you going to tell Recker?"

"I'll tell him what we know. There's no connection between them and the kidnapping or murder." Lex got up and said, "I'll be back. Save my seat."

She visited her place of solace, the ladies room.

When she returned to her partner, Pressley rushed into their cube. "This may have something to do with the kidnapping. Early this morning, there was a car fire in a vacant lot near Rikers. It was a limo. The fire is out, but remains of the car contained at least two badly burned unidentified bodies."

Lex and Gil, within minutes, were in transit to Rikers Island. As soon as the squad car crossed the bridge, Lex saw uniformed police at the scene, and Gil parked on the grass. The limo was still smoldering, and the air smelled of smoke.

The detectives sidled up to a lieutenant. "Don't get too close.

It's warm."

"I see," Lex said as Gil coughed and covered his mouth. "Did you see the victims?"

"Not closely. Firefighters removed them about an hour ago, and they were taken away in ambulances."

"Could you tell if there were two or three?"

"Male or female?"

"Your guess is as good as mine."

Lex examined the vehicle from about five feet away. "Not much left but it was a limo. Despite the char, it was black."

Gil walked around the vehicle and began coughing again. "The plates are melted like a marshmallow."

Lex took a few pictures, and then she and Gil left the scene.

CHAPTER 52

Waking from a bad dream, Westbrook screamed. His nightmare about Svetlana dying seemed so real. Sitting on the edge of the couch as sweat drenched his pajamas, he came back to reality, but he still didn't know if his wife was dead or alive. He also worried he would end up in prison for Lawrence's death, a crime he knew he didn't commit.

His phone beeped, and he read the message.

It's time. It's you or her. Load the gun.

Either way, you will never see Svetlana again.

He barely finished reading when a second message came through.

The choice is yours.

You can go to jail, accused of killing Lawrence, or you can take your life and make up for the crime you did commit.

You have less than 24 hours to ponder your decision.

His first reaction was panic, then he again called Recker. "Josh, I got new messages. Threats. Her life or mine. I'm staring at that gun."

"I cancelled my important meeting. I'll be right over. Don't do anything stupid."

"Josh, hurry."

Westbrook was sinking fast. Randomly pacing throughout the apartment, he tore at his hair and pulled at his sleeves. When the attorney rushed in, the author was in dire straits. "Help me, Josh. You know I'm innocent. I need to get Svetlana back, but I can't go to jail. The whole world is caving in on me." He pointed to the gun and bullets on the dining table.

"I see them. It's time to let the detectives know," Recker said, pulling out his phone.

Lex answered the incoming call.

Recker said, "Detective, I'm at Westbrook's. He received a package this morning containing bullets along with a message saying he should kill himself with the gun to free Svetlana, or he could go to jail for the crime he didn't commit or the one he did commit."

"Do you understand that last part?"

"No. I came here to make sure he is safe and to help negotiate the return of Svetlana. The Lawrence case is on the back burner."

"Don't hang up. Something happened earlier. A limo was set afire near Rikers, and two victims were discovered. It could be the limo the abductors were using."

"Svetlana?"

"We don't know. The bodies were badly burned and haven't been identified yet. Is that Westbrook in the background? He doesn't sound good."

"He's really strung out."

"Keep him away from the bar."

⚊⚊⚊

Lex saw Neil Gerstein approaching the captain while she was speaking with Westbrook's attorney. The agent carried a black briefcase and Lex shortened the call. "I have to go. Stay with him. Let us know if something happens."

Gerstein waved for her and Gil to join them. "Can we go to the conference room?" he asked.

They entered the meeting quarters, and Gerstein didn't waste time. He opened his briefcase, pulled out a folder, and placed it in front of him. Flipping it open, he showed the group a photo of the 9/11 memorial and pointed to the name Margaret Westbrook. "Do you see that name?"

Lex said, "Yes. Westbrook has a photo of it. His wife died in the attack. She was in the north building."

"You think so? That's your first mistake. She was never in

either building that day. She did work for an advertising company named Cadbury and Lyons, but she was off that week."

"What? How did her name get etched onto the memorial wall?" Lex asked.

Gerstein said, "Many people who died were never truly identified. Several names on that wall were given by employers and relatives who knew individuals in those buildings. We spoke with the CEO of Cadbury and Lyons. Their firm had been in the north building. Now they are on Park Avenue. They never gave her name to the media or fact finders. It had to be Westbrook."

Lex looked at Gil. "Is that the crime he committed?"

Gerstein asked, "What are you referring to?"

"It's the message Westbrook got this morning. It referred to a crime he committed and one he didn't commit."

"That's interesting. Essex Westbrook and Margaret Rutledge Westbrook, who by the way was known as Greta to friends, lived in Westport, Connecticut. Margaret disappeared that fateful day and was never seen again."

"Wait. You're saying Margaret was home, and he killed her?" Lex asked.

"Hang with me. She definitely wasn't in those buildings. We spoke with neighbors, most of whom did not live there at that time. However, one woman, Nicole Santacasa remembered seeing Margaret who was wearing jogging clothes. It was around seven-thirty that morning. Nicole had always taken her dog for a walk at that time. Then, later that afternoon Nicole was sitting on her porch and saw Westbrook's car drive by. He was driving, but a woman she didn't recognize was in the passenger seat."

"Jillian Stemple," Lex said.

"That's our guess."

"Why didn't Nicole report it then?"

"It's not uncommon. She didn't want to get involved."

Another reason Margaret couldn't have been in the twin towers was that it takes an hour and twenty minutes by train to get to Grand Central, and there are no trains that early to Penn Station. It takes an hour and forty minutes on a good day to reach Manhattan by car. It would have been impossible for her to be there. The north building was crashed into at eight forty-six, the south tower at three minutes past nine."

"This is crazy," Lex uttered. "So, that's the crime he committed but was never arrested and Jillian was his accomplice."

"Yes, that's what we believe, and later Jillian ended up in Niantic for dealing drugs. Would you like to take a guess as to who her attorney was?" Before anyone could offer an answer, he said, "It was Joshua Recker, who somehow swung her a plea deal for twenty years rather than her receiving a much steeper sentence."

Gil was dumbfounded. "We never suspected that."

Lex said, "Tomas Costa was Jillian's son. We're sure Westbrook was his father. She didn't put the father's name on the birth certificate after naming the baby. We found the document in Bridgeport. The baby's name was T-H-O-M-A-S. It appears he was adopted by a family named Costa, and we think they changed the spelling to T-O-M-A-S. It was Tomas who purchased the drones, the phones, and the listening devices. It looks like the kidnappers got rid of him because he was a threat. He was talking to us. We also know about Jillian. They killed her after her finger was cut off."

Gerstein said, "Here's what we know. You are right about the Costas. Their names are Miguel and Carmine, and they live in Puerto Rico. I should say their last known residence is there, but we can't find them."

Benzinger knocked on the door, and Pressley opened it. "Sir, this message is important. It's about the car fire. They have identified the victims from their charred passports." He handed the note to the captain.

"It's them, Miguel and Carmine Costa," Pressley said.

Then it dawned on Lex. "Oh my God. He's with Westbrook. Recker is with him now and has a gun. The lawyer killed Lydell Lawrence and planted the evidence to frame his own friend." Lex said, "It's the Costa family. It's Jillian, as well as Recker."

"Get over there," Pressley said. "I'm calling now to have uniforms get there promptly."

"Wait, one more thing," Gerstein said. "The house Westbrook owned in Westport: he sold it a couple of months later to police chief Anton Willians and then moved to New York. We contacted Williams, explained things and he's agreed to let us dig up the yard. We suspect Margaret was buried there."

Lex swiftly rose. "Let's go," she said to Gil.

"I have to get back to the FBI Building," Gerstein said as he was leaving.

CHAPTER 53

Gil drove frantically to the Grand Truman with the squad car's flashing lights and siren engaged, allowing them to cut through traffic. As soon as they got there, Lex spotted black and whites as well as an ambulance. Victor said, "Police are inside. What's going on?"

"It's Mister Westbrook," Lex said as she and Gil hopped out of the car.

"His attorney left here a while ago."

Gil asked, "Do you know which way he went? Was he carrying anything?"

"It's strange because I never parked his car. He had two suitcases with him, and he sped out of here, but I didn't recognize the car."

Racing toward the hotel's door, she murmured, "Damn it."

The detectives rushed to the elevator and rode up to the author's suite. When they arrived, the door was open, and four uniforms were inside, as were EMTs. Westbrook's body was prone, face down, on the blood-stained carpet. "He's dead," a paramedic said.

Careful not to step in fluid, Lex walked to the EMT closest to the body. "He was shot above the temple," she said.

"The gun is by his side," Gil noted.

Lex closely observed the body and weapon. "Recker wanted it to look like suicide."

"I doubt Recker went back to his office," Gil said. "And he apparently still has Svetlana."

"He?" Lex asked. "What about his wife and partner, Jennifer? Someone has to be with Svetlana. Why not her?"

An earth-shattering scream interrupted their conversation. Claudia and Benton Kimball were peering into the suite. His wife lowered her head and Benton inquired, "What happened?"

"Go back to your unit, please," Gil said.

Lex called her boss. "Westbrook is dead. Recker shot him, and the valet said he saw him leaving here a short while ago."

"Gerstein is on the other line. I'll connect him," Pressley said.

Lex quickly caught him up on what had happened. "I'm putting out an APB on Recker's plates as we speak," the FBI agent responded.

Lex said, "No. Cancel it. The valet said he saw Recker drive out of here in a vehicle other than the one he normally sees. We'll be with Pressley at the precinct."

Lex and Gil rushed to be with their boss and waited for an update from Gerstein. Ten minutes later, he called, and Pressley put him on speaker. "We're nearing Recker's residence in Scarborough. He may or may not be there."

"Keep us updated," Pressley said.

A half hour elapsed before Gerstein called again. "We are just leaving Recker's house. There is no one here, but according to a neighbor, he and his wife have another residence on Sheepshead Bay. We have the address, and I'm on my way there. Hopefully, the crew I sent over will find them."

As Lex, Gil, and Pressley sat idly, the FBI was in action. There was little to do while time passed. Pressley hit the speaker when the phone finally rang. Gerstein said, "We're at Sheepshead Bay with other agents, and Svetlana is here. She appears to be shellshocked but seems okay. Relieved to be free. We have Jennifer Recker in custody and put out a revised APB. His car is here, and he is driving his wife's BMW."

Lex stood while breathing heavily. "Thank the Lord, Svetlana is alive and free."

"We'll find Recker. He's a kidnapper and a killer. Tomas Costa, Jillian Stemple, Lydell Lawrence, Miguel and Carmine Costa, and now Essex Westbrook are all dead because of him."

With several resources having the new APB, Recker was sought after with tracking devices. The BMW was located, and they homed in. Gerstein provided the update. "We are tracking Recker. It appears he is driving toward Teterboro. A team of agents will be there soon."

"Thanks," Lex said.

ᐱ

Recker reached his destination, parked the car, and walked as fast as he could. Wheeling the suitcases to the plane, he said to the pilot, "Let's go. Make it fast."

The attorney took a few steps toward the airplane's ladder, and a team of FBI tactical agents swarmed the runway. A loud voice sounded, "Hold it right there." Three lawmen pointed rifles at the attorney.

Recker stopped, looked around, and saw two more rifles aimed at him and the pilot.

"You're not going anywhere," the lead agent shouted. "Both of you, get on the ground."

The stunned pilot hit the pavement along with Recker. After being cuffed, they were pulled upright. "I didn't do anything," the pilot stated.

A rifleman said, "Stay put."

Recker asked, "How did you find me?"

Gerstein said, "We were at your house on Sheepshead Bay. Svetlana is free, and your wife is in custody. We tracked the car."

A buzzing noise echoed over the area, and he looked up. "You're kidding. You tracked me with a drone, a fucking drone?"

"Yes, sir." Gerstein read him his rights and arrested him. "You're going to love prison."

Agents questioned the pilot who was not involved in the scheme, he was released.

CHAPTER 54

ex, Gil, and Pressley met Gerstein at the FBI building. "Svetlana spent the night in a guest room," Gerstein said. "We have a therapist with her. She's very shaken and disoriented. It's been a long siege that wasn't supposed to end up this way, but it did."

"May I speak with Svetlana?" Lex asked.

"Yes, but I think the therapist should stay with you."

Gerstein rapped on the door before opening it. "Detective Stall would like to chat with Svetlana."

The therapist nodded, and Lex took a seat beside the distraught Svetlana. "I'm sorry for what has happened."

"Yes, it's so bizarre. It all started with a letter I got, and then I went to Izzy's. I never should have gone. In the beginning, they only wanted money and then something happened. They kept watch over me all night and day. Joshua Recker, of all the people. How could they have done this?"

"I don't know, but they did. Have you given any consideration as to where you may be able to stay?" Lex felt compassion for her.

"I don't have family here, so I'm not sure where to go. I can't bear the stress of going back to Grand Truman. I heard a lot, but Essex killing Margaret is very hard to take."

Svetlana began to cry.

Lex handed her a tissue. "I'll be right back."

She left the room, stood in the corridor, and made a call. Explaining the story to Clark Fullerton, he agreed to Lex's ask. When the detective again sat beside Svetlana, she explained her plan. "I just spoke with Clark Fullerton, and he is making a suite available for you at the Rembrandt. He said not to worry about the fee."

Svetlana wiped her eyes. "That's kind. I appreciate it."

The therapist reached out for Svetlana's hand and said, "I think she's had enough for now."

Lex moved close to Svetlana. "Please don't hesitate to call me, and I hope you don't mind if I check in with you every now and then."

"Thank you."

Lex rejoined Gerstein, Pressley, and Gil. "I'm going to keep tabs on her. It may take time, but she's strong, and I'm sure she'll get through it."

Gerstein said, "Recker and Jennifer will go up on federal charges. We should begin digging at Westbrook's old Westport residence in the morning."

"It's been a long, hard ordeal," Lex said.

"It all began with Jillian and Margaret," Gerstein said. Apparently, Margaret found out about Jillian and her husband. She was going to divorce him, but he didn't let that happen."

Lex asked, "Why the kidnapping?"

The FBI agent leaned forward. "Recker told us he was concerned about Westbrook going to the police about Margaret. Westbrook was sometimes loose with his words after he's had too much to drink and had said that he was going to turn himself in for killing Margaret. Recker knew he would be implicated. As for the money, Recker was silently angry that back then he was forced to sell his boat, actually, his yacht, to a judge for a hundred bucks. He aimed to get back money for that loss, as well as being paid for all the free services he'd provided Westbrook over the years. It's crazy. Recker didn't intend to resort to violence, but the whole kidnapping, ransom scheme began to go south."

"It sure did," Lex said. "He became a killer."

"Yes, but from the start, Recker wasn't sure what to do with Svetlana. He never intended to hurt her. The unstable Jillian got high enough to cut off her own finger."

"How insane," Lex said.

"Back then, Recker knew Jillian was not going to keep the baby, and he found out Tomas was adopted by Costas. Westbrook was never made aware of that."

Gil shook his head. "Amazing."

Gerstein continued, "He traced the Costas and found them in Puerto Rico. They were poor and came here with the promise they would walk away rich. They believed it."

"What about Tomas and Lawrence?"

"Recker did a lot of internet searches but didn't know Thomas's name had been changed to Tomas. Jennifer is the one who located him, and fortunately for them, he was in New York. After promising Tomas a big payday, Recker got him a job at the hotel." Gerstein paused to take a sip of water. "Recker killed Lawrence, knowing it would be easy to frame Westbrook. He was aware that Westbrook was going to visit Lawrence to patch things up, so Recker asked to use the bathroom and took the comb and then went to the kitchen and saw a knife on the counter. He stuck it into his suit pocket next to the comb." Gerstein wiped his brow. Then after Westbrook and Lawrence made amends, Recker who had followed his friend, went into Lawrence's office, and attacked the agent, stabbing him and planting the comb on the floor."

Lex said, "He knew the DNA on the comb would match Westbrooks."

"He did. When he realized the money was not going to be wired, he panicked. That's when he decided to end it and run. He took Jennifer's car and never intended to take her with him."

"Where are the suitcases?" Pressley asked.

Gerstein said, "We have them in custody, but Svetlana can claim them anytime."

Lex remembered that she owed Miguel Costa's sister-in-law, Juanita, a call to inform her of the deaths of Miguel, Carmine, and Tomas. She found the number in her cell phone and stepped into another room to deliver the news.

She rejoined her comrades, let out a deep breath, and said, "What a day."

Chapter 55

Lex was seated, a latte in her hand, while Gil's half-eaten doughnut was on his napkin. "I'd rather be assigned a homicide instead of a kidnapping," she said.

Gil agreed, "So would I. Answer your phone."

Lex did and Svetlana said, "Good morning."

"Hi. How are you doing?"

"I'm as well as I can be. I wanted to let you know that I stayed at the Rembrandt last night. Betsy brought over a lot of my things. She's going back to get the rest of my belongings, and she found my ring as well. Thank you so much."

"I'm happy to hear from you. You sound better."

"I have a lot to think about."

"I understand. Listen, I meant what I said. If you ever need anything, please call me."

"Thank you again, Detective."

"You're welcome, and it's Lex. Okay?"

"Thank you, Lex."

"I take it, that was Svetlana. How is she?" Gil asked.

"Much better than yesterday. Betsy is helping her."

"You intend to keep in touch with her, don't you?"

"I do. She said she has no family here."

Later that afternoon, Agent Gerstein appeared at the precinct to speak with Pressley, Lex and Gil. Once they were all together, the FBI agent opened his briefcase and laid out a set of photos on the desk. "Take a look at these."

The detectives studied the shots. "Where is this?" Lex asked.

Gerstein said, "It's Westbrook's old house in Westport, the one Anton Williams purchased from him. Williams said his wife had a garden out back, but nothing grew there, so she had to move it. That was a clear sign something was wrong, and our crew began digging there. It wasn't long before they hit upon the grave. Now we have to get a positive ID and confirm that it's Margaret's corpse, but who else can it be?"

"It has to be her," Lex said.

Gerstein agreed.

Lex updated the agent on Svetlana. "I spoke with her a little while ago. She is settling in at the Rembrandt and is doing as well as can be. I'll keep checking on her."

"Very well," Gerstein said. "I wanted to share this information with you. Maybe we'll see each other sometime down the road."

"It better be a long, long road," Pressley said.

▲

Later that evening Lex was with Liz, and they walked purposefully to a familiar place, the old record store. As she'd always done, Lex gazed into the shop's window. *Dad, everything is fine. It's time I told you about Stefan. I think you would like him. He's handsome, and between you and me. I don't know if I will ever get married again.*

I still feel your hurt, but I also see the smile on your face. That's good enough for me.

Liz, for the first time, spoke to him. *"Hi, Grandpa. I never knew you, but I understand now why mom still comes here. And I'll be back."*

Lex held her daughter's hand, and they stepped away from the window to walk home. After Liz went to her room, Lex sat on the couch with her legs folded beneath her and placed a copy of the book she'd just purchased, *Greta's Gone*, on the coffee table. She had to hear Stefan's voice, so she called him and finally after five rings, he answered. "Lex. Sorry, I left the phone in my pants that I put on the bed before I changed. What's new?"

"Not much. Well, I can use a vacation."

"I can too. I was thinking Memorial Day weekend isn't far off.

249

How about going to Newport for a few days?"

"With you?"

"Funny, Lex. I checked out a place called the Hotel Viking. It's old and charming."

"I'd love to stay there."

"I'll book it."

"Thanks." She paused. "By the way, I googled the Viking, and their breakfast menu says they serve extra crispy bacon."

THE END

About the Author

Mark L. Dressler was born and raised in Hartford, Connecticut. A retired former corporate manager and successful businessman, he began writing in 2014.

His popular Dan Shields mysteries Dead and Gone and Dead Right are set in his hometown, while revered female detective, Lex Stall, takes on Manhattan in Dying for Fame.

Mark's riveting novels have earned him recognition by the Hartford Courant, who named him a most notable author.

His TV appearances on CT Style with Teresa Dufour at News 8 WTNH in New Haven and on Real People with Stan Simpson at Fox 61 in Hartford have solidified his stature as one of Connecticut's favorite authors.

Additionally, Mark has been honored by Boston Children's Hospital for his charitable donations from partial proceeds of his books.

The author is a member of Mystery Writers of America as well as the Connecticut Authors and Publishers Association.

Mark's books are available on Amazon in Kindle and paperback. You may also purchase his books from any bookseller, including Barnes and Noble, Walmart, and Target.

Follow Mark on Facebook at:
www.facebook.com/MarkLDressler
Email him at mark.dressler17@gmail.com

THE MARK L. DRESSLER MYSTERY COLLECTION

THE DAN SHIELDS SERIES
(The detective who breaks all the rules)

DEAD AND GONE (2017)

Dan Shields is drawn into the gang world when a drug bust goes wrong. Police, as well as gang members, are killed, and the money is nowhere to be found. Dan soon confronts the thug who shot and nearly killed the detective six years earlier. The savvy sleuth follows a twisted path leading to an unexpected discovery that stuns the entire police force.

DEAD RIGHT (2019)

Dan Shields and powerful attorney Angelo Biaggio engage in a game of life and death. It was the lawyer's car that had struck and killed a twelve-year-old boy on a city street. Without stopping, the vehicle sped away from the scene. As the detective homes in on the driver, the lives of Dan, and his family are placed in grave danger.

DEAD WRONG (2022)

Dan Shields goes to college and investigates the killings of security guard Christine Kole, and DJ Gordon Gunderson while the student is airing his weekly music show. Dan is confronted by the undergraduate's combative, aspiring politician father, who leads the detective down a path of truths and lies. Sorting facts from fiction, Dan uncovers a scheme that entails more than he could anticipate.

At the same time, the overworked detective tries to untangle the Halloween evening killings of two men whom, at different locations, are dressed in Batman costumes. Dan ponders whether these deadly shootings are related and soon discovers the answer that sends him into dangerous territory.

THE LEX STALL SERIES

(Manhattan's tenacious female detective)

DYING FOR FAME (2020)

Lex Stall draws aim on an edgy suspect who had discovered Fredrike Cambourd's bullet-riddled body in the artist's Manhattan basement studio. The person of interest has an alibi, but it soon crumbles, and she is determined to get to the truth. What Lex discovers is more than she could have imagined.

Note: Dan Shields makes a cameo appearance in this story.

WRITE TO THE END (2024)

Lex Stall seeks to find the kidnappers of author Essex Westbrook's wife, Svetlana. A hefty ransom is demanded as Lex tries to convince the reclusive, alcoholic novelist not to hand over the money. The antsy man does not listen to her and decides to obey the hostage takers, but he and Lex are stunned when an unforeseen event turns the case upside down.

Made in the USA
Middletown, DE
11 August 2024

58402835R00154